Tail Whip
of the
Black Dragon

John Andes

HAVAH
PUBLISHING

Tail Whip of the Black Dragon

Published by:
HAVAH Publishing
Ashland, OH
Havahpublishing.com

Address all inquiries to:
John Andes
c/o HAVAH Publishing

ISBN: 978-1-64751-016-9

Editor and Interior Layout Design: Amy Rice
Cover Designer: Geremy Woods

Every attempt has been made to source properly all quotes.

Printed in the United States of America

First Edition

> ## "Come not between the dragon and his wrath."
>
> ~William Shakespeare, *King Lear*

4

Everyone, from ancient wizards to school children, knows that even if they lop off the head of dragon, they must be leery of the whip of the dragon's tail...the lethal tail whip.

"They say dragons never truly die. No matter how many times you kill them."

~S.G. Rogers, *Jon Hansen and the Dragon Clan on Yden*

I

"Daddy! Daddy! Don't! Don't hurt mommy!"

As the small plaintive cry faded into the corners of the living room, the sound was masked by three reports from a 9mm handgun. The entry holes in the woman's forehead and chest were dime-sized while the exit wounds were the size of a saucer. Bone splinters, brain matter, and blood sprayed the wall and furniture behind her. The female's form momentarily convulsed and collapsed onto the couch where she and her family spent hours watching TV. She slumped next to her daughter; the girl's chin balanced on her chest as she sat in a large pool of blood covering the cushions. Both women wore no expression... four eyes closed ... two mouths agape. The telephone kept ringing, but the man refused to answer... again. The incessant ringing expressed the frustration of the caller.

"Daddy. Daddy. Why did you hurt mommy? Mommy, get up. Get up!"

From outside the house, a bullhorn blared as police tried another way to contact the shooter: "Mr. Brankow. Mr. Brankow. What happened? Are you okay? Is your wife okay? How about your children?"

The questions coming from the front of the house caused Eliot Brankow and the boy to look toward the door. With one arm, Eliot grabbed his son under the arms, hoisted the boy to cover his chest, and walked awkwardly toward the front door... the phone continued to ring, unanswered.

"Mr. Brankow, we don't want anybody to be injured. Please come outside and talk. Father O'Brien is here. He wants to talk to you and your family. I am sure we can work all this out to your satisfaction. We just want to help."

"Eliot. This is Father O'Brien. How can I help? May I talk to Mary? Is she alright? Please come out so we can talk this through. How are Alex and Maria? Are they okay? Please send them out. I just want to help you solve whatever is troubling you. I know you are a good man. I know God loves you. You know God loves you. Please come out so we can talk."

Strategically stationed behind patrol cars and two of the trees lining the middle-class neighborhood street, Buffalo PD ESU sharpshooters trained their weapons on the door and windows of the living and dining rooms in front of the house, awaiting the signal to fire.

"We're coming out. Don't shoot."

"That's great, Mr. Brankow. Now we can talk this through. Come out very slowly. All we want to do is talk, face-to-face."

Eliot checked his two Glocks to be sure they were loaded and unlocked. He gripped one in his left hand and stuffed the other in the rear of his waistband. Holding his son before him, he struggled to inch open the door. He peered at the assembled force prepared to either accept him or bring him down like a wild animal. Turning back inside, he glimpsed his face in a mirror. Spittle now coated his lips. His mouth looked covered with vanilla icing. His eyes red and glazed... his skin ashen. Sweating profusely, he felt on fire. With his foot, Eliot slowly pushed the door completely open, the boy-shield ushered in front onto the small two-step stoop.

"Mr. Brankow, just relax. We want this to end peacefully."

"Peacefully, my ass."

With those words, Eliot pushed his son to the right into the rose garden nurtured and loved by the adult woman now dead on the floor. The boy stumbled and fell to his knees. With his right hand, Eliot reached into his rear waistband and removed the concealed Glock G30S, the twin of the gun in his raised left hand. He aimed in the general direction of the police gathered and commenced indiscriminate fire, getting off two rounds each from his right and left hands before the police responded. The sharpshooters didn't wait for the order to fire. The defensive response was overwhelming, and bullets cut into him and the front of the house as if the slugs were a sheet of hail blown by a stiff wind. The wooden door and frame splintered while bricks chipped away by rounds that didn't find their human target, but many bullets found their target. Eliot bounced about like a marionette and tossed backward, his contorted mass crumpling backward into the open doorway. Police are trained to fire their weapons to suppress the threat of deadly force until it is no longer a threat. Eliot Brankow was no longer a threat. They stopped shooting.

"Cease fire! Cease fire!"

Heavy silence covered 3412 Woodmere Drive, Buffalo, New York. The reports of the police sharpshooter rifles had echoed through the neighborhood. Violence… starting out as a personal one-on-one inside the home… ends as an impersonal ten-on-one slaughter outside.

"Sergeant Miller echoed orders: retrieve the boy… take him to the EMS bus and make sure they get him to the hospital immediately. Father, please ride with the boy; it may help calm him down." Pointing to other officers, he said, "You two, confirm the kill. The rest of you, once they give us the 'all clear,' we'll enter the house."

Captain Stankiewitz directed a contingent of four officers to step over the body and into the living room. The Captain and one officer surveyed the living room slaughter, while the other three inspected every room in the house for other possible family members or another shooter. The shouts of 'clear' were welcomed sounds to the Captain.

What he saw in the living room made him uncomfortable. Not that he hadn't experienced murder scenes before, but the two women seemingly posed on the couch triggered thoughts of his wife and daughter. He willed himself not to tear up. "Where is the Crime Scene Team? I want this house processed and sealed off now, damn it, now! Is the ME here? I want the bodies examined with all dispatch then taken downtown. I need to be sure there's nothing hinky."

* * *

Lunch at his desk consisted of soup du jour, a bottle of water, and a brownie from the cafeteria, plus a sandwich from home. His lunch meal was not always sufficient for his six-foot, two-hundred-and-five-pound body. At this stage in his life, he enjoyed eating and drinking...perhaps a little too much. A full mop of hair hints of a younger man. David wonders if the love of certain foods is genetic. He smiled as he unwrapped his peanut butter and honey sandwich. His dad took a PB&H to his office during planning season for his clients. Dad had spent fifteen hours a day, six days each week, for six weeks at the office, developing materials for each client's marketing for the next year. No time for family or to take a weekend off for his beloved golf. But as his dad said, those six weeks helped pay for the family's yearlong living and the three-week summer vacation. Peanut butter. He could see his dad's face. *Stop,* he thought. *No time for reverie.*

He had to review the contents of the package delivered yesterday to his townhome. The cover of the package: Decorated with colorful stamps of various sizes confirming its point of origination...the island of Eleuthera in the Bahamas. Eleuthera. The name lifted David's spirits and he felt the dream within reach: That of retiring to an idyllic world to fish and swim in the sea, write the great American novel, and be normal again. Normal is a concept that heretofore existed sporadically and vaguely in his mind and in loving conversations with Rachel. Rachel Vincent, the woman who shared his retirement dream and had helped make their dream become reality. Slowly, his mind drifted into another place.

* * *

Ten years prior, David was transferred from FBI field work out of the home office in Washington, D.C. to an analyst position in the Kansas City office. He transferred without a wife, friends, and only a little self-respect. He understood the synonym for the transfer: Banishment. He had friends in power at the Bureau. They protected him from dismissal while they touted the importance of his role as Special Agent for Interagency Communications. As a newly created position within the safe confines of the Federal Government, there would be little pressure or stress. They told him it would be a comfortable launching pad to retirement.

The CIA, NSA, and HSA were also required to create a functional position like David's in their agencies to break through the *Chinese Wall*: The ego-driven paranoid barrier that kept agencies from talking with each other and sharing vital information. As a result of the 9/11 attack, the Senate Oversight Committee demanded interagency sharing of information. To help keep the country safe, every agency would have access to the same information. There would be no secrets. In reality, David knew he could share only the information he was given, and it would be the same with the other agencies. Directors and section chiefs were the arbiters of what sensitive information they wanted shared. He knew from firsthand experience that very questionable information, potentially damaging information to an agency, or information that had not been confirmed by three independent sources was held back from the sharing process until the appropriate issue was resolved. This could be weeks or forever.

Secretly his powerful friends told him to take the post, keep his head down, and enjoy the benefits of being a seasoned Federal Government employee: Decent salary, great health benefits, numerous PTO days, and a valuable pension. In reality, his new role was a place to hide. His name appeared on email reports, but he was faceless to field office personnel and to a few section chiefs within his own building. In the last ten years, he received one promotion and was the Senior Special Agent for Interagency Communications...but, alas, he is a dinosaur. All other senior special agents in the Kansas City office, as well as his counterparts throughout the country, are younger than he, some young enough to be his children. Their roles are simply rungs to help them climb the ladder of authority and success. David remains stationary on the ladder. Somewhere around the middle...never to go higher. He will only stop climbing with retirement and will never be a section chief. Not sad about his lot, he's comfortable and his retirement isn't threatened. He occasionally plays the *What If? Game,* a game he can never win.

The reason behind his geographic move occasionally flashes through his mind. Bad memories. In a firefight with right wing zealots in the hills of Virginia, he killed a fourteen-year-old girl. In reality, David bore no blame. It was a tragic accident in the middle of a bad situation. The girl's uncle, parents, and brothers were barricaded inside one of two large log cabins in a very rural county somewhere off several dirt roads. Two banks in a neighboring county had been robbed and three people were killed during the robberies. The heavily armed criminals had escaped. Their trail led to an obscure and well-fortified compound.

The town's policemen and four county sheriff's deputies had the fortified compound surrounded but had yet to begin proper negotiations, having never before faced a standoff. There were no negotiators on either force. Those inside had fired several warning rounds at local law enforcement who were forced to keep a low profile. From that moment on, nothing was done to get the robbers to surrender, except pleas from a police captain that went unanswered. The locals were in a wait-and-see-mode: Waiting to see if law enforcement would simply give up and leave.

When David and the other federal agents arrived, the quiet standoff was in its third hour. The federal forces took command of the situation and sharpshooters were dispersed, in a perimeter away from the locals. David was one of the sharpshooters and this was his first opportunity to exercise his special training and talent. From his position about one hundred yards from the two cabins, he saw a figure with what he thought was a gun run from the main building toward the second cabin. The activity caused an ill-advised reaction from the local authorities. Several shot wildly in the direction of the girl, the cabin, and the door from which she ran. People in the main cabin returned fire.

David shot and killed the girl: One shot, one kill. David was well trained. The shooting produced great lamentation from inside the cabin and after an hour of negotiations, the rest of the family surrendered. When the Bureau examined the young body outside the house, they found a piece of wood with a key attached beside the girl. Despite the absence of a gun, it was a righteous shoot. From his distance to the girl, David could not be positive she wasn't holding a gun. He could not take the chance. In the aftermath, David thought himself a killer of a child slightly younger than his own and suffered occasional night sweats about that shot and that girl. Her name was Joleen Ray Jergin.

David discussed the event and his feelings with a Bureau psychiatrist who prescribed a twice-daily low dose of alprazolam. Once, he tried to explain the incident and his painful reaction to it to his children but was unsure they fully understood. Thus, his anguish remained, diminished, and the images less frequent as the years passed. He stopped the prescribed meds after two years. He hated how they made him feel physically.

To avoid the undue and awkward scrutiny of a public investigation and hysteria created by the right-wing media, the Bureau felt it best if David and the girl's death were swept under the rug. He was transferred from D.C. to K.C.: A Midwest place to blend in with Midwest faces...new faces. A place to hide in plain sight.

Jennifer, his wife, announced that she would not leave the glamour of the D.C. power center. She wanted to stay where she would be seen by people who mattered in society and her name and picture on the pages of Sunday paper with all the political glitterati. Her father, Winthrop Bashere, a high-profile lobbyist for oil interests, was (and is) a pompous scion of the influential Bashere family from Dallas. He wanted to avoid getting any shit on his shoes.

It was Winthrop who encouraged her to stay near her parents and play the faux role of the abandoned wife. But, in reality, it was David who was abandoned. He knew she was having an affair with a young attaché from Spain. Her parents learned of the affair from the pictures David provided them prior to the divorce. Winthrop Bashere cried the photos were altered and thus libelous, threatening to go well over David's head to have him dismissed with no benefits. David called his bluff when he threatened his father-in-law with going public with the pictures. Thereafter, everything was kept hush-hush. Nothing was said to the wife and family of the attaché from Barcelona. The threat of going public with the facts about her marital infidelity was powerful leverage over his wife. The move to K.C. made easier by the fact that David's children, Bill and Dorothy, were in boarding school and came home only for holidays and the summer.

Without love and respect, there was no reason for David and Jennifer to stay together. Jennifer, always the drama queen, was driven by needy social acceptability. She had selfish reasons to be a desirable single woman in Washington and no reason to get on the wagon train and head west with an agent winding down his career. In the settlement, he gave her everything in the house, paid off the final six years of the mortgage, packed his bags, and began a mid-life do-over. Prepared to work hard, keep his head down, and look past the unfortunate and bizarre circumstances to life in a new environment.

* * *

14

After five years in his Midwest environment, David met Rachel Vincent at a mixer held by a couple living in the same gated town home community. Rachel, a widowed mother of two college-aged boys, was a successful financial advisor and became his financial advisor.

At first, their relationship was strictly advisor-client and imperceptibly morphed over a few years. He was smitten by her dark eyes and warm honest smile that manifested the kindness of her soul. Her black hair cascaded gently to her shoulders and her trim well-toned body belied her age. The first time they held hands, he felt like a kid again. The first time they kissed, his heart rate increased noticeably...the first time they made love, he felt he was exploring a new adult world.

With Rachel, David felt respected and loved, emotions absent from his psyche for years. She never criticized him, or his behavior, and they talked about everything that concerned them. Her past was kept under wraps. He thought it strange she never volunteered any information about her divorce, former husband, or children. He never asked because he respected her apparent need for privacy.

Once they discussed his evening drinking—too often heavy—a result of his overbearing supervisor and tedium of his work. She did not nag but was concerned for his health. He opted to control his unhealthy reaction to the negative office environment with exercise. Rachel was happy he worked out thrice weekly. They tried to attend a yoga class on Wednesday evening and Saturday morning, and each had space in the master bedroom closet of the other's apartment. That first step took quite a while since they wanted to play it slow.

One Saturday night, after Rachel created an Asian Fusion meal, they made a commitment to each other and their future. Marriage would happen after they both retired and were living in their tropical paradise.

Despite what he spent to pay off the D.C. house mortgage, David had retained a modest amount of his individual retirement nest egg, and his government pension was untouched. The amounts in these two accounts, plus additional growth to his pension and monthly additions to his two IRAs guided by Rachel's expertise, produced enough money for his portion of their dream.

* * *

Clearing his head and returning to reality, he decided he had indulged in too much of *what was* in his life. Daydreaming serves no purpose now. He needed to focus on his immediate future. Slowly opening a large mailing envelope, he tried to savor every second. Handling the package delicately…almost fondling the envelope…his anticipation was sweet. Knowing what was inside… photos of his dream house on the beach of Eleuthera, Bahamas. He removed four 8 x 10 glossy photos, the promotional DVD, and an eleven-page stack of paper clipped together with obligatory sticky tabs indicating areas requiring a signature.

He and Rachel would sign and initial the contract tomorrow after dinner then send the contract and a cashier's check for $750,000 as the initial down payment for their dream. The second payment of $750,000 came due when they retired and moved into the house. A unique arrangement but necessary to secure their dream. They were not going to let their dream house slip from their collective grip. With the second payment, they would start on the road to happiness and never look back…no mortgage hanging over their heads.

Tomorrow's signing would be an important ceremony and reading the contract thoroughly required him to *work through lunch* and deliver the document to Rachel's office before five today. He reviewed photos of the house with the beach in front and woods in back and studied the floor plan. Three bedrooms with accompanying baths and he'd have a space for his second love… writing the great American novel. Rachel would keep her painting supplies and her work in progress on an easel in her den. The dining area, located off the massive kitchen, was pleasing to Rachel. Her love of cooking demanded a large kitchen, and she was pretty good at it. She'd already ordered cookbooks and spices of the Caribbean. She teased him about the need to *go native,* though David isn't sure she fully understands all that that expression entails. Their nearest neighbor is a quarter of a mile down the beach. Occasional nudity, full or partial, may not be totally out of the question. Just not in the kitchen—the home of sharp instruments or spattering grease.

"David, to my office please."

"Yes, Barbara."

The boss commands: He obeys. Section Chief Barbara Wilkins did not like the fact she was, as she has said to others many times, stuck with dead wood. She won't give David a merit raise or recommend him for promotion, so he receives only the yearly COLA. She can't stop that and can't fire him, risking the wrath of his highly placed friends back in D.C., who might make her life a living hell, demote her, or dismiss her out of retaliation. But she can lean on him and make his job time uncomfortable. Toward this end, Barbara has made micromanagement an excruciating art form. If a report is due within twenty-four hours of receipt of information, she wants the report within twelve hours and will look over David's shoulders hourly until she gets the report. Then she will attempt to criticize him for an incomplete job or shoddy work. Often her criticism is offered in front of others. David simply ignores her acrid comments…he has a bigger concern: Getting out alive.

She earned the nickname, Black Dragon or *Heisedelong.* It didn't matter that supervisor and supervised don't like or respect each other, they are stuck with one another like a couple in a bad marriage, stuck together for the children. David's been there and understood completely. Plus, she needs someone to handle the unglamorous minutia and monotony of interagency communications. Someone who will not push for field service, someone who will not make waves. Someone content with waiting for the final bell, and David fits the description. His retirement couldn't come soon enough for both of them and when mid-summer arrived, he'd get out from under the evil lady warden.

She watched him close his door and waited until she could interrupt his private time with a meaningless conversation in her office. He replaced everything in the envelope and locked the package in a desk drawer.

At her doorway, "Ms. Wilkins, how can I help you?"

"We need to talk."

Her brusque, threatening, and loud response is evidence of how she bristles at his public and phony deference. Not rising to acknowledge his entrance, she barely looked up from her desk.

"I need an update of your work. I need to know what you are doing, or not doing, as the case may be. I have a meeting upstairs in an hour. I know the higher-ups will ask about the productivity of everyone in my section. I fear they may be looking to trim the non-productive fat and show a leaner meaner Bureau to the Senate Oversight Committee. So, what have you done lately?"

After years of her verbal abuse, he was immune to her empty threats. He replied, "The issue with the delay in the reports from the Seattle Field Office has been resolved. We will be getting reports on a weekly basis from now on. After the resolution of the issue in Seattle, we will go deeper into the small markets to ensure the new process is viable there. We are testing a faster system of information dissemination to the CIA, NSA, and HSA, as well as state and local authorities. As you recall, I copied you on all the correspondence dealing with this new procedure. I attached a copy of the process to the email. I'll resend it if you wish. No longer will we have to wait two to three weeks to get the reports and bulletins into the right hands. The test of the procedure will be downstream in Tampa, Buffalo, and San Diego. We'll have an

18

answer as to its effectiveness and ease of operation within two months. Recently, we have experienced delays and some minor omissions in the bulletins from the CDC. We are digging into this and hope to have answers and a recommended course of action on your desk within the month. That's about it except for the three hundred types of communication that we review, edit, process, and redistribute each week. Do you need copies of these documents? Is there anything else I can help you with?" *Check and mate.*

"No, that will be all for now."

Standing in her doorway he said loud enough for others on the floor to hear, "You're welcome, ma'am."

He knew she hated it when he called her ma'am, because she is at least thirty years younger than he and never lets people forget she is the youngest female to be promoted to section chief in the Bureau. The use of the deferential ma'am is his small attempt to mind fuck the Black Dragon. Walking through the bullpen of cubicles, he whispers so those near to him can hear...*Heisedelong.* With each utterance, he received a smile of acknowledgment from those who know what he is saying and why.

He recalled the other whispers about the Black Dragon: How she was able to rise so rapidly within the system because she slept with nearly everyone two or three levels above her...men and women. The other rumor is she has every tryst at her apartment on DVD. But these are rumors...rumors are normally baseless and fomented by jealous rivals.

She doesn't have many friends in this office and section chiefs in other offices view her work ethos as being solely self-serving. In her present situation, she reached a massive roadblock. She can't use the alleged sex extortion tactic any longer because those above her have heard the rumors and don't wish to confirm them. They don't want to be another notch on her bedpost. However, she receives positive file notations for organizational productivity and operational efficiency, and she is financially well rewarded.

She is rewarded for the work of David and his team…or is it hush money? She has become increasingly frustrated in her present role and unloads her frustration on the personnel she oversees. On more than one occasion, David has smelled the strong odor of alcohol on her breath first thing in the morning or immediately after lunch. The odor comes through despite the consumption of numerous breath mints.

She has serious problems. But they are not his. Back to his working lunch.

* * *

Pouring over the contract of sale was not difficult. It's tedious, like trying to find termite crap in a mound of ground pepper. Gradually, he got into a work zone but was shaken out of his concentration by the noise of his compatriots in the bullpen. As he opened his door, he saw agents looking up a several large screen TVs. He walked to the nearest cluster and saw police cars, ambulances, and fire trucks surrounding a crumpled flaming mass of metal. There are men and women in uniform scurrying about, lifting and carrying small bodies from outside a bus that is overturned at the side of a city street to waiting ambulances. The bus looks vaguely like an overturned turtle. He hears the staccato accent of an English-speaking Spanish reporter: *"At approximately four pm, here in Madrid, several unknown people attacked a school bus loaded with children heading home after their day at St. Ignacio School. The assailants fired several RPGs into the bus, overturning it, and setting the fuel in the tank ablaze. The assailants then sprayed the vehicle and its helpless riders with automatic rifle fire. A spokesman for the school indicated that there were twenty children on the bus when it left the school. As of now there is no way of knowing how many were on the bus when it*

20

was attacked. I must warn you who are watching this on-site report that what you are viewing is very disturbing. Behind me, you can see the bodies of several children apparently killed as they struggled to escape the inferno that had been the bus.

"Approximately twenty minutes after the attack, the following video was emailed to a local TV station. We have no way of confirming the authenticity of the announcement, but we can report that the masked spokesperson in this video is surrounded by flags and banners that suggest he is a member of the jihadist organization known as The Flame of Allah... ولهب محمد *We have been able to translate the message into English with crude subtitles.*

"'This is a warning to infidels. You are witness to the purifying power of The Flame of Allah. This sign of purification is shown to you because you have sinned against Allah and his chosen people. You have invaded our holy land, desecrated our cities, and perverted our youth with your evil ways. Today you have the first taste of what you have visited upon us for the past one hundred years of illegal Western and Zionist occupation. We have shown you how easy it is for us to bring the purifying Flame of Allah to your homes and families. This is a warning: Withdraw your aggressor armies, pay $100 billion U.S. to us for the damage you have caused, and pledge never again to assault our land. If you do not heed this warning, we will visit our wrath upon all of your cities. Your children will pay for what you have done. We will attack until your will to dominate us is crushed. Future purification will take many forms and be visited to many places. Take heed. Fear us. We do not fear you, nor do we fear death in this struggle. The lives of your children are in your hands.'"

Stunned by the carnage and the threat from the hooded male, the clusters are silent. Section Chief Wilkins stood imperiously in front of her office overlooking the bullpen. "Ladies and gentlemen. Pay close attention. I have just gotten off the phone with Washington and have been assured that our people are assisting Spanish authorities in investigating the situation and tracking down the craven cowards who perpetrated this heinous act. We have been urged to increase our diligence. This means we must comb our resources looking for chatter, website announcements, and any anomalies in the communications of Muslims, as well as any homegrown radicals. Review all information within the past ninety days. Look for any possible connection to *The Flame of Allah*. All section chiefs and above will convene tomorrow at eight am in the large conference room to discuss what has occurred in the last ninety days. Now, get to work and dig deep. Overlook nothing."

The Black Dragon has commanded. She would be looking over everyone's shoulders as they worked to ensure their work was up to her ever-changing and demanding standards. David knew he'd have to sneak out of the office to deliver the package to Rachel's office before five. He needed a reason to leave and return before six and called his team to his office: "We need to review everything we have and get updates from other field offices then meet at seven pm tonight. Send urgent messages to all your field office contacts requesting they give you an up-to-the-minute accounting of any and all terrorist activity of any kind. Please stress you must have this information by 6:45 pm, our time. We'll pour over their input to determine what anything indicates or means so that we can dig deeper before we go home tonight. Tell your contacts after their initial report, you will be re-contacting them by eight-thirty our time to discuss our further needs. They are not to leave their posts until after your second contact. Ms. Wilkins is counting on us to make her look good. I don't need to tell you the gravity of the situation or how important our work will be to her. We won't let her down. The cafeteria is closed, so I will spring for dinner. Just write down what you want from Dolly's Deli. I need your food orders by four. Any questions?" His team is thorough and rarely grumbles. They will dig, dig, and dig some more. Troupers all.

* * *

After scouring the minutia of the sales contract for anomalies and faced with the pressure of the events unfolding internationally, David needed to scrub his mind before the team's evening sit-down. To clear his mind, he used the same numerical and verbal games he enjoyed during his workouts. Mental gymnastics can be just as refreshing and invigorating as a physical workout, clearing his mind of facts unrelated to the event at hand.

The numerical game is to add the digits in a long series, such as the serial numbers on all the bills in his wallet and reduce that result to a single digit. The resultant number is either favorable or unfavorable. Final numbers 1, 2, 3, and 6 are favorable, while the numbers 4, 5, 7, 8, and 9 are unfavorable. He grins at this comical twist on the philosophical thesis of *reductio ad absurdum*. He cannot give a rationale for the designated moral values. They just are. Of course, these favorable and unfavorable designations have no real influence on his life. It's just a game. There is no way for him to know his fate. His fate is determined by actions: Some he can control; most are beyond his control. He also knows that in life it doesn't matter how many times he gets knocked down, it only matters how many times he gets back up. That's what drives him toward his future.

The word game is more fun. In the game he has to think of words that have a similar sound but are not related. He then constructs a tabloid headline from a minimum of three of these words. He starts: If the police investigate the appearance of a birth control device in the stairwell of a high-rise building, they would be looking at the "Condominium Condom Conundrum." If the police were aggressively exhuming the corpse of a well-known criminal, they would be "Diligent Dillinger Diggers." These two seemingly childish games make him smile and occasionally chuckle. Inside of twenty minutes his mind is clear, and he is

ready to focus on the onslaught of facts and opinions from his
team.

II

"Dinah, what have you uncovered?"

"Our Tulsa listening post reports a sprinkling of recent chatter, four weeks old, from The Strength of Allah. No specific mentions of the event in Spain but an urging of preparedness for the struggle with the aggressor. Nothing heard in Seattle, Los Angeles, or Philadelphia as of yet. I suspect they will have something for me when I call them again."

"Robert?"

"Cleveland and Minneapolis note a similar type of situation at a mosque in each city. Each mosque experienced larger than usual attendance at a recent prayer meeting. Both prayer meetings were held two days before the Madrid massacre. The Imam at each meeting prayed for peace and understanding but his prayer was spiced with words that seemed out of place. The words and phrases, *Western infidels, one hundred years, Zionist occupation, reparations, youth, purification* appear to be anomalies for messages of peace and understanding. And oddly, these same words can be found in the diatribe of the spokesman of The Flame of Allah. I believe there is no such thing as coincidence. These findings warrant that we dig deeper."

"OK. Great. I think you're onto something. Margaret, what have you uncovered?"

"There seems to be the expected amount of internet activity from the extreme right-wing factions and splinters like Defenders of Liberty, The Good Shepherds, and Our Land. And here's a new one, Liberty Belles. It appears to be an all-female group of radicals who are hardcore. Not sure of their sexual orientation, but I can guess. I need to dig deeper here. Boston, Buffalo, San Diego, Birmingham, and Phoenix report cyber outcries to get ready for the Muslim invasion because 'our government has sold out to the Zionists.' I have not yet heard from San Francisco and Pittsburgh, but I will."

"See what more you can learn from the four reporting offices and kick ass with the uncooperative ones. Stress the urgency of our situation. It's important that we have all information, in hand, by daybreak tomorrow."

The preliminary meeting progresses with reports of undistinguished activity or none at all.

"Thank you all. Good work so far. Now, get back to your contacts and re-confirm what they have told you. Also, mention what you heard here to get their juices flowing. Tell them we need their updated input by eight-thirty, our time, so we can reconvene at nine to create our final preliminary report. The final, final report must be issued by seven am, after you've had one more early contact with the other offices at six am, our time. They'll be contacted for one last time, by you, at that time. If they whine and complain, tell them to take it up with Director Strathmore. At six-thirty, I will review any new input and your final conclusions. At seven, the final report will be made available to Section Chief Wilkins. My guess is this is only the beginning. I'll be in my office accessing international contacts until then if you need me."

* * *

26

"David, I need to know your progress so far in information gathering. What have you determined that might be useful?"

"Preliminarily, ma'am, we have a little chatter. Both Muslim and radical right are saying nothing unexpected or concrete. We are going back to our contacts to expand upon what they told us."

"How soon will you have a final report to me?"

"When it's final. ETA: Your desk, seven am."

"What's taking you so long?"

"As you know, information gathering is a process with many moving parts. It takes time to get the information from numerous and diverse sources. Then we have to analyze the information and often go back to sources for clarification. As you also know, it is impossible to accelerate information gathering from the other end. Unless contacted by our section chief stressing the urgency of cooperation, our contacts at various field offices treat information gathering, of this ad hoc nature, as a nuisance not critical to their job. They think they are obligated to report weekly, not overnight."

"I want your guarantee that the final report will be on my desk by seven. Is that clear?"

"Yes, ma'am."

David knows that the Black Dragon would never call her counterparts at other offices and attempt to apply pressure to get what she wanted. He knows that she knows the other section chiefs would politely listen to her urgent request (her demand), and then ignore it as a rant driven by her desire to look better than her peers. She tried the bullying tactic once before and it became true Karma. It sunk its teeth deep into her ass.

* * *

International sources report substantial internet activity and phone chatter, but nothing among ex-pats. Just the usual clamor from homegrown radicals with only loose connections to Middle East warring factions. The second string.

The second meeting at nine pm, for the creation of the preliminary report, reveals only two new items. First, the Detroit field office reported a flyer distributed by young men standing on several street corners in the Arab neighborhood of the city. The flyer touched on the core of the message from The Flame of Allah but in softened tones and stressing non-violent public disobedience for better housing, jobs, daycare, fewer police patrols, and more self-governance. Second, the Albuquerque field office reported cries to mobilize, stockpile food and weapons, and monitor local Muslims and their mosques. The cries came from the Free Cowboys, a dispersed group of men and families throughout the Western ranch lands that initially wanted the U.S. Government to just let them alone to ranch and farm. They refuse federal subsidies. This loosely knit organization has radically morphed and now wants a wall built around the country and 24/7 drone flights to keep illegal migrants out, as well as a shoot-to-kill order for all border guards. David finds it interesting that they now want the Federal Government to protect them.

The team is excused for the night and reminded to be back in the office before six am to create a final report.

* * *

David's phone rings as he is turning the key in his front door. He answers without fumbling.

"Hey sweetie, how was your day?"

"Rachel, it was an expected clusterfuck in reaction to the mess in Spain. Nothing I can't handle."

"Do you want me to come over?"

28

"Under normal circumstances, that would be great. But I have to be in the office by five-thirty, and I really just want to have a few drinks and collapse. I wouldn't be good company. Besides, I'll see you tomorrow when we sign the contract that locks in our future. I'll be in a better mood tomorrow."

"I gave the contract a cursory read, and it seems OK. We're on our way. If you really don't want me to come over, that's fine with me."

Fine is the one word that man never wants to hear from his significant other because it means just the opposite and is most often a not-too-subtle threat. If a man does something wrong and he apologizes, a response of "that's fine" means the female is seriously pissed and will seek some form or diabolical retribution. David lived under this Sword of Damocles for many years. So, Rachel's response was disconcerting.

"Are you sure you're OK with that?"

"Yes, I'm sure. See you tomorrow. We'll have a great meal, sign the contract and take the big step toward our future together. I send you kisses all over your body to give you a hint of tomorrow. Sleep well."

"Thanks, sweetie. You, too."

That was an interesting female version of the carrot and the stick. He smiles and pours a healthy measure of Balvenie Doublewood into a short glass. He then splashes in some room temperature bottled water. He takes a large sip of the nectar as he undresses and turns on the bedroom TV. Regardless of the channel, it's all Madrid, all the time. There is a wide spectrum of commentators and pundits pronouncing their usual speculation of the event in Spain and what it means to the U.S. The right wing wants the U.S. to deploy troops and bomb the suspected terrorists back to the Stone Age. They are demanding information from the DOD and the Pentagon. Their hints that our government is hiding something are not thinly veiled. Another sip and another channel. The left wing calls for increased diplomatic efforts, creating a

29

stronger Middle Eastern coalition, and sanctions against the nations that support terrorist activities. Another sip and another channel. Before he gets involved in the Libertarian point of view of non-involvement, David's breathing becomes deep and slowly rhythmic. His eyelids droop. The freshly cleaned linen sheets feel cool against his body. He's wrapped in the arms of Morpheus.

The alarm startles him at four forty-five. He is groggy. Hitting the off button, he notices the half-consumed drink and the remote control on the bedside table. The TV is off. Sometime during his sleep, he silenced the prattle. He eases out of bed, still naked, and now partially tumescent. He pads to the kitchen for coffee, which is starting to brew. He pours a big mug of a special Jamaican blend he orders from an importer of teas and coffees at the mall, then he heads to the shower. The caffeinated beverage and the room temperature shower water attempt to bring him back to life. Shaving in the shower, as he has done for decades, allows him to slowly lower the temperature of the water for a more bracing effect on his body and mind.

Dressed, he's back in the kitchen for a breakfast of high-protein cereal and fresh fruit. The cost of oranges and bananas is staggering in the heartland due to transportation from Florida or California. Everybody wants a slice of this economic pie. Regardless, David must have a banana and an orange several days a week. Finished and out the door in twenty-five minutes. The drive to work will take less time than usual because of the absence of traffic at this early hour. He flashes back to his conversation with Rachel. She was in a snit because she had offered herself, and he had rejected her. He must make it up to her tonight with love and kindness. The phrase, "it's a tough job, but somebody's got to do it," makes him smile broadly.

* * *

"OK, team. Let's construct the final report we send to those in authority. Have we learned anything new since last night? Margaret?"

"We have reports of more email and a little bit of phone chatter from some of the usual right-wing groups plus a new one, Protectors of Freedom. They are located in Sioux City. The strange thing about the chatter from various groups is that despite the geographic disparity and divergent creeds of the groups, they appear to use similar language in their communications. Phrases such as: 'Secure America,' 'for the people,' 'decayed government morals,' and 'reclaim rightful place as leader of the free world' appear in one combination or another in the communications from all the groups. It's as if they are reading talking points from a script…a generic script. If there is a generic script, it would come from an overarching group influencing this loose confederation of self-indulgent whackos."

"Margaret let's not get ahead of ourselves. The similarity of phrases and terms is interesting, but I see a conclusion like an overarching organization with a connection to these cults as being an ill-advised quantum leap. First, there is no history of a single overarching right-wing organization influencing the words and actions of the numerous, fractured, geographically divergent, and isolated cults throughout the country. They are referred to as splinter groups or cults for two reasons, size and divergent ideology. Second, because of the differences in the creeds, from white supremacists to survivalists to Posse Comitatus to the Suburban Vanguard, I seriously doubt any one of the groups would listen to, or be influenced, by an overarching organization that does not walk in lockstep with their very specific myopic creed. I am sure that those above my pay grade would summarily dismiss your point as a misinterpretation of the facts because we ignored the proven historical precedents. Therefore, I don't think your hypothesis should be in the conclusion section. You may include it as an anecdotal observation but that's all. Anyone else?"

31

"But, David, if I may. We see the Muslim faith as an overarching force guiding and driving the Imams in Cleveland and Minneapolis, as well as the flyer distribution in Detroit. Why is it illogical to assume that there could not be a parallel type of structure guiding and driving the various right-wing splinter groups?"

"The Muslim activity noted in those cities is in line with a centuries old religious belief system which has been twisted by the interpretation or misinterpretation of the Koran by local Imams. Internationally, this same type of misinterpretation, a seriously perverted one, sets a single goal for various tribes to wage war against and defeat the West, i.e. the U.S.A. This is an overarching engine shared by millions, regardless of whether they are Houthi or ISIS on the Arabian Peninsula, al-Qaeda in Afghanistan, or The Flame of Allah in northern Africa. Also, remember that these diverse terror groups share two common activities: They proselytize in the name of their faith with the goal to rule the world, or at least a large portion of it, and they hate those who stand in their way...westerners.

"Now back to our right-wing groups, there is no conquer-at-all-costs proselytizing evidenced in their activity. More important, there is no single faith that the various groups espouse. They each have a parochial approach to their little world. The activity and ranting of each faction in the U.S. is based on each cult's sectarian credo which is rarely, if ever, even partially shared by other groups. Regardless of the credo: Freedom from the tyranny of the Federal Government, White Power, or anti-Semitism, these domestic groups have no interest in cooperating with each other. I suspect that if you put a leader of each of these whacko groups in a room, they would likely kill each other, rather than allow another group or a national force to assume the mantle of leadership over all the groups. So, as you can see there is no parallel. Let's move on."

Silence. No one wanted to come to Margaret's aid. It is better and safer for everyone to just do their jobs and not make waves. They have learned this tactic working for the Black Dragon.

"I can report that our international friends have little or nothing to report. These are what I think the recommendations should be:

> A. Increase surveillance of the mosques in Minneapolis and Cleveland;
>
> B. Determine who is attempting to proselytize and organize the Arab population of Detroit;
>
> C. Ascertain more about the activities of the right-wing groups–Liberty Men, The Good Shepherds, Our Land, Protectors of Freedom, Free Cowboys, Defenders of Liberty, and Liberty Belles.

"I'll let you fill in the rest of the report with details of your work and the cooperation of your contacts. Margaret, be sure to include your discovery and hypothesis based on the phraseology. But do so only as anecdotal observation. I need the final report by six fifty-five, so I can email it and hand deliver a hard copy to Section Chief Wilkins. I'll spring for breakfast after eight. Thanks all of you."

* * *

David arrives at Rachel's at five-thirty. He is tired but excited to be with his lover. Evening darkness is commencing. An expensive bottle of wine in one hand and a dozen roses in the other. Corny but they've worked in the past as peace offerings.

"You didn't have to, David."

"I just wanted to show you how much I care. Last night, I was selfishly thinking only of myself, a sort of pity party in my head."

33

"Well, I was volunteering to take your mind off your woes in my own special way. Now, that has to wait until after dinner." They kiss and hug like friends and lovers taking and giving the strength in their souls.

"Now that you mention it, what's for dinner?"

"Kansas City comfort food: a full rack of ribs, cole slaw, thick cut French fries, and baked beans. All the things we love but don't always love us. We'll wash all of it down with Yuengling Lagers so cold they will numb your tongue. It all awaits us on the table. We can save the wine until after dinner when we sign the deed. It'll be a celebration."

"I see you laid out your best Irish linen napkins." A large roll of paper towels sits on the table between them.

"Smart-ass. Now let's over-indulge."

They each get half the rack and heap the sides on their plates. During the first fifteen minutes, a beer is needed to calm the food heat and spices. Except for chewing and minor slurping sounds, the feral attack on the meal is conducted in silence. They don't even look at each other. Suddenly, David looks at Rachel and laughs.

"What's funny?"

"We must look like we were in the movie *Tom Jones*. Remember the scene where Tom is eating a meal with the woman he met at the inn. They are voraciously attacking their food. They're hunched over plates mounded with food. And they're shoveling it into their mouths. Fat drippings and spices cover their chins and cheeks. The eating, almost a competitive sport, builds to a frenzy. Suddenly, Tom looks at the woman across the table. Just as I am looking at you with lust in my eyes. He stands, comes to her side of the table, takes her hand, and pulls her to a bed chamber. I see barbeque sauce on your lips and chin. So, stop eating and give me your hand."

"You're kidding. What are you doing?"

34

David walks her down the hall and gently pushes her onto the bed. There commences aggressive kissing and thrashing, frantic clothes removal, and energetic lovemaking. He is a beast let loose from the cage of a bad workplace and two weeks away from his love. She wants to be conquered and thus actively gives of herself. Her body parts are massaged and kissed. Breathing becomes intense. Moaning gives way to near screaming from his throat. His exhaustion is total as he collapses onto her waiting bosom. She tenderly clutches him. The fire of his lust has self-consumed. Ten minutes of in-synch rhythmic breathing and they are back to the moment.

"That was different."

"That was good and what I needed, beautiful wench. But we deserve a second helping?"

"Are you up for it, stranger?"

"Surprisingly, yes. Or I will be in fifteen minutes. And amazingly without the little blue pill. It must be my bedmate. Let's take advantage of this opportunity. At my age, it may never be here again."

"Allow me help you get ready."

With her help, in a short time he is ready. The second helping is slow and tender. His lust has been transformed into the ebb and flow of tender contact with his beloved. He reaches nirvana but does not stop until she does. This is his expression of love for her. He withdraws. Eyes closed; she faces the ceiling while he buries his head between two pillows. His arm is over her breasts and wrapped around her rib cage as if to hold her forever.

"Remind me to serve that meal again. David, I hate to be mundane but what about the food?"

"In a few minutes, we'll go back to the table and replenish the energy we just depleted. Remember how you said that when we were living on Eleuthera we could go native. Going native means no clothing, or maybe just a loin cloth. Tonight, we will test the appropriateness of that look. We will wear nothing more than underpants."

"You're as crazy as a teen. Here? In my house? What if someone sees?"

"No one will see, and yes I am teen-like crazy. But that's your fault. I have never felt as alive and unencumbered by the small minds and the demands of others as when I am with you. I love you more than you can imagine."

"I love you, too. OK, then, it's back to the meal on the dining room table and hope that we're not interrupted by a member of the homeowner's association, a Girl Scout selling cookies, or a Jehovah's Witness."

Two large toothy grins tell the joy of the night.

* * *

The night is oil black. Those walking on the ground in areas outside of towns and cities can see only a few feet in front or to either side, even with the aid of lanterns or flashlights. The four pilots flying high above can see only the small flickering lights of substantial population clusters. These are not the targets. The two targets and the courses to reach them from one continent to another have been confirmed by friendlies. There will be limited communication between the four planes until they approach their respective targets.

The first target is a tiny fishing village in the Northwest section of Libya, east of Zawareh. Because there are numerous fishing villages in this area, a laser-like strike is critical. It would do substantial political damage to obliterate peaceful fishermen and their families in a village which is not the assembly point for terrorists. This type of collateral damage would be a bad result of their efforts. Two 18C-Hornets peel off over the Mediterranean before the Libyan coast. They descend to a firing altitude. The two other planes stay aloft and head south southeast.

As the first two planes near their target, a fire breaks out on the dock. The pilots must give the friendlies that lit the fire time to get out of Dodge before the Sheriffs arrive. Two minutes is all they get. Two fingers flick the safety caps on weaponry triggers.

"Vengador Dos. Vengador Uno. Soy listo. Copier?"

"Vengador Uno. Copier. Soy listo."

"En mi marca."

"Copier."

In a small warehouse at the land end of the pier, three men look up from their work, rush to the window, and stare at the twenty-foot flames at the far end of the pier. They are in a quandary. Do they stop their tasks of bomb making and gun loading and rush to extinguish the fire? Do they continue their work to have all ready for the boat leaving tomorrow morning at six? They remain in the warehouse to meet their obligation to Allah.

A baby is fidgeting in a crib beside the bed of her parents. An old man stirs as if urged awake by some impending event. The village is quiet and dark except for the bright signal fire. The two-minute escape time is up.

"Vengador Dos. En mi marca. Cinco-cuattro-tres-dos-uno. Marca."

Two fingers flip two toggle switches. Simultaneously, four AGM-84E Standoff Land Attack Missiles hurtle toward the dock and surrounding buildings. The planes veer left and head back over water. Behind them hell has been visited upon the enemy. The tiny village is nearly vaporized, and the shoreline has moved about forty meters inland. Hunks of burning wood are thrown high in the air. No one on or near the dock survives the blasts. The two pilots don't look back. Damage assessment is not their responsibility. They just create damage. The red and orange circular insignia of the Spanish Air Force on the tail of both planes is illuminated by the rising twisting fireball.

The target for the second set of 18C-Hornets is many kilometers south, southeast in the Northwest area of Chad. In the barren wasteland between Bardei and Faya, there are several military camps: Breeding grounds for the displaced fanatics who wish nothing more than to kill and destroy all that is evil...the West. Each camp has its own identity. These identities are based on the inhabitants' country of origin and the misguided ranting of local Imams. The differences are slight, but the nuances are significant enough for the fanatics in one camp serving their Imam and Allah to try to be more devout than fanatics in other camps. It's almost as if they are playing a deadly game of competitive religious adherence. All the camps have a single enemy and a common deity, so they do not fight each other. But they never band together to fight the common grand evil. Each wants to be the one that defeated Satan.

The target camp is designated as FA-24. By destroying this camp, the government behind the jets will eliminate one band of terrorists and send a clear message to the other camps that they are vulnerable to elimination. It takes the planes approximately ninety minutes from the Mediterranean coast to enter the desert kill zone.

"*Vengador Tres. Vengador Quattro. Soy listo. Copier?*"

"*Vengador Cuattro. Copier. Soy listo.*"

"*En mi marca.*"

"*Copier.*"

The target camp is an array of tents encircling a mud-slab single-story structure. The camp is quiet. Lanterns hang from poles outside several tents. Six men, each with a large dog of mixed and angry heritage, patrol the barbed wire perimeter of the camp. A cold wind whips around the tents and building causing the sleeping residents to tighten the blankets around them. Suddenly, a rocket is fired from behind a berm approximately four hundred meters from the camp's center. The explosion and bright light create panic among the guards. Their dogs bark wildly and awaken those not soundly sleeping in the tents. The flare remains above the camp for ninety seconds.

"Vengador Tres. En mi marca. Cinco-cuattro-tres-dos-uno. Marca."

Two fingers flip two toggle switches. Simultaneously, four AGM-84E Standoff Land Attack Missiles hurtle toward the camp. The planes veer left and head back toward the sea and beyond to the safety of another continent. Behind them, hell has been visited upon the enemy. The explosions rip a football field size crater in the sand. Humans, dogs, and structural elements are vaporized by the fireball. The explosions and fire can be seen by other camps many kilometers away. The two pilots never look back. Damage assessment is not their responsibility. They just create damage. The red and orange circular insignia of the Spanish Air Force on the tail of both planes is illuminated by the rising twisting fireball.

III

"Good morning. This just in, to San Diego KSDN Your News Now: Police have been called to Northwood High School on Rolling Hills Road where it is reported that a student with a gun has fired the weapon several times. It is yet to be confirmed whether the student has hit any fellow students, teachers, or administration. We believe the student may be holding hostages. For all the details of this unfolding story, we take you live to our feet on the street and eye in the sky for up close and personal

coverage. On the scene is Brenda Goodmill. Brenda, what can you tell us?"

"Well, Victor, what we know from speaking with several students, as well as a teacher, who were all evacuated from the school, is that a student, a junior at Northwood High School named Lisa Marie Buenaventura apparently brought at least one handgun, perhaps two handguns, to school today. At approximately 10:30 this morning she became very erratic: Raising her voice in class and waving the gun or guns over her head. One of the students in her class at the time said that Ms. Buenaventura threatened to kill everyone, students and teachers alike. I now have the opportunity to speak with a teacher who was in a classroom next to Ms. Buenaventura's. Darnell Williams is that teacher. Mr. Williams, what can you tell our viewers?"

"Well, I heard this loud yelling and what seemed to be a commotion caused by students in the classroom next to mine. I told my students to be still and I went out of my classroom into the hall. I went to the next classroom and looked through the small window in the door. There I saw a female student standing on a desk seat waving her arms violently. In each of her hands, she held a gun. That's when I heard the loud pop-pop-pop that I assumed was gunfire. I did not see if the gun fire had struck anybody. I quickly got back to my classroom and told my students to leave their desks, exit the room, and walk rapidly down the hall to go outside. Those are some of my students over there."

"Thank you, Mr. Williams. And now we will hear from Jessica Brown, a fellow student in Ms. Buenaventura's class. Ms. Brown what can you tell our viewers about the incident in the classroom?"

"Well, it was like real scary, ya know? Lisa Marie like just jumped up on her chair and started screaming and pointing guns at everybody. Man, she was actin' like crazy, ya know?"

"Can you recall what Ms. Buenaventura was saying at that time?"

"She was, like, really angry. Angry at the teacher, Miss Jennings. Angry at the school. Angry at her mom. She was going to, like, kill all the people that made her angry. She fired a couple of shots into the wall, like, right over the head of Miss Jennings. That's when Lisa Marie, like, told us to get the fuck out of the classroom. We were, like, scared and didn't need a second invitation. All of us, like, ran to the door. The doorway got jammed but we all got out and ran down the hall and outside. By then, the school resource guard was, like, running to the room to see what was going on. We were watching him run down the hall from outside. When he, like, opened the door, we heard two more pops and he fell back into the hall. It all was, like, really scary."

"Thank you, Miss Brown. Now I will try to get some information from the police captain who appears to be in charge. Captain Fogerty, what can you tell our viewers about the present situation and the events that led up to now?"

"We know the student in question is Lisa Marie Buenaventura. We know that at least one person, a school resource guard, James Milton has been shot. We do not know his condition. We do not know if anyone else has been shot. We believe there may be at least one other person remaining in the classroom with Ms. Buenaventura. That person is the teacher, Ms. Anita Jennings. We do not know her condition. We do not know if anyone else is in the classroom."

"What are your plans to diffuse the situation?"

"We are presently making sure everyone has been evacuated from the school. Once that has been established, we will attempt to contact Ms. Buenaventura to ascertain her mindset and her demands if any. We will attempt to determine if anyone is in the classroom with her. To establish contact, we will insert several of our officers into the school and position them near Ms. Buenaventura's classroom. Now, if you'll excuse me, this is an active crime scene, and all non-essential personnel are being ordered to stay behind the yellow tape. So please, you and your

41

cameraman must retreat to the prescribed safe distance. Thank you. Officers, get all these people back to the tree line and run the tape." "Well, that's all the information we can get for now. Back to the studio. Victor."

"Thanks, Brenda. We turn to our eye in the sky with Your News Now Chopper 10 and Rafael Torres. Rafael, what can you report?"

"Thanks, Victor. Hovering over the school, we can see the students, teachers, and administration being herded under the trees behind the police crime scene tape while the police are standing in a line between the school and the crowd, which is approximately fifty yards from the school's main building. I see the police purposefully deploying at the main entrance and at what may be the windows to Ms. Buenaventura's classroom. We cannot be positive of their motives, but the action of containment seems logical. Kind of a wait-and-see approach while they attempt to contact Ms. Buenaventura. That's what we can see at this time. If there is aggressive movement on the part of the police, we will let you know. This Rafael Torres in Your News Now Chopper 10.

"Thank you, Rafael. Now back to Brenda at the scene. Brenda, are there new developments?"

"Yes, Victor. A police cruiser just arrived and in it was an adult woman believed to be Lisa Marie's mother. She is walking this way. Mrs. Buenaventura, what can you tell us about your daughter and her emotional situation?"

"It's Mrs. Jackson. And all I know is that Lisa Marie is a good girl. She has never been violent. I just don't know what happened. It would not surprise me if her father, my slug of a former husband had something to do with this. Now, please take the microphone out of my face. Have you no decency? I have to talk to my daughter."

* * *

42

"Fox One? This is Fox Two. I am in position thirty feet from the body in the door. What is your position?"

"Crawling on the floor about to reach the corner in the hall. My objective is to reach a position with a visual on the door. I'll be in your line of sight in ten seconds."

"Command, Fox One and Fox Two are in position. We are in visual contact with each other. We are ready to attempt verbal contact with the student."

"Fox One and Fox Two, you are good to go."

"Fox One, take the lead. I'll follow."

"Roger that, Fox Two."

"Lisa Marie? Are you OK?"

A long silence. "Yeah, I'm just peachy. Who the fuck are you?"

"Pete Jones. I'm here to see if you need anything. Do you need anything?"

"You're a cop. And what I need is for you and your storm troopers to go the fuck away. Is that clear?'

"What can I do to help you?"

"Like I said, leave."

"May I speak with your teacher, Miss Jennings?"

"That ain't gonna happen. She's dead."

"I'd like to talk to you face-to-face. Will you come into the hall?"

"You have got to be kidding. I am safe and secure in here."

"Do you want some water? Or something to eat? I can get it for you."

"Thanks, I don't need anything except for you to leave."

"May I come in, so we can talk to each other and not yell at each other?"

"If you try to come in, yours will be the second body in the doorway. Is that clear?"

"Your mother is here, and she would like to talk to you. I'll bring her into the hall."

"I don't want to have anything to do with that bitch. Is that clear?'

"I understand you are upset. Many teenage girls get upset with their mothers."

"Upset! Upset! You have no idea how fucking upset I am. That bitch tossed my father to the curb when she found a guy who would give her everything she wanted: A big Beemer, a house in the hills, and lots of drugs. My dad loved her and worked hard to provide for the two of us. But it was never enough for the greedy bitch. So out with the old and in with the new. She even wanted me to change my name. I told her bullshit. I wanted to live with my father, but her new man hired a vicious lawyer who convinced the court that my mom and her new man could provide a better living environment for me. Better living environment, my ass. Her new man was always offering to massage my neck and shoulders when my mother was not around. He tried to kiss me lots of times. I caught him watching me when I was in the outdoor shower. He even offered me X. I think he wanted to pimp me out to make money to buy the drugs my mother demanded. He's a damned perv. He caved in to her every wish, regardless of the cost. He just sold more drugs. So, no, I don't want to see or talk to the bitch."

"Command, apparently Miss Jennings, the teacher has been killed by Ms. Buenaventura. So, including the resource officer, that's at least two down. We asked about the mother and were told a defiant no. We will continue to negotiate, but the subject seems to be increasingly agitated. I fear our entry will result in a…"

"Here I am, motherfuckers, and here are my answers to your annoying questions."

The girl springs through the door to the classroom leaping over the body of the resource officer. In each hand she holds what appears to be a snub-nosed .32. Waving her arms, she searches for

44

something or someone to shoot. Her hands scan up and down the hall. Lisa's face is ashen, her eyes glazed, dried spittle covers both lips, and she is sweating profusely. She spots Officer Peter Jones, prone with his assault rifle aimed at the room's entrance, and fires wildly in his direction, shooting over his head. He returns fire with deadly accuracy. Officer Brendan O'Malley also opens fire. Both policemen get off several rounds each from their ACRs. Lisa Marie is struck from both sides and spun around like a rag doll. Her arms flail as she attempts to return targeted fire. Her last shots go into the hall's ceiling. She crumples to the floor. In ten seconds, there is silence.

* * *

The giddy couple boards the plane from Kansas City's MCI to Miami's MIA in the early afternoon. Arrival is scheduled for six thirty-five pm EST. They will spend the night at the airport Marriott where they will change from big-city-escape to vacation clothes to their idea of appropriate island garb. At seven am the next day, they will board a flight to Lynden Pindling International Airport, Nassau, Bahamas. From the airport, they will take a taxi to Prince George Wharf and board a deep-water ferry for the ninety-minute trip to Eleuthera: A pleasure cruise for many, and a method of bringing consumables to the smaller island for retailers. They'll need to slather SPF 30 sunblock on the pale exposed parts of their bodies for this last leg of their trip. They'll ride on the top deck to drink in all the joy of the Caribbean air and sun.

Rachel held his hand on each leg of the flight. They stared lovingly at each other like honeymooners. Occasionally, they would kiss the other's cheek or forehead when they were seated. When they applied the sun block to one another, they chuckled.

"If our children could see us now, they would be embarrassed."

"Not mine, Rachel. My two would applaud what I am doing and with whom I am doing it. I've told them often how much I care about you and how much you mean to me. They want me to be happy, and I am happy."

"David, dearest, you make me happier than I thought would be possible. Even more than I think I deserve. Come here. Face me and rub the sunblock on my back while I kiss you."

"You deserve all the happiness in the world. Now, how could a red-blooded American male deprive you of a back-rub happiness?"

Her kiss is warm and deep. She holds him as if she would never let him go.

"Rachel, we'd better stop. People are staring."

"Who cares? They're just jealous. Hey you, strangers! This is my man and I love him. We are embarking on an overdue adventure and a life together smothered in happiness. We will grow old together. He will get fat from my cooking. I will serve him drinks on our porch, and we will make love in the moonlight and sometimes in the sunlight."

Her pronouncement garners smiles and applause from the other passengers on the ferry. Having been told of Rachel's pronouncement, the captain blows the boat whistle several times. The couple is truly on a love adventure. After the boat is well underway, other passengers congratulate them and shake their hands. The happy couple stands at the railing and stares into their future.

The first stop in Eleuthera is Premier Island Estates Realty, a four-block walk from the harbor. There they pick up keys to their dream house and a copy of the signed paperwork. Car rental is not possible, so they hire a taxi. Although the vehicle looks like an old clown car, they hope it has been deemed safe by some governing body. David notices many people on bicycles or motor scooters. There is no speed limit on the island roads because no one could go over thirty on them. This is life in the slow and casual lane. The second stop is the food market where David and Rachel buy bare necessities for dinner and breakfast. David thinks how expensive the necessities are in paradise. But, if that's the price for eternal happiness, it is well worth it. Fresh fruit, vegetables, and fish are not expensive. More shopping tomorrow. As the taxi wends its way around to Double Bay Beach, the overhanging trees kiss the roof and flowering undergrowth gently rubs against both sides. David's heart is beating rapidly, and his breath is shallow and strained. The sheer excitement of the reality is damned near overwhelming. He looks at Rachel. He sees tears of joy.

There it is. Their three-bedroom castle. And there is the water. And the trees. It's perfect. David lets out his best attempt at a rebel yell, grabs Rachel, and they run to the beach. Felix, their driver, carries suitcases, groceries, and wine to the front porch. In ten minutes, the loving couple comes back to Felix.

"We will need you to pick us up tomorrow and take us to town for shopping and looking. Can you be here around ten?"

"Yes, around ten. I will be your guide. I know the best places to shop. My cousins' places."

"Do we pay you now or would you prefer as we leave the island?"

"Please pay me at the end of each day I serve your transportation needs."

"OK. This is for today, and this is because we are happy with the service."

Felix is happy for the happy couple and happy they are reflecting their happiness in the excessive tip they gave to him. He departs. David unlocks the door and turns to Rachel. As she begins to step toward the opening, he swoops her up in his arms and carries her across the threshold.

"No one ever did that for me before."

"I never did it for anyone before. Does that make us virgins?"

Their giggles become laughter. Back on the porch, they each grab a suitcase and carry it to the master bedroom. David then brings the groceries into the kitchen. He plugs in the refrigerator and pours water in two ice trays. He stocks the larder with cheese, crackers, island fruit, coffee, rolls, and milk for tonight and tomorrow morning. Rachel is walking throughout the house opening windows and propping open doors. The breeze off the water is cool and clean. It clears out the staleness of the house almost immediately. David hears a large thump from the bedroom followed by the sound of something heavy being dragged on the floor. Concerned, he looks away from the shelves holding the plates, dishes, and glasses and sees Rachel pulling and pushing the master bedroom mattress through the house. She looks at him and smiles impishly.

"Moonlight, baby. Moonlight tonight."

It is in his best interest to help, and he does so. Plop! There the mattress rests beneath the ceiling fan on the veranda.

"Oh, beautiful maiden, how about our first swim?"

"I'll get our suits from the bedroom."

"Suits, my ass. Remember about going native?"

"What if our neighbors down the beach spot us?"

"Hell, they're too far away to see. Besides, they would be envious that I am with such a beautiful and adventuresome woman."

"What about towels?"

"We'll dry off as we walk back from the beach. Ready. Set. Strip. I'll race you to the water!"

Clothes are hurriedly removed and tossed on the floor. The race is on. Today, they play. Tomorrow, they work, videoing and taking written inventory of everything.

Having purchased the home and land, lock, stock, and barrel, they want to be assured that their total purchase is in the house when they move in a few months from now. There will be renters coming next week. David and Rachel will share the rental income with the present, now co-owner. The lovebirds plan to use their share of the rental income to purchase whatever they need during their first month on the island. They will need personal transportation and the larder must be well stocked with staples...particularly wine, beer, and scotch. David is looking forward to drinks at every sunset.

Three days of cataloging, dining on fresh fruit and broiled fish, and sipping wine as the sunsets rush by. Their work completed, they close up the house, return the keys to the real estate agency, and start the multi-stage trek to their home and work. On the flight from Miami to Kansas City, Rachel rests her head and pillow on David's shoulder. He wonders why the trip back to work feels like it is taking a half day, while the trip to the island felt like it took three days. The disparate emotions of dread and pleasant anticipation alter man's sense of time and distance. Did Einstein know that? He grins. The words of a ballad echo in his mind as he falls asleep...*love's more wonderful the second time around.*

* * *

Sitting in front of his computer, back at work, David thinks how nice it would be to have an overnight work gnome, a character that would deal with the astronomical number of emails, most of which are senseless reminders or requests for things that the sender is able to find without David pointing the way. The mythical worker would come into David's office and work second shift, from six to midnight. But alas, he does not have such a kindly figure to assist him. So, he must deal with the 274 emails, either sent to him directly or on which he was a member of an extensive list. The latter sent by someone attempting to look smart or cover his ass. If David does nothing else, properly going through and reading all the cyber mail would take a full two days. So, to shorten the task, he will look at the subject and quickly delete any correspondence that he knows is unnecessary. There are real issues that arose during his week away. These require his attention.

"David, please come to my office."

The familiar command of the Black Dragon, with all its joylessness and implied threat, makes David's stomach tense. He walks through the bullpen nodding to his team as they welcome him back. He whispers, "*Heisedelong*." His team hears him. No one comments on his recently acquired tan.

"We'll meet in my office after I meet with the Black Dragon. In about thirty minutes."

Standing at attention before Barbara's desk, he is a dutiful soldier reporting as ordered. "David, I need to know what you and your team have been doing in the past week."

"As I'm sure you are aware; I was on a brief vacation. So, I did no Bureau work. I plan to meet with my team next. They will bring me up to speed. Then I'll send you a recap of the meeting. Will that suffice?"

She looks up from the papers in front of her and she delivers a small scowl. She has been trumped by the truth and is powerless to reject it. She is not happy that she can't rattle David. "That will be all. Except, I expect your recap before noon."

"When it is ready." His pushback widens her scowl.

* * *

"OK, ladies and gentlemen, tell me what has happened since I last gazed at your comely countenances. Robert?"

"Welcome back, David. Nice tan."

"Thanks. Please continue."

"As you recall, there are mosques in Cleveland and Minneapolis in which the respective Imams prayed for peace and understanding, but each prayer was spiced with words that seemed out of place. The words, '*western infidels,*' '*one hundred years,*'

50

'Zionist occupation,' 'reparations,' 'youth,' 'purification' were part of the diatribe of the spokesman of The Flame of Allah. This past week each of the mosques suffered physical damage. Two windows in the Al Akbar Mosque in Minneapolis were broken, pig's blood was splashed on the door, there was urine found in the fountain in which the attendees wash their hands, and anti-Muslim graffiti was spray painted on the walls inside. A total desecration of a holy site.

"We did pick up some chatter from two new hate groups. Pure American and White Pride claimed knowledge of the mess in Minneapolis but neither group claimed responsibility, although each did praise 'their brothers in arms who seek to cleanse evil from the land.' They each used the exact phrase. As we have seen before, in the world of right-wing groups, a similar key phrase in the communications from different groups could indicate some form of connection."

"But only a connection between groups with a similar purpose and creed. Most likely the second sender of the hate message copied the words of the first. Can you determine which of the hate groups issued their message first?"

"Unfortunately, not."

"OK, then let's chalk up the similarities to timing. Agreed?"

"Agreed."

"What about Cleveland?"

"The Abu Akbar Mosque in Cleveland was firebombed. The damage was substantial, but no one was injured. The building is being repaired. And after four days, no chatter. No happiness at the Muslim misfortune. That, in and of itself, is strange. Normally, some group would send a message praising an event as severe as a firebombing. This leads to the assumption that the firebombing could have been the work of someone other than a homegrown hate group. The local field office told me that there is an ongoing power struggle among several mosques. This is a struggle to bring more local Muslims under the control of like-minded Imams and thereby increase the strength of the radical Muslim community in Cleveland. Our field office reports that Tariq Raqmani and Hussein Abandi are two Imams who appear to be leading this consolidation effort. They are both radical Shiites. The mosque that was firebombed housed a liberal, almost progressive Sunni community."

"Interesting. We need more in-depth information on the activities in these two cities. OK?"

"Yes."

"What about the right-wing groups we heard from before?"

"Nothing new from the Defenders of Liberty, The Good Shepherds, Our Land, and the Liberty Belles. I did find out that the Liberty Belles are based outside of Philadelphia in Valley Forge. Their leaders are unidentified as of now."

"Thanks."

"Boston, Charlotte, Birmingham, Phoenix, Seattle, San Francisco, and Pittsburgh report no new activity since their reporting after the Madrid incident."

"So, Minneapolis with its vast Somali population and Cleveland with its possible power struggle are the only hotspots as of now. I'll send a recap of this information to Ms. Wilkins. Thanks for your work."

"David, how is Eleuthera?"

"Margaret, it's more beautiful than I remembered. Thanks for asking."

One hundred and fifteen emails deleted. More tomorrow and Monday. The weekend is necessary so David can be prepared for the pressures of tedium and Barbara's harassment. Having just gotten a tip-of-the-tongue-taste of the paradise that awaits him within a few months, he must steel himself against the frustration of not being there and diligently work within the system. A key administrative job is to recommend his replacement. Robert?

Margaret? They are the most senior and arguably the most qualified. Regardless of his recommendation, Barbara will have her own strong point of view. She will want a lap dog not a lead dog, and certainly not someone with connections above her. Dinah? Jacob? She will definitely fight to keep the promotion in-house. A transfer would have no allegiance to her or fear of her.

This project will require combing through the previous evaluations and the work files of the four in his group. Completed, he will make his recommendation simultaneously to Barbara and her supervisor, Assistant Director in Charge of Operations, Fletcher Wilson. Maybe the other three ADs also. One last mind game with *Heisedelong*. David is reminded of the line from a play he saw many years ago in D.C. in which the protagonist said… "I'm not afraid of dying, if I could just roll over once in a while and kick some son-of-a-bitch in the ass." He smiles at this childish attitude. Saturday is for shopping and chores. Rachel is coming over for a swim and dinner. This time they must wear proper attire. It's a community pool.

IV

The phone on the nightstand is on its fourth buzz when David responds.

"Hello. Yes. Yes. I see. I'll be there right away."

"David, what was that all about?"

"That was Fletcher Wilson the AD over my group. It seems that Barbara Wilkins has died. He will give me all the details when we meet at the office within the hour."

"Jesus, sweetie. If the Black Dragon is dead, her condition won't change by daybreak. Why must you go into the office now…it's three fifteen? It's pitch dark."

"Something strange about her death that requires immediate attention. I'll be back for breakfast. Go back to sleep. Luvya."

"Luvya back."

Odd. This is the first time that Rachel called Barbara the Black Dragon. On top of that, she was flippant about her death interfering with his life. He never realized how Rachel felt about Barbara. He never asked, and she never said. Did he fail to notice Rachel's hints? Did she dislike or hate Barbara? Was her feeling based on how Barbara treated him? Was it out of jealousy that the work as dictated by Barbara always came first? Subjects for a later discussion.

He badges through the main door, past the security desk, and onto the elevator where he badges to the top floor. The ride takes seconds. The hall lights are dim, but there is an abundance of light emanating from the open double doors of the main conference room. He enters the room crowded with senior agents, supervisors, section chiefs, and assistant directors. David is not the last to be seated at the table: Mitchell Davis, the ADO of Operations, lives farther from the office and Jack Strathmore, the Director, is already in his office which is connected to the conference room. David can hear Jack talking on the telephone. There are several people whispering, but no one in the conference room talks aloud as they strain to hear what Jack is saying. There will be time for talking when they know what they are supposed to know. Enter Jack.

"Thank you all for coming to the office on such short notice and at this ungodly hour. Let us begin. This is what I know:

About an hour and a half ago, I received a call from Commander Anderson of the Kansas City, Missouri-Kansas Major Case Joint Task Force. He advised me that upon responding to a 911 noise complaint, two officers found Section Chief Barbara Wilkins dead in her townhouse. The officers determined who she was by examining the contents of her wallet and they notified their superiors. Through the proper chain of command, the information came to me. A few minutes ago, I was told by Commander Anderson that while the locals would conduct the investigation, we at the Bureau would be kept in the loop during the process. They will give us information once it has been verified. No rumors or suppositions. This case is too critical. He also indicated that they might reach out to us for technical expertise and support. But he would know more about any area of needed cooperation later today.

"Commander Anderson said that they would strive to keep the event out of the newspapers and off the TV. But he could not guarantee a complete blackout because they are required to note the incident in the press. They will keep it to the Police Blotter. On this point, over the next few days any inquiries about what happened or the identity of the section chief that you receive from the media or anyone outside the Bureau must go through Emily Knapp. For those who have never met or worked with Ms. Knapp, she is Deputy Director of Community Communications in D.C. And she is good at her job of controlling what the public knows and thinks about the Bureau. She is more protective of the Bureau than a wounded tigress of her cubs. She has been known to publicly eviscerate anyone in the media who besmirches the Bureau.

"Everything for the external communities goes through her. That's an order not a request. If someone is found to have leaked any information to the media, and I mean anyone in this or any other office, at any level, they will be summarily dismissed…fired on the spot with no severance benefits. Is that clear?

"The details about how Section Chief Wilkins died were unclear as of ten minutes ago. It seems that she was bludgeoned to death. The officers on the scene found a brass candelabrum resting on the floor near her head. It was covered with blood. The apparent murder weapon is being processed for DNA and fingerprints. Now here it gets quite dicey. This information is for this room only. Barbara's head was caved in so deeply that her eyes were found outside of their sockets. She was found on the floor naked, except for long black leather gloves and a black leather corset. Her breasts suffered several shallow cuts and she had what appear to be cigarettes burns on her buttocks. All of this appears to be an indication of aggressive sado-masochistic activities. Given these facts, the police are checking out the bars that cater to the rough trade. This step of the process may take a few days. It's their primary investigative avenue at this time.

"The murder was vicious and crime scene ugly. But if we lose control of the facts, and the information gets to the media before we can temper it, slant it to a gruesome murder and away from any deviant lifestyle, the entire event and the Bureau's connection will become ugly in the eyes of the public and the Senate Oversight Committee. As of now, the position of this office and the Bureau will be that Barbara Wilkins, a section chief, slipped getting out of the shower and hit her head on the sink's countertop. The blow stunned her but did not kill her. She staggered to the living room of her home to find her phone and call 911. The pain overcame her. She started screaming, lost consciousness, and collapsed. She bled out on the floor. We will stick with this story until the local police determine the acceptable truth that we can relate to the public. Is all that clear?"

"Yes, sir." Spoken in unison like good soldiers.

"To reiterate, we're to cooperate with the police, if and when they ask for our assistance, keep our mouths shut and our

56

heads down, and refer all external inquiries to Emily Knapp in D.C. I'll now take questions."

No one wants to get any deeper into the subject. They'll just follow the marching orders.

"David?"

"What do we...or I tell my team?"

"As little as possible. Tell them no more than I just told you. She slipped and hit her head as she fell. She bled out. Tell them that work must go on. Tell them to refer any inquiries to you so that you can refer them to Emily Knapp. Advise them of the importance of silence. And also tell them that you will be the acting section chief. To all in this room, David will be the Section Chief of Interagency Communications until we can determine a suitable long-term replacement for Barbara. I anticipate that process to take months. Until then we have a very capable acting section chief."

"Thank you, sir."

"I will make a general announcement Monday morning. As I learn more, so will you. Again, thanks for coming in so quickly. I remind you that we can ill afford to have this personal tragedy, with all its twisted social overtones, reflect on the Bureau and this office. So, do your jobs and let me and the other directors do theirs. Good night...er, that's good morning."

* * *

"Sweetie, what happened? You look like crap."

"Thanks for the kind words. The death of one of our own creates great stress among those close to the dead. That's me and my team. That's why I look like crap. Barbara Wilkins died an ugly and unfortunate death. The initial indications are that as she was getting out of the shower, she slipped and fell, hitting her head on a bathroom counter edge. This did not knock her out. But she must have been woozy and numb from the impact. She had the strength to stagger into the living room in an attempt to reach her phone. As the numbness of the blow wore off and severe pain took over, she started crying loudly and collapsed before she could dial 911. She bled out where she fell. The crying aroused her neighbors who called 911. The officers had to break into her townhome. They found her in a pool of her own blood." David marches to the Bureau's drummer.

"Good God, that's horrible. I hope she didn't suffer much."

"More than likely she suffered severely, but for only a few seconds, until she lapsed into a coma as she bled out. The local police have opened an investigation. It's in their hands now."

"What does this mean for you and your team? I have to believe the higher ups already have a game plan."

"Business as usual for us. I have been named 'Acting Section Chief' until they find a suitable replacement for Barbara. They will have to be thorough because the Interagency Communications Section is under the watchful eye of the Senate. Jack Strathmore will reach out to all the directors to create a talent pool. This will take time. In the meantime, I have been entrusted with the authority and responsibility because of my experience and knowledge of the section's operations. Now you know all that I know. Sorry, if all that sounds like company speak. I'd like to change the subject for now. I need to process all that happened and all that is about to happen. Next week will be very different at the Bureau."

"Sure, sweetie. Let's have breakfast and relax with the paper."

"What's for breakfast?"

"Morning comfort food for my man: ham, eggs, biscuits and gravy, grapefruit juice, sweet rolls, and coffee."

"So that's what was in the bag you brought."

"You just read the paper outside on the patio. The air outside is cool and clean. Little or no pollen. The season has not yet started. I'll bring you breakfast when I have created it. Now, scoot."

David opens the paper to the Police Blotter in the Metro Section. There is a three-sentence blurb about an unidentified woman found in her townhome. She died from a skull fracture. The residence is in Pine View Estates. A small, but dangerous thread of information for any diligent investigative reporter has been provided. There will be a call from this reporter once he or she tracks down the name of the victim and more details are made available from the police. Next week will be the first opportunity to tell the story that isn't. That's Emily Knapp's job, not David's. The cover-up is in full swing.

* * *

The Monday briefing meeting was different than all previous ones. There were no personal questions, tears, or even faux shock. David detected a hint of relief.

"What do we do now?"

"Work as usual. I'll function as the interim section chief until the big boys find a replacement for Barbara. You will be required to keep the information machine running at top speed. Dig into every matter, as I know you can. I encourage you to question everything. I want your best work. I want your best judgment. This is your time to shine and garner the credit. I won't look over your shoulders. If we disagree, convince me. If you can't convince me, I will make the call. Now, I want you to get back to your sources at the other field offices and gather more information. The issues we reported recently are ongoing and evolving. I want us to stay ahead of them before they evolve into messy and uncontrollable situations."

"Will you be moving into Barbara's office?"

"No, Margaret, I am comfortable in my cave. Besides, I will be retiring soon, and an office move would just be a waste of time. But occasionally, I will sit in her office and review files that must stay there. Excuse me, I'd better take this. It's Assistant Director Wilson."

He waits to speak until his troops have left his office. "Yes, Assistant Director, how can I help you?"

"I just got off the phone with Director Strathmore. It seems that Barbara has no next of kin anywhere in the country. She has worked in this office for her entire career, so there is no trail outside our system. We hired her out of Northwestern. She got to Northwestern from a private school that gives educational breaks to foster children. The foster parents can't be found. There is no record of any blood family. The emergency contact telephone number she entered in the HR system is a disconnected number. Jack had somebody look up the address of this person and found the address on the form to be an abandoned warehouse. She was truly off the grid. She was a chimera. So, it is up to us, you and me, to identify the body and sign the requisite forms. I have a copy of her badge ID for use at the coroner's office. We leave in twenty. Meet me in the parking garage, level three, aisle A, space 321. See you then and there. Oh, yes, better tell your team that you will be out of the office until after lunch. We don't want them to think they lost two section chiefs in two days."

David thinks that's strange. The trip to the coroner's office and identification of the body should take no more than two hours. They should be back well before lunch. Why the extra time? Assistant Director Wilson drives an Audi R8. Wilson knows everyone knows how expensive the coupe is, but as he explains it… "This is my one extravagance in life because life is too short not to have one extravagance." They arrive at the coroner's office in twenty minutes. It was supposed to be a thirty-five-minute trip. Wilson's high testosterone level, a six-speed transmission, and risky driving bordering on psychotic, shortened the time. David is too concerned about Wilson's driving for office talk or social chitchat. The identification takes fifteen minutes and then they're back in the car.

"David, Jack and I want you to know that we are aware of the great job you have been doing these past few years under extremely trying circumstances. We appreciate your productivity and your attitude of cooperation. We decided to say thank you in a special way. Effective immediately, and retroactive to all of last year, you will be bumped two pay grades to the level of a senior section chief. You'll receive all the back pay from the beginning of last year in a separate deposit within two weeks."

David asks himself...*What the hell is that all about?*

"I don't know what to say, except thank you."

"We thought a little extra income might get you ready for your retirement to Eleuthera."

"It will certainly help. I really appreciate it. Now, I have a question."

"Shoot."

"Where are we going if not back to the office?"

"Next stop is 1456 Meadow Brook Lane in Pine View Estates. We are going on a hunting expedition. I'll explain when we arrive. Now, tell me about your island paradise."

As David pours out his dream, he can't help but wonder about the big raise and what Fletcher hoped to find at Barbara Wilkins' home. Why the gift? Why the hunt? How will they gain entry to a crime scene under the control of the Kansas City Police? The trip seems to be over before he can describe all the details of his soon-to-be home on Eleuthera. Wilson's federal bumper sticker wards off police who think about ticketing a speeder.

There is a large bright orange paper patch connecting the front door and door frame...*Crime Scene. Do Not Enter.* Entry requires cutting the patch and thus violating the integrity of the crime scene. Wilson cuts the patch with his pen knife and peels away the two pieces. Mysteriously, he has a key to the house.

They enter. The living and dining rooms are orderly and tidy, except for the blood stain on the carpet.

"OK, we're in. Now, what are we looking for?"

"We are here to prove or disprove the ugly rumors about Barbara's sexual escapades with members of the Bureau. We are here to determine if there is a camera hidden somewhere in the bedroom and if Barbara retained any record of her alleged sexual romps. Simple and direct. Now, let's start digging."

David now realizes that the unheard-of pay increase is meant to buy his silence as the Bureau attempts to sanitize its dirty laundry outside of public scrutiny. They gingerly walk around the large dark brown stain on the living room carpet and the crude outline where Barbara's contorted body laid. They go to the orderly bedroom. While Fletcher starts looking through drawers and lifting furniture, David enters the walk-in closet to the right of the bed. An obvious place for a hidden camera. There he spots a small step stool she must have used to get to items on the top shelf. He turns to the wall common to the closet and bedroom and sees a single short shelf about a foot below the ceiling. Using the step stool, he climbs and examines the shelf. It is dusty due to lack of attention, but there is a faint outline of an object that once was on the shelf but has since been removed. On the wall in front of the outline, he sees light from the bedroom coming through a hole the size of a dime. He can't see on what the hole is focused so he inserts a ballpoint pen.

"Fletcher, look at the wall to the right of the bed. Near the entrance to the closet. Up near the ceiling. See my pen protruding from a small hole. I found a shelf beneath the hole and the vague outline on the shelf of what could have been a camera. She could have recorded what was happening on the bed very easily from that vantage point. Her process would have been simple. She gets whomever she is with all hot and bothered, excuses herself to get into the appropriate garb, steps into the closet, turns on the camera, and records her performance for posterity."

"Great work, David. I'll bet she transferred her activities onto discs and replayed them on the DVD player next to the TV at the foot of her bed. We're on to something. Now, we have to find the camera and the discs. You stay in the closet, and I'll go back over the bedroom more closely now that we know what we are looking for."

David searches behind the dresses, skirts, blouses, and suits. The clothes stretch the entire length of the closet: Over twenty linear feet of clothes. Clothes for every occasion and every season. Most likely, she bought new clothes each season saving only a few items from year to year. She was a clotheshorse. David was aware his boss had a figure that called out for tailored clothes. The number and diversity of items reminds him of the countless items his former wife required. They hung in two walk-ins. His closet was a small one near the bathroom. An uncomfortable memory. He pokes around on the two shelves above the hanging clothes. Bags and small boxes containing jewelry and scarves. The thirty or so shoeboxes on the floor provide a bizarre treasure trove. Sex toys of different types and sizes for different genders. Several looked like they required batteries to be functional. There were various rubber masks, two riding crops, a nylon cat-o'-nine-tails, a ball attached to a strap for a mouth and head gag and restraint, numerous vibrators, various lengths of nylon rope, three bottles and two tubes of ointments, and a spy cam but no discs.

"Fletcher, you're not going to believe what I found. Come in here and look."

"Jaysus! It looks like the accoutrements of an S and M dungeon. She was a sicko for sure. No doubt about it. We need to take the SIM card out of the camcorder. Any discs?

"No discs. How about you? I'll remove the SIM card and put everything else back where I found it. It will look as if no one was ever here violating the integrity of a crime scene and rummaging around for socially damaging evidence of the deceased's sexual proclivities."

"Easy, David. We are seeking to protect Barbara's name, as well as the image of the Bureau. Besides, whatever we find is most likely not be germane to Barbara's homicide. Whatever we find would be just dark facts that need not come into the light of inspection by a hysterical, misguided public."

"If you say so."

"I say so."

The brusque exchange and subtle threat confirm David's suspicion about the goal of this digging exercise and the hefty raise. This triggers anxiety about his involvement. He has been bribed to be is a good soldier and follow orders, or he will suffer the implied consequences. He follows orders.

"Did you find anything in the chests of drawers?"

"I came up empty. I need to re-check the bedside nightstands."

David goes about returning items to their rightful place to disguise the intrusion.

"Bingo! David, I found a bunch of discs hidden under a false bottom of the second drawer of a nightstand. She kept them nearby, so she could relive her adventures and use her sex toys when she was alone at night. The DVD player and 40-inch TV screen were there for a reason and it wasn't to watch MSNBC. Come here and tell me what you make of the markings on them."

They both stare at the numerical markings on the discs.

"Sorry Fletcher, the numbers mean nothing to me. Maybe when the discs are viewed, the codes will become clear. How many discs are there?"

"Twelve. Hopefully, that's all. I'll search some more while you straighten up the closet. We don't want some nosey detective stumbling onto crime scene that looks altered."

Back on the floor of the closet, David flashes on the numeric codes: 10, 19, 5, 17, 15 and 6, 23, 12, 12, 14 were the two he could recall. He approaches the code deciphering considering Occam's Razor: the simplest answer to a problem or puzzle is most likely the right one. He views the numerical code in the context of the alphabet. David guesses the first disc contains the images of Jack Strathmore because J is the tenth letter of the alphabet and S is the nineteenth. He guesses that the second disc contains the images of Fletcher Wilson because F is the sixth letter and W is the twenty-third. He surmises that the last set of digits of each code do not represent letters. They could be dates that the discs were created: May 17, 2015 and December 12, 2014.

The dates of two sexual adventures. Those bastards! They gave David a big raise before he began digging into their sordid past because they wanted him included in their effort to hide evidence. They're counting on him to go along with their devious plan to protect his job, newfound increased income, and pension. Hush money and a threat behind the bribe. Carrot and stick. In their warped minds, they must have thought the cover-up would not really hurt anyone, and a whitewash would help everyone. From David's point of view, a cover-up would destroy his integrity and that's everything. Being a good soldier is one thing. Blindly following illegal and immoral orders is another. Several Nazis at the war tribunals tried this approach and it didn't save them. David's emotional state is racing from angry to anxious to panicky. He must put a damper on this strong emotional evolution, lest Wilson and Strathmore take actions against him. But how can he put a damper on the truth?

As he is returning the items on the floor, he discovers a laptop computer tucked behind two of the larger boxes. He turns on the computer and opens it to a file entitled, 'Fun.' Within 'Fun,' there are what appear to be copies of the twelve files. Are these copies of the individual discs Fletcher uncovered? He checks the dates. Yes! She kept a back-up. Good FBI training. Not password protecting the computer shows her arrogance. Wilson will want this, and he will get it. David picks up the laptop and feels a small envelope taped to the bottom. Inside the envelope is a flash drive. He inserts it and, on the screen, pops a duplicate of the 'Fun' file. This version of the file contains the same files with codes as in the computer. There are files that start ten-nineteen and six-twenty-three. If he knew about the flash drive, Wilson would want it, but he will not know about it, and therefore, he won't get it. David wants leverage in this dangerous game he is now playing. He's just not sure how he will use leverage.

"Are you done with your housekeeping? We'd better be going."

"All done. I found this laptop. You may want to have our techies look at it. It may contain more damning evidence."

"Not a good choice of words, David."

Fletcher retrieves a second police crime scene patch from his jacket and applies it over the space of the original. How did he get a police patch? Are they involved?

The drive back to the office is icily quiet.

* * *

Midnight in the oil-rich fields of the Middle East right after the guard change. There is no moon, so the sky is absolutely black, except for the sparkle of stars. It looks like a dancehall ceiling. Then, the explosion. Sergeant Daniel Fulker was disintegrated by the explosion. Pieces of the small truck, which carried the mass of explosives, were found forty meters away. Shreds of one tire and a piston. Shards of the side mirror and a twisted ignition switch. The blast lifted the side wall of the embassy compound about six inches off its foundation, bowed it in toward the buildings, and turned the concrete reinforcing rebar into lace. The lattice encrusted with chunks of concrete fell into the courtyard. No one saw the three running figures dressed entirely in black from head to calf. They wore tan combat boots and carried RPGs. They were kneeling in the wall's maw before the dust settled. The three blasts thrust one highly explosive and two incendiary shells into another wall. This time it was a building

66

that housed the soldiers and a few administrators. The collapsing walls and fire claimed forty-eight of America's best and brightest.

Some of them wanted to be in the Middle East: in Chadar. Chadar is a strategic military point to the north of Basjar, home of the bully of the world, el Jahdiq...savior of the downtrodden masses and leader in the campaign to carve out his own caliphate. All of the American soldiers were proud to serve. They knew there would be some tense times with the threat of real danger. No one, from top to bottom, was vaguely prescient of this event.

* * *

Precisely ninety seconds later, a small, smoke belching pick-up truck pulled up to the gates at the military barracks adjacent to the United States Embassy in Riatta, the seaport capital of Qratri. Riatta ships about one fourth of the area's oil to the U.S. for refining. Oil from pumping stations of several countries. One guard at the gate leaves the booth for a bathroom break and the other stays in air-conditioned comfort to call the Officer of the Watch. Before the guard reaches the OW, the rusted bucket of smoke blowing inefficiency arrives and the driver is off and running. The immediate explosion catches him about twenty-five meters from ground zero and throws him, ablaze, another thirty meters onto a large truck parked across the boulevard. The guard in the booth vanishes in the fireball. The booth disappears in the fireball. The gate disappears in the fireball.

Alarms sound and pandemonium reigns. From the back of the truck rush five bodies dressed in black from head to calf. They wore tan combat boots. They kneel beside the truck and fire their grenade launchers. All the projectiles strike the first-floor front. The wall, weakened by the shock wave of the first blast, slides to the ground like mud down a hill. The entire face of the three-story building has gone away, revealing twisted pipes and air-conditioning ducts. The four-sided rooms are now three-sided open boxes. The furniture, drapes, and bed linens are on fire. Smoke encases the entire building. Five bodies scurry, like rats, back into the truck as it pulls out and heads south. The alarms blare and orders are barked from top to bottom. Perimeter secured. Full battle alert. Just sixty seconds too late. The digging will commence shortly. Sixty-three dead.

* * *

Approximately six hundred kilometers to the east, over some of the fiercest mountains and most barren desert the world, is another time zone. At nearly midnight, real time, a small pick-up truck bumps and weaves its way through the undersized streets of Najret. Najret is a city state that controls the oil within a two-hundred-kilometer radius. What is pumped from Najret is exported from Riatta. Food, clothing, medicines, and all manner of necessities for this landlocked center of wealth come through Riatta back to Najret. The relationship between the two governments is one of extensive dependence, and it can be contentious. Their faith in Allah and hatred for the western world are the bonds that hold them together.

The truck is stopped at the crest of a hill on the partially paved road that leads directly to the American Embassy and military barracks. Two men exit the truck and make ready a bomb. One activates the detonator. He leaves hurriedly, and the driver reenters the cab. The wheel is lashed right and left to keep the truck on target. A crudely crafted piece of metal is wedged under the old accelerator to keep the engine roaring. The onslaught begins. About one hundred meters from the gate, the pick-up's driver leaps from the cab. The truck hurtles on toward its appointed target. The crash and blast are simultaneous. In the dark night, the fireball can be seen for several kilometers. For those in the know, it is not an oil storage tank explosion. The blaze, smoke, and flying debris are perfect cover for the second vehicle: An old army truck grinds its way to the much-enlarged gate opening and pauses. The tarpaulin on the building side of the truck is raised and six bodies become visible. They are dressed in black from head to calf. They wear tan combat boots.

Their firepower is unleashed on the interior building. Six RPG launchers. Three rounds each. What was a wall is now rubble. What was behind the wall is now more rubble. In less than three minutes, the tarp is lowered, and the truck stumbles off into the flame-lit night. One hundred and thirty-seven are lost under the aggregate of concrete, rebar, furniture, and metal doors. The U.S. Army may never find all the bodies, just lots of parts.

* * *

The scenes are replayed by CNN, CBS, NBC, Fox, and ABC as networks are picking up feeds from international crews. Those brave enough and given permission by local tribes and regional armies to cover this part of the world, are at each mini war zone. The scenes play over and over as if on a loop. The reporters speak in broken English. Hand-held cams bob and weave through the soldiers and wreckage. The night has been darkened further by the smoke and ash in the air. The cameras can offer only tight perspective. High-intensity lamps on the cameras are not sufficient to light a width of more than ten or twelve meters. No panoramic shots of the destruction are available because there are no klieg lights. The pictures shift from one devastation to another to another. Is one carnage worse than another? They all look alike. They were meant to.

The two-star commanders of each fortress are saying nothing. The top General for this Middle East theater of operations is saying nothing. The Pentagon is saying nothing. The White House has scheduled a briefing for eight am Washington time. The visuals replay and the words are repeated. After an hour, the shock has begun to wear off and the pain diminished. How many times can the audiences at home hear about and see the butchery before they stop caring? Do they ever stop caring? The body count rises with the sun. Soldiers and medics scamper about in the background. Officers are directing heavy equipment to lift pieces of the structures from the bodies. Faint calls for the medics can be heard in the background. The outcome is predetermined, but the medics must try nonetheless.

* * *

Ladies and gentlemen: The President of the United States.

My fellow Americans, within the past twenty-four hours, three of our embassies in the Middle East have been attacked and many embassy officials and military personnel attached to the embassies have been killed. As of this time, we do not have irrefutable proof of the perpetrators of these heinous crimes. We have asked our friends and partners in the region to assist us with information gathering so that the criminals can be brought to justice. We have sent additional military personnel to the region to protect those Americans still there. We have opened up back channels of diplomatic access to secure the names and locations of the responsible parties. We have placed all embassies in Europe, Africa, and Asia on high alert and are posting additional military personnel to those embassies. Rest assured, your government is doing everything possible to find the attackers and to bring them to justice before a legitimately appointed court. We are working with all dispatch and will have updates for you as we learn more. In the meantime, our thoughts and prayers go out to the families of those men and women killed in the attacks. I will not take questions at this time. God bless the U.S.A. Thank you.

The news is chilling to everyone throughout the country and particularly in the law enforcement agencies. David wonders…What's next? That question is answered at the noon hour via a network TV interview with Barry Nelson, the former governor of Texas. This strident neocon has been a consistent adversary of the administration and a leader of a growing group of ill-informed people seeking to blame the President for every ill that befalls the nation and its people. During his time in Austin, and afterward as a private citizen, he has railed against the federal government's general energy, economic, and foreign policies. Many of his recent attacks have been against the President and not the amorphous federal government. His public tirades are more ad hominem than de facto. He never met a fact he couldn't misquote or ignore if it didn't fit his agenda.

I am appalled at the weak-kneed reaction of the President. The desert thugs just slaughtered more than five hundred American citizens on soil that is as much American as if it were in downtown New York. Yet, all he does is wring his hands and talk about diplomatic and legal solutions. I say, we treat this event for what it is...an attack on America. I say we approach these heinous crimes as the good book says... 'an eye for an eye.' I say the thugs have just declared war on the United States, and we should respond with force so great they will never think of trying something like this again...if they are even alive after our justified response. Our embassies were in the region with the agreement of the appropriate governments. Their space was protected by treaty. Yet these same governments allow their lands to be the home of camps from which these criminals attack the U.S.A. I say, we don't go through diplomatic channels or back channels. I say, we tell the governments of the region to give us access to these camps, so they can be destroyed. I say, that if the governments balk at our demands, we replace those who are complicit with the thugs, with those who will be our friends. I say, it's time that we get tough. Thank you.

Is he standing on his usual blame game soapbox or is he really calling for war?

V

"David Drummer."

"Mr. Drummer, this is Wendell Peterson of the *Star*. I just got off the phone with your boss. He told me you were the go-to guy if I needed some background information on the murder of Barbara Wilkins. Now, I have just a few simple questions. Some points that need clarification before I write the piece for the *Star*'s many readers."

"Mr. Peterson, you spoke to Charles Brown and he told you to contact me. Is that correct? Have you spoken to the police?"

"Yes, sir. I have spoken to Charles Brown and the police. The police said that the FBI was cooperating in the investigation. I wanted to be sure of the facts about Ms. Wilkins they gave me. I just got off the phone with Mr. Brown. He said you would be glad to help me with information."

"Well, Mr. Peterson or whoever you really are, my supervisor is not named Charles Brown. In fact, there is no one in this office named Charles Brown. So, you must be sadly mistaken. I applaud your motive for information gathering but not your tactics. That said, since the Bureau strives to cooperate with the media, I will give you the name and telephone number of someone who will be able to supply you all the information you and your many readers deserve. Have a pen handy? Her name is Emily Knapp. She's in Washington, and her telephone number is 202-555-5555. With that, I bid you good-bye."

David has just fed raw meat to the tigress. He hopes she will dispatch this reporter to the nether region quickly. Back to the emails. After a numbing hour, another call interrupts his non-productive work.

"David, can you come to Jack's office?"

He recognizes Fletcher's voice and the urgency in it. No need to respond. Just hang up and go up. During the brief elevator ride, David wonders about the SIM card from the camcorder, the discs, and the computer. Where are they now? Who has control of them? So long as David has the flash drive and its contents, he has some measure of protection of his life for the next few months. Protection against any backlash from the cover-up. The elevator doors open, and he stares down the long hall. All the office doors on the right and left of the hall are closed. Secrecy. Executive Administrative Assistants are sentries to the closed doors and the secrets behind them. As he approaches Director Strathmore's door, his path is verbally interrupted.

"May I help you?" Her tone is condescending...almost threatening.

"I'm David Drummer. I have an appointment with Director Strathmore."

The icy woman does not look at David. She scans her computer screen in an attempt to confirm his statement. "I don't see..."

Suddenly one of the double doors opens and Fletcher Wilson's smiling face pops out. "David, good of you to come so quickly. Come in. Jack and I are about to start a meeting that will impact you and your team. Jack, David's here. We can start."

As he is ushered into the realm of the holy one, David turns to the icy woman and gives her his best plastic, all-tooth smile. A smile that clearly says *fuck you, bitch*. He feels more rambunctious as he nears retirement and has the flash drive.

"David, great to see you again. We're about to start a teleconference with Emily Knapp, and we think you should hear what she has to say. Emily, I have David Drummer and Fletcher Wilson in my office. We're ready on this end. Are you ready?"

"Yes, director. Good morning, gentlemen. This morning, I learned three things. One, Commander Anderson advised me that there have been some developments that shed new light on the murder. Overnight, the police arrested Fatima Johansson. Her fingerprints were a match to those on the candelabrum. She was in the system. She's being held as a material witness. They can hold her for forty-eight hours before they have to charge her with the murder. Normally the waiting time gives the detained time to contemplate the consequences of their actions. This produces cooperation giving the police guidance as they move up the food chain. Although not under arrest, she requested a lawyer. A public defender, named Louisa Cochran, visited Ms. Johansson. I'll have a reading on Ms. Cochran in an hour. Before she goes public with her client's side of the story, the Bureau must get in front of the event. That's my job.

"Two, there were traces of alcohol, cocaine, and ecstasy in Section Chief Wilkins' blood. This is not good. I'll have to tap dance around this unfortunate set of facts. It just makes my job a bit more challenging. Three, the local press has started to poke around the mess. I just got off the phone with some rube named Peterson, who claimed to be from the *Star*. He asked a lot of inane questions that I deflected. I think I temporarily closed him down. Anderson advised me that he can no longer keep an airtight lid on the crime. Gentlemen, the game is afoot.

"We have to paint a clear and favorable picture of this tragic event. Favorable to the Bureau. Regardless of who Wilkins was, or what she did in her personal life, she is a murder victim. Let me repeat that…murder victim. That will be the focus of our position. We have to make sure the Bureau is shocked that an individual with a criminal record for prostitution, drug distribution, and armed robbery…the female criminal trifecta…would brazenly attack and kill one of the Bureau's rising stars."

"Sounds good to me, Emily. What do you want us to do?"

"I just booked one of the jets to Kansas City. I leave in two hours. I'll prepare all necessary verbiage and appropriate actions for you and Fletcher before I arrive. We can discuss these

74

when I'm in your office later today. In the meantime, I'll make some calls to the media to set up a press conference for tomorrow at eight am. I assume that will be okay with you. Director, could you get someone to set up a temporary stage and have the sound system functional?"

"Sounds like you have a solid game plan. I'll take care of the setting for the press conference and order food, so we can have a working dinner when you arrive. Fletcher and I look forward to seeing you. I'll have a car at the airport. Where will you be spending the night?"

"Director, please be sure Commander Anderson is at the working dinner. The locals and the Bureau must speak with one voice, or at least look like that. I made reservations at the airport Marriott. See you in about five hours. Good-bye."

The screen goes black before Jack can respond.

"David, as you can see the situation is in good hands. You needn't worry about anything. Just go about your business, keeping everyone in the field and the other agencies informed of the critical information your team acquires. I'm sure there's plenty to tell the other agencies that's more important than this mess. So, there is no need for you to stay late or plan to come back for our working dinner. Most likely, Emily will want me to stand beside her tomorrow morning. That's about it. Thanks for coming."

Summoned and dismissed in less than ten minutes, an obvious show of power over David's life and livelihood. They jerked him like a hooked fish on a line. They think they can do that because they think they own him. Disconcerting to say the least. Given that he has the flash drive, their actions are stupid, but they don't know it, and he won't tell them. On the elevator ride downstairs, David feels a substantial tightening of his stomach. His mouth is dry. Back to work.

* * *

"Robert, come in."

"David, I have uncovered something that needs further explanation. I was going over a communication from the CDC in Atlanta. They report two recent cases of rabies: One in Buffalo and one in San Diego. Both individuals died in police shootouts. So, the cause of both deaths is presently listed as gunshots. However, when the CDC reviewed the findings of the local coroners and the tissue samples in both cases, they determined that the brains of each individual were so decomposed from the rabies virus that death was imminent without the gunshots. The really bizarre part is the local coroners reported no animal bite marks on the bodies. So, the CDC is at a loss to explain how the rabies virus infected the two. The report from the CDC reads like it came from a textbook. They don't condemn the coroners' reports, but they are at a loss to explain the rabies. The technical part is dry, as you would expect. Take a look."

Rabies may spread through exposure to infected domestic farm animals, groundhogs, weasels, bears, raccoons, and other wild carnivores. Small rodents, such as squirrels, hamsters, guinea pigs, gerbils, chipmunks, rats, mice, and lagomorphs, such as rabbits and hares, are almost never found to be infected with rabies and are not known to transmit rabies to humans. The Virginia opossum is resistant but not immune to rabies.

Transmission between humans is extremely rare. A few cases have been recorded through transplant surgery. After a typical human infection by bite, the virus enters the peripheral nervous system. It then travels along the afferent nerves toward the central nervous system. During this phase, the virus cannot be easily detected within the host, and vaccination may still confer cell-mediated immunity to prevent symptomatic rabies. When the virus reaches the brain, it rapidly causes encephalitis, the prodromal phase, and is the beginning of the symptoms. Once the patient becomes symptomatic, treatment is almost never effective, and mortality is over 99%.

Rabies can be difficult to diagnose, because, in the early stages, it is easily confused with other diseases or with aggressiveness. The diagnosis can be made from saliva, urine, and cerebrospinal fluid samples, but this is not as sensitive and reliable as brain samples. Cerebral inclusion bodies called Negri bodies are 100% diagnostic for rabies infection. If possible, the animal from which the bite was received should also be examined for rabies.

"The disease normally takes time to kill...sometimes a month. During the two weeks up to death, the symptoms are obvious. But as far as the police were able to determine, there were no physical symptoms of the disease the week before each shooting. The fact that these similar cases were discovered three thousand miles apart further muddies the water. This is too strange. If you agree, I'll do more digging."

"Yes, please get to the bottom of this anomaly. Contact the CDC, the police departments in Buffalo and San Diego, and the corresponding coroners. Tell them that they should dig deeper. But before you do that, gather your compatriots and come to my office. I want to tell you all something."

Is Robert chasing a chimera? Is he trying to show his diligence and suitability for promotion? David checks his voicemail. Two angry messages from Peterson of the *Star* and one inquiry from a Ms. Beckerman at Channel 8 News. They'll have to wait for the press conference. His team enters.

"Please close the door. What I'm about to tell must be kept secret until tomorrow morning when the world will know what you are about to learn. Barbara Wilkins did not die from a slip in the bathroom. She was attacked by a woman, Fatima Johansson, who is being held by the local police. Barbara did bleed out but the blow that opened her skull came from behind.

Why Fatima killed her, we don't know. Fatima Johansson has an extensive criminal record that includes a great deal of violence. Tomorrow morning Emily Knapp, Deputy Director of Community Communications, will hold a press conference in front of our offices during which she will explain Barbara's death from the Bureau's perspective. It was murder, plain and simple. She will stress that regardless of Barbara's personal life, she was murdered. All of the focus and conversation must be on the event and not the why. I urge you all to listen to what Emily Knapp has to say, particularly how she handles the media. You should watch how she deals with the pressure of the questions and be prepared to answer any questions from your peers in field offices. Be prepared to answer those questions the way Emily answers the questions that come to her. But, if you receive questions from outside the Bureau, refer the individual to me so that I can refer them to Ms. Knapp. Thanks for your work and have a good night."

He gave them the top line information in the hope that Emily's press conference will fill in the blank spots. Now, home and Rachel.

* * *

"Rachel, wanna come over for a cookout?"

"Tonight? Kinda jammed at the office. I have three nervous clients whose accounts are not growing as fast as they hoped. Can we make it tomorrow?"

"I have two ears of corn, two baking potatoes, a two-pound, two-inch thick T-bone, and a six-pack of ice cold Yuengling. Waddaya say?"

"I'm surprised you bought so much food before inviting me."

"Actually, you were not my first choice, but the three different women at the Adult Congregate Living Facility, over on Rosewood, were so excited about the dinner that the facility was

78

serving tonight...hamburgers, mashed potatoes, and succotash, topped off by lime Jell-O for dessert that they turned me down. That meal is perfect for their dentures in their ninety-year-old jaws. They were afraid my corn on the cob and steak would be too difficult to chew."

"Gawd, you're terrible. Don't forget, you'll be there sooner than you want to be and much sooner than I will be."

"No, I will never be that way. I'll be with the love of my life, whoever she is, on an island in the Caribbean. She will chew my food for me and spit it on my plate like a mother bird, and I will eat the pre-chewed food like a baby in the nest."

"That is disgusting. Let me alter the trajectory of this conversation. Are you OK?"

"I'm fine. I just really, really want to see you."

"Fine, my ass. I can hear something in your voice. OK, to save you from yourself, I'll let you cook for me and feed me."

"Thanks."

"See you in an hour, plus or minus."

Why is it when men say *fine*, it does not have the same implied threat as when spoken by a woman? Is there a double standard in communication? While the grill is slowly heating, David retrieves the flash drive and inserts it into his laptop. He scans the 'Fun' file for the video that contains the images of Jack. Scanning the numerous video files, he wonders why a woman with Barbara's intelligence would use such a childish numerical code to designate the material on each disc. He opens Jack Strathmore's video. There, in all his naked splendor, is the Director of the Kansas City Office of the Federal Bureau of Investigation. With a little hand and mouth coaxing from Barbara, the games begin. Apparently, Jack likes to be spanked with a special paddle and gently whipped. He enjoys anal probes and licking her boots and kissing her anus. Too much ugly information. David abruptly closes the file.

He finds and opens the Fletcher Wilson video file. Fletcher likes to be bound, wrist to ankle, and whipped aggressively with the cat-o'-nine-tails while bent over. The whip strikes his buttocks and his delicate man parts. Barbara unties him, yanks him over to the bed, tosses him on his back, ties him to the bedposts, and rides him. She slaps his face and pinches the flesh on his chest and arms as if he had been bad. Again, TMI. These videos would end the careers of each male lead. Careers that would end in disgrace and the loss of accrued benefits, as well as the loss of wives in very messy, costly divorces. Playtime can be very expensive. Saved by the bell, David closes down the peep show of discomfort.

"I'm here to be fed."

"Rachel, we have to talk."

"No one ever likes to hear that."

"Let me rephrase that statement. I have to tell you some things."

"If it's about the three old ladies at the home, I forgive you."

"No. This is serious."

"Is it about us? Do you want to back out?"

"No, damn it. Let me finish. It's about work. I want to tell you something that's going on at the Bureau."

"Sorry for being sassy. You know you can tell me anything."

"Yes, I know. Here's the weird, good news. I was told today that as the interim section chief, I'll be getting a raise. Not the normal raise, but I am being bumped two pay grades. That's a big bump. A lot even for the remainder of my time at the Bureau. And here is the weirder, good news. My raise is effective from the beginning of last year to the present. That's really a ton of extra money. A single substantial deposit will be made into my bank account in less than a month. Fletcher told me it was for all my great work under very trying circumstances. The big bump will help as we get settled in our island paradise. But, and here is the big but, I am afraid that the money is hush money, or a bribe, if you like. A bribe for me to keep quiet."

"Congratulations. A bribe? Quiet about what?"

"I'll explain. Here is the weird, bad news…"

For the next thirty minutes, David tells Rachel as much as he knows about the videos and how they were acquired and his fear about what is transpiring at the Bureau. His words spew forth like water from a broken main. His sentences seem to run on without punctuation. And often without him taking a breath. The volume of his voice steadily increases. It is never modulated. He started the monologue as a baritone and finishes as a tenor. Almost screaming. She is silent, stunned by the accusations and innuendos, as well as frightened by the disquieting performance of his rant. When he is finished he is quiet but trembling. Exhausted, his shoulders are slumped, and his head is bowed.

"David, relax and breathe. Take ten deep breaths. Calm down. This whole mess has you very agitated. You need to be calm, so we can discuss it. You're sweating. Here, wipes your face with these napkins. Let me feel your pulse. Crap! Your heart rate is near one hundred and forty. You have to be careful to not stroke out on me. I'm not a nurse or doctor."

He smiles feebly as he mops the moisture manifestation of his anxiety. Rachel is quite concerned with his physical reaction to the telling of the situation. She rises above her fear as she gently touches his arm while she hands him a bottle of water. He takes a few swigs, then gulps half the contents. She lovingly holds his hand. In five minutes, his breathing is back to normal, but he is still pale. He looks lovingly at Rachel, the way he used to look to his mother for comfort. Rachel's words and gentle tone are soothing, just like his mother's were, years ago. Her touch affirms her caring for him and her concern about his present condition. She delicately initiates the next phase of the conversation: A simple Q and A session to get answers while avoiding a return of David to his distraught state.

"First question: Are you OK? Can you talk more about this mess?"

"I'm better than I was, and yes, I want to talk about it with you."

"Second question: Have you seen the alleged videos?"

"Yes, and they are disgusting. The actions of the parties involved are normally seen in very sleazy porn magazines and movies."

"Third question: Have you looked at any other files?"

"No, I have no idea who the other stars in Barbara's videos are."

"Fourth question: Do you have the flash drive?"

"Yes. It's in a safe place."

"Fifth question: Do you have any idea what this Emily Knapp will say at the news conference?"

"Not the details. She will attempt to focus everyone's attention on the fact that Barbara was murdered. I suspect she will do a good job of painting Ms. Johansson as pure evil, while generating sympathy for the admirable and highly respected civil servant, Barbara. She will aggressively distance the Bureau from Barbara's deviant lifestyle."

"Sixth question: Do you think Jack and Fletcher fear your knowledge of the illegal entry to Barbara's home, their hiding of evidence, their entanglement with Barbara, and the video files?"

"No. I don't know. I'm not sure. I'm confused. I think they think they bought my loyalty. I think they think I will keep my mouth shut about the hunting expedition and what Fletcher found. They don't know what I found and kept. They know I've committed major funds to the property in Eleuthera, and I need my pension benefits to live out my dream. They are banking on my need for money to force me to follow their marching orders and keep a lid on the illegal entry and retrieval of damning evidence. I think they think I will not reveal their cover-up of evidence about Barbara's lifestyle that would result in the two of them being summarily dismissed with no benefits and no wives. At least, I hope all of that is true."

"Seventh question: When will dinner be ready?"

"Shit! I was so tied up in knots that I forgot. I'll put the potatoes on now, the T-bone in thirty minutes and the corn on in twenty minutes."

"Eighth question: What do you want to do about the situation?"

"I'm not sure. I don't know. I'm so confused. There's a large part of me that feels I'm holding a live grenade that will explode if I release the spring handle. And I'm not sure I have the strength in my right hand to keep the handle squeezed. I need someone to grip my hand closed so that I'm safe...so that we're both safe. I am afraid that if I give Jack and Fletcher the impression that I'm not a real team player who will keep his mouth shut; they might summarily dismiss me. They are powerful, and they could and would do that for self-protection. I am afraid that they may think I would share information about the break-in and cover-up with you. Therefore, I am also concerned that you could be in jeopardy because they have no hold over you like they think they have over me. I think this is something we both must deal with to protect ourselves. The bottom line is I'm not sure of anything dealing with Jack and Fletcher. I don't know what they know or think. I cannot be sure what they will or won't do to protect their livelihoods. I'm optimistically speculating what I think they think."

"Ninth question: Do you know that I will do anything to support and protect you?"

"Yes. I'm counting on that."

"Final statement on the subject: I do not want to view the video files. I am afraid if I cast my eyes upon such craven sin, I will be turned into a pillar of salt. It happened before, ya know, to Lot's wife."

Sardonic hyperbole is an honest and caring way a lover can break the fierce grip of anxiety in a partner. They both smile. Rachel's smile is tempered by her concern about David's answers. They have a strange pattern. With each question, his response again became louder and its pitch higher. Similar to his verbal cascade during his explanation. She fears he is stressed to an unhealthy level, and the slightest probe could set him off.

"Dinner will be ready shortly. Let's not speak of this for a few days…after we've had a chance to digest it and develop fresh thoughts and a course of action."

* * *

"Ladies and gentlemen, thank you for coming here today. My name is Emily Knapp. I am the Deputy Director in Charge of Community Communications for the FBI. I've been asked to speak to you today about a tragic event that occurred in your city within the past week. The Section Chief of Interagency Communications was brutally and senselessly murdered in her home by a woman who has a long and sordid record of crime.

"Section Chief Barbara Wilkins was savagely beaten by one Fatima Johansson. Ms. Barbara Wilkins was a rising star in the Kansas City office of the FBI. Her career trajectory was outstanding, if not spectacular. Her future with the Bureau was bright. At the other end of the spectrum, Ms. Johansson has been arrested for prostitution, drug distribution, and armed robbery. I will now give you the details of the crime: Somehow these two women, of opposite moral characters met, most likely, at a restaurant. During their conversation, Ms. Johansson must have decided that because of Ms. Wilkins' good taste in clothing and her expensive jewelry, Ms. Wilkins would be a good target for robbery. Ms. Johansson then used her considerable street charm to

84

hustle an invitation to Ms. Wilkins' home. It is likely that when the two women were in Ms. Wilkins' home, an argument developed. Before Ms. Wilkins could force Ms. Johansson to leave, a scuffle started. Because of her street toughness, Ms. Johansson overpowered Ms. Wilkins and crushed her skull with a candelabrum.

"Police responding to a 911 call of verbal disturbance, discovered Ms. Wilkins body and the candelabrum...the murder weapon on the floor. Subsequently, the police arrested Ms. Johansson based on forensic evidence from the crime scene. The Kansas City, Missouri-Kansas Major Crimes Joint Task Force, under the capable leadership of Commander Anderson initiated the investigation. It is on-going. Ms. Johansson is presently being detained as a material witness. She will be formally charged today, and thereafter she will await arraignment and trial. Now, I'll take questions."

"Wendell Peterson of the *Star*. Ms. Knapp, if the investigation of Section Chief Wilkins' murder is being conducted by the police under Commander Anderson of the Kansas City, Missouri-Kansas Major Case Joint Task Force, why is a federal agency conducting the press conference? Are you trying to cover up something?"

"Thank you, Mr. Peterson. As you can see, Commander Anderson is standing alongside me. We at the FBI wish to cooperate fully with local police officials. Federal and local officials are in lockstep in this investigation. I am here because one of the brightest agents in the Bureau was savagely murdered by a private citizen of this city. We have extended the hand of cooperation in the areas of investigative manpower and technical expertise to Commander Anderson to use in any way he deems appropriate. Next."

"This follow-up question is for Commander Anderson. Commander, the preliminary medical report indicates that Section Chief Wilkins had suffered multiple slash marks to her breasts and multiple alleged cigarette burns to her buttocks. How can you explain this?"

"We believe the cut marks and cigarette burns were administered post-mortem. We believe that Fatima Johansson vented her fury on the lifeless body of Section Chief Wilkins. Fury driven by the frustration of finding nothing of value to rob from Ms. Wilkins' house. This is supported by the fact that the officers responding to the 911 call found the house a mess, ransacked in an apparent effort to find something of value to steal. However, the investigating detectives found jewelry and a substantial stash of money hidden in a compartment within a small bedside chest of drawers. Obviously, Fatima Johansson did not find what she was looking for, became enraged, and took out her anger on the body of dead Section Chief Wilkins. Next."

"Sheree Beckerman, Channel 8 News. Commander, it is my understanding that your team of detectives learned of Ms. Johansson's identity from owners and patrons of various downtown clubs that cater to those members of our society who favor sado-masochistic activities. If this is accurate, it would explain the notation on the initial police report that the victim, Section Chief Wilkins, and I quote, '*was found naked except for long black leather gloves and a black leather corset.*' Given this, is it reasonable to assume that Ms. Wilkins and Ms. Johansson went to Ms. Wilkins' home for some form of S and M activity? Somehow the sex games went horribly wrong, and Ms. Wilkins was murdered?"

"Commander, I'll take this question. Ms. Beckerman, despite your insinuations and besmirching innuendos, you have failed to ask a question about the murder. The facts of this case will prove incontrovertibly that Fatima Johansson savagely murdered an agent of the FBI. That is the single focus of this case. This section chief's personal life, her life outside the workplace, is of little or no consequence to the fact that she was murdered. I'll take one more question."

86

"Bill Springer, Channel 13. If Section Chief Wilkins was involved in a deviant lifestyle, common sense would dictate that she could be susceptible to undue influence by forces outside the FBI. She could be blackmailed, and that blackmail could impact any case in which she was involved. How can the public trust FBI agents or section chiefs who lay themselves open to blackmail?"

"Mr. Springer, Section Chief Wilkins' responsibilities within the Bureau were in the area of interagency communications, not field case work. Since 9/11, all the federal agencies involved in protecting the public have worked diligently to share information about terrorists, domestic and foreign, so that the tragedy of that September morning would not recur. Section Chief Wilkins headed a team that was responsible for receiving, analyzing, and distributing, in a timely manner, all pertinent and appropriate information to other appropriate agencies of the federal government. So, you can see, she would not be susceptible to blackmail by any outside source from doing her job in the most professional manner. Thank you all for coming. Please feel free to contact Commander Anderson if you have any further questions."

The temporary stage empties rapidly. The glare from federal to local is not disguised.

"Commander, you have a leak. Close the fucking thing, or I'll make your life a living hell. I want no more shit thrown at the Bureau. Do you understand?"

Sheepishly, the six-foot three, two hundred forty-pound man with the impressive title walks toward his waiting car. He has just been horse whipped by a slight five-foot two-inch woman.

VI

The man hesitantly enters a large room that is dark except for the flickering light of a TV. On the screen are a white man and black woman who seem to be involved in some form of aggressive close contact action. They are naked. The floor and the walls of this room are made of stone and are cold. The room appears to be a dungeon. There is no furniture in the room except for a slightly raised wooden platform sitting in the middle of the space. The large board is covered with fluid dripping off its edges. In the soft light, the man can barely discern the composition of the ooze. He squints to get a clear, detailed picture and sees feces in thick dark red-brown fluid. As he abruptly averts his gaze, he sees eleven pale human forms hanging from manacles on two walls. There are seven male forms and four female forms. All are naked, and their heads are downcast as if in shame. They have small cuts on their chests. Against the third wall rests a tripod holding a video camera. Next to the camera are two large spotlights that are turned off but are apparently focused on wooden platform. He stops and stares at the equipment.

His attention to the camera and lights is interrupted by soft moaning. Pain or pleasure? He's not sure. When the stranger turns to find the source of the sound, he sees the man and woman who had been on the TV screen are now on the platform. He is face down in the ooze. She looks like she is riding him. The woman has a black corset covering the upper portion of her torso. Her black gloves are elbow length. Her motion is rhythmic and frenetic at the same time. She is slapping his buttocks and the back of his head. Occasionally she extinguishes a cigarette on his thighs. Does he struggle out of pain or is he writhing in pleasure? Does he relish the inflictions and his degradation? The intruder can see a broad, evil grin covering the lower half of the woman's face. Her subject's eyes are closed, and his face is contorted: partial pleasure and partial agony.

The intruder turns to walk away from the ritualistic event toward the door he used to enter the large room, but he cannot find the door. It is not located on the walls with the hanging human forms. It is not on the wall with the tripod. The intruder is becoming anxious. Where the hell is the door? Where the hell is the door? Suddenly, the black woman rises from her position of dominance and comes to him. She does not speak or smile. She simply motions her head in the direction behind the intruder. She is visually telling him to turn around and go back. Mysteriously there is a large opening in the wall where none existed before. As he begins to exit, he stumbles. He has stepped on a small arm, the hand of which is holding a stick from which hangs a key. He notices chipped polish on the small fingers. The arm is not attached to a body. The stranger can tell by the blood pulsing from the torn bicep that the arm has been recently and violently *removed from a small body. He grasps the arm in an effort to reattach it, but he can't find the body to which it belongs. Suddenly the arm wiggles from his grasp and escapes beneath the large platform in the room like a snake.*

David sits up. His pillow and the sheet beneath him are damp with sweat. His heart is racing and causing a pain in his chest. His breathing is labored and shallow. He throws back the covers and slowly staggers naked to the bathroom. As he drinks a glass of water, he notices his ashen face and dark circles around his eyes. The dream has had a horrible impact on his countenance. He is trembling. His hand can barely hold the water glass, his legs are soft, and knees bent. He cannot return to bed.

He puts on running shorts and a T-shirt and heads to the kitchen for ice. Strangely, he feels the need for ice in his water. Standing in front of the freezer, he realizes he's overly warm, almost as if he were running a fever. His forehead and underarms are damp and there are droplets of perspiration trickling down the back of his neck. He pours a big glass of water over ice and pads to the patio. He will sit for a short time, in the cold night air, to calm down. Staring at the stars, he begins to unravel the nightmare. The physical impact of the ugly thoughts and images diminishes with each level of understanding. Within thirty minutes he is cold, relaxed, and beginning to feel tired enough for sleep. He will not go back to his bed. He chooses the couch. Before he falls asleep, he vows to tell Rachel...days later. It's 2:30 in the morning.

* * *

"David, I went back to the CDC and was told that further autopsy work might shed additional light on exactly how the two victims were infected by the rabies virus. So, I contacted the Buffalo and San Diego Police Departments and filled them in...partially. They each gave me the go-ahead to recontact their medical examiners after they called the respective offices to smooth the way. Then I contacted the two MEs and explained our concerns. Within twenty-four hours each ME called me and explained that, upon further examination, they found traces of DMSO and an unknown chemical compound in the brain matter of their respective victim. The combination had been missed the first time, due to its minute level and the fact, that as a medium for something else, DMSO can take on some of the characteristics of what it is carrying. I contacted the CDC to inquire about DMSO and they sent me what appears to be a pro forma explanation of the drug or medicine or however it's classified."

Use of DMSO in medicine dates from around 1963, when an Oregon Health & Science University Medical School team, headed by Stanley Jacob, discovered it could penetrate the skin and other membranes without damaging them and could carry other compounds into a biological system. In medicine, DMSO is predominantly used as a topical analgesic, a vehicle for topical application of pharmaceuticals, as an anti-inflammatory, and an antioxidant. Because DMSO increases the rate of absorption of some compounds through organic tissues, including skin, it is used in some transdermal drug delivery systems. Its effect may be enhanced with the addition of EDTA. It is frequently compounded with antifungal medications, enabling them to penetrate not just skin but also hair and fingernails.

"I asked the CDC if DMSO could have been used to carry the rabies virus into a victim's body. They confirmed that it might have been used, but they would have to test my theory by a more exacting examination of the tissue before commenting further. I asked them if rabies carried by DMSO into a victim's system would accelerate the brain infection and damaging process. They said it that it could happen, given that the process of degeneration is based on the composition of the virus.

91

Degeneration normally takes three to four weeks. So, I think I should ask the local PDs to visit the homes of the two victims and collect bathroom items like soaps, shampoos, creme rinses, and so forth. The poison likely entered each victim's blood stream during daily bathing. This is a start. Once collected, the PDs will send the items to the CDC for analysis. I think we will find something to explain how the virus got into the victims' systems. Anyway, it's worth a shot given the strangeness of the two episodes. OK?"

"Slow down. You're making big leaps with no net. Call the local PDs and that make sure they tape off the two bathrooms as crime scenes. Don't tell them why. This will give you time to dig deeper. Then, we'll revisit this issue. Don't let your excursion into the world of drugs, pharmacology, and strange deaths disrupt your primary purpose of receiving, analyzing, and disseminating information from other agencies. OK?"

"Thanks."

David likes the concept of one-on-one meetings; he is brought up-to-date and asked for permission to proceed or for advice. He plans to have regular staff meetings on Wednesday mornings to encourage open discussion on a variety of subjects. He never liked the Monday staff meetings held by Barbara because there was rarely anything new since Friday.

"Margaret, what you have you uncovered?"

"Requests for march and rally permits."

"Is that permits to march or permits for the month of March?"

"Sorry, that was unclear. I mean permits to march in the streets of Buffalo, San Diego, and Minneapolis and to hold rallies in these cities. The permits were requested by right wing groups not normally associated with those cities: Liberty Men requested in Buffalo, Free Cowboys in San Diego, and Protectors of Freedom in Minneapolis. It seems that the Free Cowboys have assumed an urban persona. The three groups used organizational names and addresses that correspond to each of the cities.

92

Everything seems legit…strange, but legit. The date requested for the permit to march and hold a rally in the city park is the same in all three instances. Three weeks from now. That, in and of itself, is not strange, but the dates were posted on the websites of the three organizations two weeks before the permits were issued. That would mean that the groups were prescient, optimistically aggressive, or had a sympathetic friend in the city government. Those who go to the websites are encouraged to make plans to attend. There are local motels linked to each site, as well as an 800 number to call for more information. It is the same 800 for each website. Not a coincidence.

"And it gets weirder. The days are named 'Pure American Days' in the three cities. If I may reintroduce a theory of mine, it's as if the dispersed activities are being coordinated by an overarching organization. These are not picnics in the park, given by church groups. The events are hate rallies designed to stir up resentment against someone or some group. My guess is Muslims. In light of the recent attacks on our military bases and embassy outposts, Muslims are an ideal target for increased hate. Please go to the website of Liberty Men and see what I am talking about."

David goes to the site, and there he sees the usual waving American flag in the background, member notices, and snippets of reported news articles written by like-minded radicals and thus proffered as God-sent truth. In the middle of the landing page is a banner with the words "Pure American Days" in German Gothic font. Above the image is the plea to "Join Us for a Rally in Buffalo on June 23." Below the banner is the invitation to request information by calling the 800 number. The two men holding the banner are dressed in black from head to calf. They are wearing tan boots.

"That's interesting and mildly disquieting. While I may not agree with their politics, I have an obligation to ensure their freedom to assemble and speak. You also have the same obligation, Margaret."

"I know. If you go to the other websites, you'll find striking similarities. It's these similarities that lead me to believe in the specter of a force above the three local groups. If that's accurate, the threat is greater than we thought."

"I follow you. You may be making sense of all this. Dig deeper. Get answers, not conjectures. Find connections. Press your contacts in the three cities. Press them hard. Tell them your new section chief has made this a priority. Then, we'll discuss this again. Good work."

David is pleased to have such diligent people on his team. His reading of previous performance reviews by Barbara has uncovered her modus operandi of denigrating the work of Robert and Margaret while damning with faint praise that of Dinah and Jacob. What a bitch! More forms to complete. Where is the overnight work gnome hiding? He likes the power to let each member of his team function on their own, report their progress, and ask questions during their work process. He has become a manager of people and likes delegation with final authority. This is all new to him. While invigorating, the newness is mildly disquieting. Newness with its heretofore unknown responsibilities puts a new form of pressure on David. He has no one to be his backstop if he makes a mistake. His safety net is dead. His telephone thankfully interrupts his thoughts.

"Mr. Drummer, or should I call you Section Chief Drummer, this is Wendell Peterson of the *Star*. I think we need to talk."

"We don't need to talk. If you have questions, I will refer you to Commander Anderson or Ms. Knapp."

"I spoke to them in an effort to get corroboration of information at the center of the story we are running tomorrow. They gave me so much of a runaround, I felt like I was on an out-of-control carousel. So, I am coming to you. Before you hang up and go into radio silence, hear me out. In speaking with Public Defender Louisa Cochran, we determined there was something hinky about both the victim and the alleged perp. So, we did some digging.

"Both Ms. Wilkins and Ms. Johansson appear to have been frequent, if not regular, visitors to the same S and M bars, Divine Venus and The Discipline Life. This did not come as a shock to either of us. Employees and patrons of both bars remember seeing the two women together several times in the recent past. So, the trip to Ms. Wilkins' house may not have been a onetime, spur of the moment, *come to my house for tea* event. It was most likely, one in a series of events. They were seekers of strange pleasures. That's that on their relationship. It gets better. The two women in question would occasionally pick up a third woman for a night of fun and games. Not very surprising. And on three different occasions, employees of The Discipline Life recall seeing Ms. Wilkins hook up with a man and leave with him. A different man each time. And each time without Ms. Johansson. The employees were unable or unwilling to provide a detailed description of any of the men.

"Now if Ms. Wilkins was having sex with men, I think it's safe to bet that Ms. Johansson could have become jealous of her lover's trip to the other side. Given the possessive nature of many lovers, particularly unstable gay and lesbian lovers, that jealousy could have turned to rage and rage to murder. That gives Ms. Johansson a motive other than robbery. A strangely sympathetic motive, but motive nonetheless. And it reopens the issue of possible blackmail. Something that Ms. Cochran will not let go. But here is the really big question: Who were the men that left The Discipline Life with Ms. Wilkins? Can you help me here, Section Chief?"

"Your story and alleged facts lead you to numerous disparate conclusions. Most of which I can't even begin to fathom, so I won't dignify them with comments. Since I have never been to the two bars you mentioned, I am unable to corroborate any facts or suppositions. I'm sorry I can't help you because I'm not a viable source of information. OK? And with that, I bid you adieu."

"Wait. We're going to run with the story tomorrow. Are you sure you don't want to get out ahead of it?"

"I would, if I could. But I can't, so I won't. Have a great day besmirching people."

"Take my number if you change your mind. Call me anytime. It's my cell, 816-588-8989."

David replaces the telephone delicately into its cradle as if it were germ encrusted. He puts the scrap of paper with the number on it in his top desk drawer and ponders. If Peterson told these facts and suppositions to Anderson and Knapp, they must have become agitated. *Let them deal with it.*

* * *

At home, David is driven by curiosity to see who and what is on the files on the flash drive. It's like seeing a car wreck ahead on the road. Displaying the twelve video files is like slowing down and peering across the road at the mangled mess and looking for bodies. There is a mild wash of guilty relief that he is not on any of the videos, but others are. *Thank gawd.* The first four files alternate between men and women David does not recognize. Barbara is administering various forms of pain and domination to the individuals who seem to enjoy it. He doesn't dwell on any of the files and the activity long enough to become disgusted.

File five contains Barbara, Fatima, and a woman he thinks he recognizes. Studying her face, he sees Stephanie Azaub, the woman who watches Jack Strathmore's door. She is a very willing participant in the games. She even initiates a convoluted three-way coupling. David goes to another file. Files six through nine reveal no one David recognizes. File ten contains activity of Barbara and a man David recognizes from somewhere. Where has he seen that

96

partially hidden face before? The participant very much enjoys being hooked up to a dog collar and leash. He is made to crawl in front of Barbara while she whips his buttocks with the cat-o'-nine-tails. He appears to be smiling and asking for more as she increases the frequency and intensity of the lashes. David notices that an anal probe has been inserted into a crawling subject.

Where has that man entered David's life? *Shit! That's Mitchell Davis.* Their paths rarely cross. Davis hides in his domain behind locked doors and comes out only for large meetings in the main conference rooms or to meet with Jack. That's enough. The entire panoply of sick home movies is becoming too much. David must pull away. He closes the file, removes the flash drive, and returns it to its new home, his lockbox, resting beside his two handguns: The government issue Colt .45 and the Beretta 9 mm, bought years ago for his ex-wife to use in an emergency.

David's heart is beating soundly and rapidly. Perspiration has formed on his upper lip. There is a slight tightness on the left side of his chest. He must have been sitting at an awkward angle and tightened up while viewing the files. Muscles must have become tense. Time for a drink to calm down. He lifts the bottle of Balvenie 14 to slowly pour the amber nectar into the short glass and notices that his hand is trembling, causing the scotch to splash wildly into the glass. He wonders what is going on with his body. Is he internalizing the details of the recent distasteful events? Can he be suffering from stress? No, he is suffering from a new kind of ailment, *PAWS*: Pre-retirement Agonizing Work Syndrome. A smile creases his lips. He has just created a new ailment for which the only cure is to retire and move to Eleuthera with his beloved. Anyone else who suffers from this ailment will have to find their own beloved and island.

* * *

Several copies of *Kansas City Star* are on the table by the elevator in the lobby. David takes one for early morning reading. It's six fifty-five. His team will assemble by eight. There is time for him to get a jump on the day and respond to overnight messages from various parts of the country, as well as Europe and Asia. He hangs his blazer on the back of the office door. Maybe he should start to wear suits given his new, exalted position. Nah! It would be a painfully obvious knuckling under to convention. The team would immediately see it as a sham.

David unfolds the paper. Nothing with Wendell Peterson's byline on the front page. Nothing in the Metro Section. Nothing in Sports. Nothing in Home and Garden. Nothing on the Editorial page. Nothing anywhere with the reporter's name on it. Nada. Zip. Zero. Zilch. Wendell has suffered a major blackout. On one hand, for the time being, this is acceptable. But press censorship is never a good thing because it can lead to a totalitarian society. David surmises that immediately after Peterson contacted Knapp and Anderson, Anderson contacted someone high up at the newspaper while Knapp applied federal pressure on Knight Ridder/McClatchy. The double whammy killed Peterson's story about any inkling of impropriety at the Bureau. Does David get involved now? How deeply does he dive into Peterson's cesspool? Is he willing to risk his future for the truth? Without truth, there is nothing. No soul. He searches his desk drawer for the cell phone number. He takes ten deep breaths to calm his nerves and punches in the digits on his private cell phone. No sense in having anyone know or hear of this call except for Peterson and Drummer.

"Wendell, this is David Drummer. I didn't see your story in the paper this morning. What happened?"

"You know damned well what happened. I was told the story was uncorroborated and potentially libelous. It was killed before it made it past my editor. Some motherfucker did this to me and to my story, and I want to know why."

"Let's not talk now. Let's meet at my house at seven tonight. I live at…"

"I know the address. I'll be there. You had better have a believable explanation for fucking with the truth."

"One more thing: Take a circuitous route to my house. Double back a few times just to be sure you are alone."

"Christ! Do you really think someone would be keeping tabs on my activities and whereabouts?"

"You kicked shit on some big shoes when you spoke to Anderson and Knapp about what you know. They responded to your attempt to cause them major distress. In all likelihood, they will want to be sure it does not happen on your second try. So, you better be careful. If you can use someone else's car and drive a very roundabout route, we'll both be safe."

"This is beginning to sound like China or Russia. I knew I was on to something big that involved the Bureau, beyond Ms. Wilkins. I didn't know just how big the story was. I'll be there at seven."

That's it. It's done. He has just taken a massive leap out of his comfort zone. He never liked to make waves or trouble for anyone. He has never been a pot stirrer. This time is different. His ex-wife used to accuse him of being a coward. She called him Caspar Milquetoast on more than one occasion. She blamed him for never taking the initiative or the bold steps necessary for advancement in the Bureau's hierarchy. She claimed he would let people walk over him rather than say something or do anything to stop them. That's why he was never promoted. All the members of the class in which he started at the Bureau have made section chief or above. He has not. His safe approach to life is what drove her into another's bed, or so she claimed. The accidental killing of the young girl may have been a subconscious reaction to his wife's infidelity and thus was more than he could deal with. But now is different. He feels simultaneously frightened and brave. This is a new mixture for David Drummer.

More forms. Several more archived performance reviews and tedium sets in. The day is one hundred hours long. On the way home, he calls Rachel. Yes, she will join him for dinner at 6:30.

* * *

"Hey, sweetie, what's for dinner?"

"We're going out for dinner. Let me explain."

"OK, explain."

"We're going to meet someone and have a working meal. Let me make a call."

"Wendell, where are you now?"

Rachel has her 'what the hell is going on' look as she stares at David.

"Very thoughtful. Do you know the restaurant, Mangia, on East Boulevard? Meet us there in thirty minutes. Do not park in the front lot. Park in the back lot. We'll be inside waiting for you. Got that? Great. See you there."

"OK, David, what are we doing and with whom are we doing it?"

"I'll explain in the car. We'll take yours. You drive."

During the drive to the restaurant, David tries to explain the reason for the restaurant meeting. He wants to have the evil exposed, but he can't risk everything by exposing it himself. He must use a surrogate and thus stay out of the picture. What better surrogate than a newspaper reporter? David also realizes that this could be a slippery slope whereon he falls to his death because Jack and Fletcher become aware that it is he who is behind the exposure. He wants control but no responsibility. For the first time, he will have that combination. He will be in control of a massive ugly situation. He will be more than just an analyst. David's actions are being driven by his ego and not his intellect. Rachel is confused and annoyed.

"Jesus, David, you sound paranoid. Why would you be watched?"

"Point one: After Peterson spoke to Emily Knapp, my guess is that she called Jack and Fletcher. These two now must have a strong suspicion that someone may be aware that a massive cover-up is in play. And that someone is me. They just don't know the depth of my knowledge. They don't know that I know the truth. Point two: The story from Wendell and Louisa Cochran about the S and M liaisons Barbara and Fatima had with men and women was killed by the newspaper's editor. The local police do not have that kind of juice over the local media. The only one who could squash the story is someone with national power...someone who could pick up the phone and talk to the newspaper owners. Emily Knapp has such power, and she would use it to protect the Bureau and two of its senior members."

"If you are right, this is way out of my league. I'm just a humble financial advisor working in a branch office of a New York-based corporation. So, I ask, why am I here?"

"You are here because I need your strength...and your understanding. I am embarking upon a venture that is way beyond my bureaucratic experience and certainly way outside my comfort zone. I'm risking my retirement, and therefore my life with you, in an attempt to expose the lies and cover-up perpetrated by two men who are my respected workplace superiors. But I am using a surrogate...Peterson. Because this will most likely impact you, I need you to hear what I am doing to bring the truth to light. I want you to appear to be an objective observer at the dinner meeting. But in reality, you are an interested and involved party. If you want me to not do what I know is right, or if you fear for your safety, we can turn around and go back home."

"Objective observer, my ass. But I can appear to be objective when the man I love is risking everything until we leave for Eleuthera."

They are both silent. Rachel pulls into a parking lot in front of a Kwiki-Shoppe across the street from Mangia and turns off the ignition. The silence is deafening. Three minutes go by. David will not speak. Rachel has the floor. It's her decision. Five minutes go by.

"OK. Let's do this. I know you to be an honorable man. That's one of the many reasons I love you. Honor's twin is truth. So, let's get the truth out to the general public. We have almost enough money for our dream. So, fuck the bastards. We don't need their money. For us, there must be no secrets, no lies. That goes for your bosses from this point forward in this very dangerous game of show and tell. Gottit?"

"Gottit."

Rachel leans over and warmly kisses David.

"Rachel, I will tell you everything, but I will not tell Wendell everything. He will learn just enough to help him write his story. We need to hold some things back for our own protection. Plausible deniability. I'll explain after dinner. Now, let's meet our Woodward, or shall he be our Bernstein."

They sit in a booth on the long wall and order wine. About ten minutes later, an average looking man dressed in a light gray pullover sweater, jeans, and tassel loafers approaches the booth and smiles. He has dark wavy hair and a pleasant smile. "Are you David Drummer?"

"Yes. Are you Wendell Peterson?"

"Yes. And you are?"

"I am David's significant other, Rachel Vincent."

"OK. May I sit?"

"Please do. We ordered wine. Order whatever you like; this is on me."

"Thanks, David. As you can see by my clothes, I am a man of plebian tastes. I'll have a beer. What's good here?"

"When we're ready, David and I will be ordering the antipasto for two."

102

"I'll scan the menu as we talk. Do you mind if I record our conversation? Now, tell me why all the cloak and dagger crap?"

"No recording. Take good notes. Please hand me the recorder for safekeeping until we are ready to leave."

"You don't trust me. That's a helluva way to treat a compatriot."

"Let me be absolutely clear: We are not compatriots. You are a reporter, and I am a force. I am not a resource. I need protection from the shitstorm you are about to start. Plausible deniability is my protection from those you accuse. I was never here, and we never spoke."

Reluctantly, the recorder exchange is made.

"Thanks. Now, let me begin. As I mentioned on the phone, you're digging into areas that are sensitive. You and Ms. Cochran may think your investigation is collateral to the murder. But the story that you wanted to publish would have caused a great deal of pain in certain circles. It could have been a career maker for you and a career breaker for others."

"Explain. I need details."

"I don't have all the details; you'll need to dig based on the guidance I give you. If you don't dig, you won't learn everything. As I said, I don't know everything. I trust that with my little bit of help you will learn what to dig for and where to dig. Let me continue."

The conversation carries on through the meal. Between slices of pizza, Peterson takes copious notes and interrupts David's monologue, asking for expanded clarification. Ninety minutes pass and the teller is nearly exhausted. The listener looks as if he wants to go on.

"Well, now you know what I know, what I think, and where I would look if I were you. That should be enough for you to get a bigger story published. By the way, given your editor's killing of your story, how will you get him to see the truth?"

103

"I haven't figured that out yet. I am looking into alternative avenues. I could resign and sell my story to the *New York Times* or *USA Today*. Or I could leave the paper and hook up with a local TV station. I have friends in several news departments. But I'd really like to stay where I am, write the great American news story, win a Pulitzer, and write a book about the news story. Then I could retire to an island in the Pacific. I dress in plain and simple fashion, but I have grandiose dreams."

All three smile.

"Thank you for being so forthcoming. I think I see the magnitude of your risk, and I'll be careful to keep you out of my work. You are an anonymous force, not a quotable source. If I need to speak to you again, I'll call on your personal cell. Again, thanks. Have a great rest of the evening."

The three leave the restaurant and head to two respective homes.

* * *

"If you don't mind, I'll stay here tonight. I need the comfort of your body and soul."

"I never mind having you next to me. In fact, I sleep better that way. I need a drink. My head is spinning. Can I 'buy' you one?"

"That would be great. It will help me unwind. Let's sit outside with our nightcaps." Beneath the stars in the cool air, they sit close together and sip the Balvenie nectar.

* * *

There is a story on the front page of the *Star* Metro Section beneath the fold:

104

Inmate Killed at Jackson County Corrections

Last night at approximately 6:30, Fatima Johansson was stabbed to death during a melee that arose in Cell Block C-W of the Jackson County Correctional Facility. Ms. Johansson was being held over for trial in the Murder of FBI Section Chief Barbara Wilkins. Before the seven pm lockdown, guards were called to break up a fight in the women's cell block. When they arrived at the day room, Ms. Johansson was found in front of her cell bleeding from multiple stab wounds to her neck, chest, and back.

Warden Leonard stated, "Our initial investigation indicates that Ms. Johansson had made unwanted advances of a sexual nature to several of the other female inmates in Cell Block C-W. Apparently, these other inmates took offense at the advances, an argument started, and as happens many times in crowded conditions, the argument quickly escalated to violence. We have recovered the murder weapon and are reviewing the security tapes to ascertain the guilty party. Presently, because of the crowded confusion, we have numerous leads. Because we take the safety of our inmate population as seriously as that of our staff and administration, we are applying all of our available resources to resolve this matter as quickly as possible. Until the matter is resolved, Cell Block C-W will be on lockdown status."

David wonders, *When one door closes, does another really open?*

VII

Seventy-five miles outside of Taos, New Mexico, there is a group of small nondescript one-story buildings: Two are one hundred feet square, and two are fifty feet by one hundred feet. The prefab building cluster consists of a mess and relaxation hall, barracks, an administration building, and an operations building. There are no other manifestations of humanity within thirty miles of this cluster. The buildings are surrounded by two rings of twenty-foot-high electrified fence: One separated by thirty feet of ground containing tripwires and covered by a plethora of evil-looking spiked plants. There are no lights on the fences, only cameras. This compound, on the barren sandscape, is the home of the Unmanned Aircraft Vehicle Tactical Weapons Center (UAVTWC): The home of drone operations. It is also home for three-month tour rotations of the UAV Specialists, the exceedingly well-trained men and women who pilot the drones on their appointed missions.

Within the operations building are four cubicles in which sit four expressionless specialists, referred to as "Killer Techies." They call themselves KITs. Three men and a woman stare laser-focused on the monitors before them. Behind each KIT is an officer who is the communications link between someone somewhere with a drone and the KIT who will complete the mission. In this building, these four teams of two plus one overseer will be responsible for successfully neutralizing targets...men, buildings, and munitions... thousands of miles from Taos. Despite the air conditioning, the four KITs are beginning to feel the warming effect of adrenaline. The intense emotional and intellectual pressure of precision destruction from afar can cause the body to react in a normal way in this abnormal long-distant situation. It is this pressure, within the boredom of isolation, that mandates the KITs rotate out every three months. Regular technological advancements in the weaponry and the operational system require that each KIT be familiar with any enhancements before returning to his or her post.

The entire KIT force of unknown number undergoes an exhaustive year-long training and conditioning process before they are assigned to one of the secret compounds throughout the world, like the one in New Mexico. The Pentagon wants to be absolutely certain that each KIT volunteer has the acuity, as well as the approved moral compass, to rain down hell on unsuspecting combatants and collateral personnel. In the selection process of a KIT, the Pentagon looks for men and women who are not affected by the concepts of destruction and killing. Extensive video game playing time and talent in their history is a plus. This is important for the proper handling of multi-million-dollar equipment with a simple hand-held device. The moral compass is equally critical because what the KITs are doing is real killing. There are no do-overs if a target is missed. No restarts for bathroom breaks. KITs live by a modified sniper credo… "One shot…many killed."

It is zero five hundred hours in Taos and a bright hot noon in the desert countries of Africa, particularly Chadar. The assault on the unseen enemy commences. Each KIT can communicate with a handler who is behind them.

"Raptor One, are you ready."

"Roger that."

"Raptor Two, are you ready."

"Roger that."

"Raptor Three, are you ready."

"Roger that."

"Raptor Four, are you ready."

"Roger that."

"Raptor One, coming up on Target One. Do you have visual?"

"I have visual."

"Raptor Two, coming up on Target Two. Do you have visual?"

"I have visual."

"Raptor Three, coming up on Target Three. Do you have visual?"

"I have visual."

"Raptor Four, coming up on Target Four. Do you have visual?"

"I have visual."

"We are now on ready-hold."

"Roger that."

"Roger that."

"Roger that."

"Roger that."

All of these commands are predicated on the successful launch of four birds of prey. Now approaching their designated targets. When the jobs of the launch teams are completed, they casually await the successful conclusion of the missions by the KITs and the return of their birds of prey.

* * *

In four isolated gatherings of tents and small buildings, guards and dogs patrol the perimeter of the camps while men, women, and children go about their everyday activities. There is no desert breeze to cool the noon sun. The families enjoy the peace of a meal together. Later, the children will return to the makeshift school. They will continue to learn a warped version of the Koran. Women will study bomb making. They are also responsible for maintaining their households. The men will learn battle strategy and logistics, as well as train with automatic weapons and RPGs. A select few will learn the intricacies of heavier weapons and artillery, while others are responsible for upkeep of the transportation: trucks, cars, and acquired military vehicles. All adults and children over the age of 14 are expected to know how to kill and why they must kill: Eliminate Westerners from the tribal homeland, by any means necessary, to attain the goal of freedom.

* * *

"Raptor One, you have a green light."
"Raptor Two, you have a green light."
"Raptor Three, you have a green light."
"Raptor Four, you have a green light."

Four sets of eyes lock onto targets displayed on four screens. Four expensive hand-held devices are moved ever-so-slightly to bring the drone crosshairs into the center of the targets. This is the delicate part of the mission because a drone does not fly with the stability of a jet fighter. It can bob and weave or swoop and yaw almost at its own choosing. Control from so far away with no knowledge of wind currents can be difficult. But that is what the KITs train for.

"Raptor One away."
"Raptor Two away."
"Raptor Three away."
"Raptor Four away."

Four red buttons are pressed. With the simple message, four firebombs are let loose on an unseen enemy. Within three heartbeats, the bombs find their targets and four monitors flash white then show the clouds in the sky above the camps as the four drones head back to their bases. These bombs have been developed for precisely this type of mission. Each bomb contains clusters of canisters that, in turn, contain a recently developed and extremely vicious version of thermite. Each internal canister has its own detonator. When the bomb hits, it does not explode. It breaks apart and the canisters are scattered, for up to one hundred yards, in all directions. Only when the canisters hit the ground on their own are they able to work their malevolent magic...independently. The resultant four explosives each cover

110

an area the size of two football fields. Each fireball burns so hot that it turns sand into glass. Because of the chemical composition of the new and improved thermite component, the fire cannot be extinguished by traditional methods. The fire must burn itself out. These fires burn so brightly and extensively that they make the conflagration of Dresden look like an outdoor cookout. The flames will last for at least two hours. Each massive fire will be seen by nomads and people in other camps many kilometers away. The four explosions will completely erase the camps of el Jahdiq in Chadar, near Riatta in Qratri, near Basjar, and Najret.

* * *

Inside the small building outside of Taos, there are no cheers or high fives. The KITs have done what they have been trained to do. Just another day at the office. They hear a simple statement from the overseer.

"Well done."

Likewise, there will be no acknowledgment of a job well done from high-ranking members of the military in Washington. Except for the four exceptionally large burned-out holes in the desert, it's like the attack never happened. There were no survivors to report of the events. Therefore, there was no mention of the attack and obliteration in the media.

* * *

"David, I want to bring you up to speed on the rabies cases. Permit me to review the context of what we know. As we discussed, I contacted everyone in the loop: the CDC, the Buffalo and San Diego PDs, and the local medical examiners. These latter two went back and re-ran their autopsies looking for whatever might be related to rabies. They both discovered that each victim's brain tissue contained DMSO. They both sent the same explanation of DMSO which we reviewed before.

"They both admitted that the rabies virus could have been carried into the victim without an animal bite and then its effects would be accelerated...by DMSO. If that's true, the cases would have to be reclassified as murder by an unknown. So, I asked the local police to return to the homes of the teenage girl in San Diego and the adult male in Buffalo and collect every liquid, gel, and cream item from the respective bathrooms. We need every item that could possibly come in contact with the skin of both victims...soap, shampoo, creme rinse, hair conditioner, antifungal medications, and the like. Everything. Once all the items were collected, the locals were asked to forward the properly labeled items to Mary Jenkins at the CDC. She has been my contact. That's where we were before Mary got back to me.

"Mary received the items. She examined the containers and noticed nothing out of the ordinary on all the items, except two plastic shampoo bottles. There was a small mark on both bottles of *Vibrant Shampoo for Normal Hair from Beauty Brands*. This mark was a ridiculously small drop of dried shampoo. It was formed by leakage from the bottle. The small drop had congealed over, what she estimates was, a needle or pin entry. So, she analyzed the shampoo inside the bottle and discovered DMSO and a unique, high potency cousin of the normal rabies virus. She called this virus a super-rabies.

"Mary analyzed this new strain of rabies and her guess was that it is up to twenty times more virulent than the version found in nature. She guesses that someone somehow was able to intensify the virus into a super-strain. She suggested it would be like concentrating a liquid into a cream or gel. This could only have been done in a lab by an experienced chemist: not by a rank amateur or Mother Nature. She further speculates that the super-strain was mixed with DMSO and injected into the shampoo bottles now in her possession. This would explain the speed with which the rabies worked its death. If all this is accurate, and I have every reason to believe it is, we may be looking at bio-terrorism."

"Slow down. Let's not get ahead of ourselves. First, we have to determine where the teen and man bought their shampoo. Simultaneously, we have to notify the manufacturer of the shampoo about the need for a two-market, comprehensive product recall. Tell them they may not swap out the existing shelf stock for new product because we cannot be positive the product tampering didn't occur at the Beauty Brands plant. Maybe they have a disgruntled or demented employee. They must pull the product, not just from the stores where the victims bought the shampoo, but every outlet in each multi-county trading area. They need to get all the shampoo off the shelves immediately. We must tell them as little as possible to get them to do what is necessary. Second, have the manufacturer send all the recalled product to Mary Jenkins of the CDC for analysis. The important thing is that we don't want a public panic.

"We have to determine if these two incidents are isolated or are they part of a grand scheme. Right now, we must operate on the first premise. Notify the Buffalo and San Diego PDs about what we know, not what we think may be true. Have them be on the lookout for any similar incidents. Do not notify any other locals at this time. We must contain this activity as much as possible. Get in touch with your resources in the Buffalo and San Diego offices and alert them. Tell them everything that we know and what we think is happening. Have them contact the local PDs and offer assistance. Demand their cooperation. If you meet sloth or resistance, let me know, and as section chief, I will jump in with both feet.

"You've done a great job of sleuthing and working with our partners. Now, proceed with cautious dispatch. We have an obligation to protect the public from enemies of this country, foreign and domestic. But, we have an equal obligation to not cause panic. Give me a status report in three hours, after you've made the proper contacts and gotten their buy-in. I want to communicate your work to Fletcher and Jack and ask for their guidance and assistance."

David has more paperwork. He asks himself, in the era of electronic files and emails, why is there always more paperwork? Years ago, commerce was chastised for killing trees for paper. Today, he bets his office goes through a large portion of Montana lumber each year. Forms and reports take up most of his day as section chief. He is new to the tedium of creating these repetitive reports and pushing them out for review. It was never like this as a senior special agent. He's almost glad he was not promoted before now.

"David, I have a strange request."

"Margaret, whatever you ask will not be considered strange. I promise."

"I just spoke to Robert and he filled me in as to what he was doing and why. The fact that he is dealing with issues in Buffalo and San Diego interested me because, as you recall, these are two cities that plan to hold right wing hate group marches and rallies next month. I was wondering if there is any connection between Robert's issues with product tampering and right-wing marches in those two cities. If there is a connection, a gap could be that Robert has not come across any product tampering issues in Minneapolis, which is a city set to endure their own hate mongering rally. But, and this is a big but, if there is a connection between the product tampering and marches in Buffalo and San Diego, I think a connection will be found in Minneapolis. If my assessment is accurate, we should ask Beauty Brands to pull their shampoo from stores in the Twin Cities before a product tampering issue arises. Just for safety's sake. The CDC can do the same examination of the shampoo bottles from the Twin Cities at the same time they examine those from Buffalo and San Diego. If the lab rats in Atlanta find tampering with the Twin Cities' shampoo bottles, we can be sure there is some type of connection between the tampering and the hate marches."

"Or we can deduce that Beauty Brands has a demented or disgruntled employee in their plant that tampered with numerous bottles distributed throughout the country. And then, they need to close down operations, issue a national recall, and ferret out the criminal. Sad to say, that is the best-case scenario. The worst-case scenario is, if you are correct and there is a connection between the product tampering and marches in the three cities, we have a very sick and angry conspiracy on our hands. Please ask Robert to come back in here. Thanks."

For forty-five minutes, the three of them discuss and agree to the details of an action plan. They acknowledge that the faster they get information, the faster they can prevent any further poisonings. So, speed is critical. Coupled with speed is the need to have an accurate and comprehensive understanding of the full extent of the tampering, and if there is any relationship between the tampering and the rallies before David reports the issue to Fletcher and Strathmore. They need a lot of product delivered to the CDC and answers from the CDC about tampering within ninety-six hours. This will mean three shifts a day working on this project only.

Margaret will deal with the local police, and her field office resource in the Twin Cities. Also, she and Robert will team to dig deeper into the Liberty Men of Buffalo, Free Cowboys relative to San Diego, and Protectors of Freedom in Minneapolis. They'll try to learn details of any alleged relationship with each other or affiliation with a national group. Robert will re-contact Beauty Brands and have the recall expanded to include the Twin Cities. He will alert Mary Jenkins that the scope of the work has just expanded. Given the time constraints, she will have to request assistance from other lab rats.

David will contact his counterpart at the CDC to get him in the loop and request the use of additional personnel in Atlanta.

David will also contact the section chiefs in all three cities to alert them of the activity and request their full cooperation. Hell, he will demand it. They will listen to him because he is not Barbara. He has no hidden agenda. If the tampering is found in Minneapolis, the connection between the poisoning and marches might be real. However, that does not preclude a national recall, just to be sure the tampering is isolated to the three cities. If Beauty Brands wants to, or has to, recall the product nationally, the corporate position could be that there were tops that could leak or an improper dye was in the batch. It has to be some innocuous reason to keep the media out of it.

"Do you two need me to stay with you tonight as you dig?"

"Thanks anyway, dad, but we can handle it."

"I guess I deserved that."

Smiles all around. David can see that these two are excited to have a potentially huge case in their laps. They, too, are tired of processing paperwork. He is confident they will go above and beyond to resolve this matter.

"OK then. My Bureau phone will be turned on, unlike when Barbara was running the show. Also, on the back of these cards is my personal cell number. Call me on that if I don't answer my Bureau phone. I'm proud of what you are doing. I know you are too."

* * *

David dares to eat his dinner of broccoli and a chicken breast on the patio. He washes it down with two beers. The allergy season has begun. He suffers less during the evening and night. He must initiate his med taking regimen: Take the upper in the morning and the downer at night to help him sleep. He has been doing this for years. Nonetheless, he wishes to delay the pill popping process each year because he doesn't care for the way the

116

two meds make him feel. His reverie of watching the sun set is interrupted by the ringing of his personal cell. Blocked caller.

"Hello."

"David, this is Wendell. Louisa and I have uncovered some interesting facts that could be evidence of a conspiracy in the murders of Section Chief Wilkins and Fatima Johansson. When can we meet?"

"Whoa, cowboy, not so fast. What's the hurry?"

"The information is mind-blowing. We want to share it with you and see what we should do."

"If you're looking for me to hold your hand and lead you to the next phase, forget it. I'm not your native guide. If you're looking for a sounding board, come on over. We can meet tonight. But have Ms. Cochran drive and ask her to take a circuitous route. When can you be here?"

"Ten minutes. We are in the parking lot of the East more Shopping Center. And yes, we took a circuitous route. Louisa knows why. See you in ten."

David thinks that Peterson is aggressively presumptive to say the least. What good is an investigative reporter who is not aggressively presumptive? Faint heart ne'er won fair maiden. The doorbell rings.

"Welcome, Wendell. Welcome, Louisa. I was just relaxing on the patio when this pushy reporter called and interrupted my beer. Can I offer you something to drink?"

"A beer would be great."

"And you, Louisa?"

"Beer also."

"Now, what's so important that you drove to see me?"

The three settled in for a long conversation, as the sun settled into the other part of the globe.

"David, we dug into Fatima's life, past and present, and learned there had been a large cash deposit into her checking account."

"Wait. Stop. How did you get legal approval to examine her banking records?"

"She was my client at legal aid and had given me the authority to access all her personal and private information. It's fairly standard in our office. It helps us screen out those who can afford an attorney but want free advice. It also helps us develop a solid case for who legitimately needs our help. Sometimes, poverty is a strong argument in court."

"OK, hurdle number one cleared. Wendell, how big was the cash deposit?"

"Ten thousand."

"Ten grand for a supposed street hustler is a lot. Very intriguing."

"That's what we thought, too. If we could follow the money, we might find someone who would not want to be found…the money giver. But that's not all."

"As you may have read, Ms. Johansson was shanked in jail while awaiting trial. We learned from a friendly corrections office that there was only one murderer of Ms. Johansson. The stabs to the back were administered after she fell to the floor. Killer insurance. The suspected murderer is Roberta Mainway. Ms. Mainway is in jail awaiting trial for armed robbery. This is her second visit and for a similar crime. She did a five-year hitch for the first crime. She could be a two-time loser and go away for fifteen to one of the state facilities. She's a very tough cookie, and a frequenter of the downtown S and M bar scene.

"She, too, is a client of the public defender's office. So, Louisa had access to all of her personal and private records. And Louisa found that ten thousand dollars was also recently deposited into the joint checking account Louisa shared with her mother. That's a lot of money for a street tough. Louisa's mother receives Social Security Disability of $1,254 per month, lives in government subsidized housing, and receives food stamps. So, it is highly unlikely mom suddenly came upon ten grand. The deposit of cash was made two days before Ms. Johansson was murdered. I do not believe in coincidences. Do you?"

"No, I don't. But you may be getting ahead of yourself. What is the connection?"

"Follow this. Someone who wants Ms. Wilkins' lifestyle kept secret hired Ms. Johansson to kill her. When the police got to Ms. Wilkins' townhouse, they reported it to be in an orderly state. That's on the official written report. It was not ransacked as proffered by Commander Anderson at the news conference. So, Ms. Johansson's mission was to kill Ms. Wilkins, make it look like a sex game that got out of hand, and leave town immediately with the ten grand. But she decided to stay. We'll never know why. She was subsequently arrested. That made the person, or persons, who hired her nervous that she would reveal who hired her. Then the same person, or persons, that bought her services as a killer decided it was in their best interest to have her silenced. So, this same person, or persons, hired Roberta Mainway to kill the killer. She took the job because it looked like it was a good deal for her mother. When convicted, she wouldn't see her mother for a long time, except through plate glass on Sundays. In fact, there was a good chance that her mother would die while Roberta was in prison. Her mother could use the money to enhance her meager existence. Louisa knows Roberta. She's tough, and she will never give up the people who hired her for fear that the money will be taken from her disabled mother."

"I hear what you are saying. But you have not given me any clue as to who is involved in the conspiracy. Where is the trail from the money to the killers?"

"We know that. That's why we need your help."

"Here we go again. I told you in the beginning that I was a force not a source. I gave you all the information I had and what I thought the other evening over dinner. The Bureau is not in the business of solving crimes of a local nature. That's the purview of the local police. If the murders were crimes that crossed state lines, we would get involved. This is not such a situation and is therefore outside my sphere of influence. I can't help you. Sorry. Would you like another beer?"

"Wait. Won't you even think about what we uncovered and help us?"

"As they say in all TV murder mysteries, follow the money. That's my advice."

David's guests are crestfallen. He thinks Wendell and Louisa were hoping that he would jump up, yell "Eureka!", and save the day. That isn't going to happen. No further conversation between Wendell and David is going to put his dream with Rachel at risk.

"No thanks. We must be going. Sorry to bother you."

They are not happy campers. Tough shit!

* * *

It's three in the morning when David sits upright in bed. His eyes are wide open. He's not sweating as a result of a bad dream. That's good. He has a big and risky task ahead of him. He knows what he has to do, and he knows that he has to do it now. He also knows that this is another perilous step on the slippery slope of his own doing. He plans it to be his last. Padding to his lockbox, he removes the flash drive and inserts it into his laptop. He downloads eight videos…not the ones containing images of anyone at the Bureau. The four starring Jack Strathmore, Fletcher Wilson, Mitchell Davis, and Stephanie Azaub will remain in his lockbox as insurance. He then downloads the eight videos from his laptop to a second flash drive and erases the eight from his laptop's memory. He finds a suitable envelope for mailing his gift. Writing with his left hand to look like a child's handwriting, he addresses the envelope, tapes it closed, and applies too much postage to ensure delivery. Later this morning, before work, he will drive to a post office on the other side of the city and mail the

120

envelope. In two or three days, Wendell Peterson will get another injection of information. He will have enough trails to follow to keep him busy for weeks. Maybe months. At least until David is safe on Eleuthera.

Staring at the mailer, David wonders if he should do this. Should he feed Peterson snippets of information over time? Is he trying to be some form of puppeteer manipulating Peterson's investigation? Should he tell all and run the risk of ruin? He answers his own questions: Yes. No. No. No. He is standing at the top of a slippery slope looking into the abyss. He can't deny the wonderful feeling of power. The feeling is, as everyone has told him, like a drug. It creates euphoria: A high that is short-lived. Thus, it also creates the psychological need for a longer and higher euphoria. He is unaccustomed to this feeling. The fear of unintended consequences both invites him and repels him.

Could the feeling of power become frequent and intensified to the point of burnout just like with a junkie? Could he be dependent upon the process and the feeling of power to the exclusion of honest feelings, just like a junky? Yes, and yes. He is leery of what he sees himself doing. But he must do what he knows is right. What would Jennifer, back in D.C., think of her Caspar Milquetoast now? Would his children be proud of his newfound inner strength and actions or would they chastise him for manipulating someone? He stares blankly at his path like a zombie as he walks back to his bed. He vows to tell Rachel how he is very slowly taking his last steps on this slippery slope. He is not sure why he must confess. Emotionally exhausted, he falls into a heavy sleep almost instantly.

VIII

"Are you crazy? David Eugene Drummer, have you completely lost your mind? Do you realize you are playing with very serious fire: Fire that will do more than burn your hands, it will consume your body? Why in gad's name did you do it?"

David is about to suffer Rachel's wrath. The depth of her displeasure is manifested by the fact that she used his complete name when calling him out for stupidity. His mother used to do that when he had done something very wrong, for which there would be substantial punishment. He looks chagrinned.

"David, by sending the files to Peterson, you're encouraging him to dig into the lives of private citizens. If he is any good at investigating, he will expose their seamy side to public ridicule and possible violent reactions like dismissal from their jobs or ugly divorce. You may be responsible for ruining the lives of eight people. How thoughtless?"

"Wait a minute. I did what I did to make damned sure Jack and Fletcher cause us no harm. Besides, Peterson is a big boy: He can take care of himself. This is the logical scenario. Peterson enlarges the pictures of the willing participants in Barbara's games. Armed with the photos, he and Louisa revisit the S and M bars downtown. They ask employees and patrons if the people in the photos can be identified. Some, if not all, are identified. The participants are found and questioned. Since no one in my office is in the photos, they are immune from Peterson's investigation. Thus, Peterson has a solid story about K.C.'s deviant underbelly with no mention of the Bureau. Maybe, front page of the Sunday edition with pictures of the bars but Jack, Fletcher, Mitchell, and Stephanie will not be seen or mentioned.

They will believe they have just dodged a huge bullet. They feel safe. When they feel safe, you and I will be safe. It was a planned diversion. That's why I did it."

"What if Peterson goes to the Bureau and asks if Jack or Fletcher can identify anyone in the photos?"

"He has no reason to contact the Bureau. And if he does, Emily Knapp will cut off his balls."

"What if Jack and Fletcher question where Peterson got his information about the other participants?"

"Peterson will not mention the files or that the information was spoon-fed to him. He will tell anyone who asks that the identities of the eight participants came from his diligent digging at the clubs. He'll want to take full credit for such a fine investigation. Remember his desire for a Pulitzer. Not sharing credit with an anonymous source or in this case a force makes the story all his. That's why reporters use the moniker, 'Anonymous,' when quoting a source. His objective, and his ego, will prohibit him from sharing credit."

"What if Peterson rightfully guesses that the files on the flash drive came from you, shortly after he asked you for help and you turned him down? Then, you become a source."

"So, what? I am still anonymous."

"What if he inquires if there are other files? Files of more people? What if he asks if there are files of people you wish to protect, like people at the Bureau? If he gets a bug up his butt, he will ask, and ask, and ask again."

"If he goes down that path, I will deny, deny, deny. He will be told he has the complete library and that's final. He has no way of proving otherwise."

"How can you be sure Jack, et al., will feel they are in the clear?"

"Because Fletcher most likely believes he and I retrieved all records of Barbara's games. He is in possession of said records. The flash drive was a backup of a backup. Fletcher is not smart enough to dig to that level. His self-inflated ego won't allow him to think an underling is smarter than he is, and that the underling would withhold information. More than that, if Jack, Mitchell, or Stephanie thinks Fletcher held back on his evidence discovery and has leaked the files, the three of them will turn on Fletcher like ravenous wolves. Jack will drive the bus over him, back up, and drive over him again."

"What if Fletcher tries to throw *you* under the bus?"

"My position is that I didn't know what we were looking for but when I found any items of interest, I turned all of them over to Fletcher like the good soldier Jack wants me to be."

"I still think you're crazy but you're my crazy. I stand by you. But please promise to share any more stupid ideas before you put them into action. Not post facto. Gottit?"

"Gottit."

"Tell me again what Peterson and Cochran told you."

The retelling takes about ten minutes. Then Rachel takes over: "So, Peterson and Cochran see a conspiracy. People hiring a killer to kill a killer. Bizarre, but possible. The two ten grand deposits can't be a coincidence. They are too close together in time and the recipients are similar in their lifestyle. Also, as you have schooled me, in crime there is no such thing as coincidence. The deposits were made in cash, so they can't be traced. Who has twenty thousand in cash just sitting around in a shoebox? Or who can scrape together that amount of cash on such short notice?"

"My guess is that one or more of the eight participants could have that amount of money. The cash had to come from a single source. I doubt any of the eight would collude. Most likely, they don't know each other. Maybe one who was bored enough to play with Barbara is also rich enough to pay for the murders. Peterson will find the source of the funds and expose that person."

"I can see how someone on the videos might know Fatima, if they frequented the clubs. They could contract with her to kill Barbara, if they were worried that Barbara had videos that could destroy their other world. If they feared they were being videoed during playtime, so that Barbara could blackmail them, then they would want her eliminated. That's plausible. But, David, who would know Roberta Mainway to be a potential killer? Another criminal or a cop? And how did that person know that Roberta was in jail, in the same cell block as Fatima? Criminal or cop? My non-FBI guess is that a corrections officer or someone in administration at the county facility relayed that information to a party asking about Fatima. That would mean the police are involved. That means Anderson has shit on his shoes. Gawd, I'm thinking like a Federal Agent."

"Yes, and as Knapp said, the federal investigators and local police are joined at the hip in this situation. That would mean that Emily Knapp has shit on her shoes also. She must know what is going on and how to deal with it. And I'll bet the silence of people down the line in the corrections facility was bought."

"As we get deeper into understanding all the events, we see a lot of money being thrown around. So, I go back to a basic question…who has that kind of money?"

"Beyond a possible rich patron of the spanking and punishment playtime, I'm sure Strathmore has accumulated reasonably large investments that can be liquidated. Plus, he has discretion over the petty cash account of the Bureau. Ten grand here and ten grand there would not be missed until the yearly audit in September. That would give Jack plenty of time to replace the funds."

"How did Roberta get the murder weapon?"

"The same individual who told the interested party about her presence and how to use her street skills carried the weapon into the jail and to the day room where he or she gave it to Roberta."

"Holy, crap! There are so many moving parts, I need a scorecard to tell the players and how they are involved. Now, the police are up to their chins in it. If what you believe is true,

126

Commander Anderson must have his fingerprints on the affair. If that's true, Emily Knapp knows. If she knows, Jack knows. My best danger sense tells me that they are all complicit in the murders. This is a cover-up of massive proportions. David, you may have stepped into a bed of fecal quicksand, from which it will be difficult to extricate you safely and cleanly. And by you, I mean we or us."

Rachel notices David's left hand is hanging limply by his side and his breath is labored. She must not let David know that she is concerned. So, she does not mention his physical reaction to the Q and A session.

"We'll be fine. I have the flash drive as leverage and insurance."

"This playing God or puppeteer stops now. I'm serious. For your own good, you must have no more contact with Peterson. Let him bring this mess to an end, without any more of your involvement. Let Peterson do whatever he does. Assume a low profile and stay out of everyone's way. Hide in plain sight. Gottit?"

"Gottit."

"Let's change the topic from frightening to promising. How soon should we put our homes on the market? And how much money will we net?"

The evening progresses amicably, although Rachel is beginning to be very worried about David's health. He has lost weight and his skin has become ashen. He has less energy, and his breathing is shallow and strained.

* * *

"David, Margaret and I want to provide a status report of our progress."

"Go, Robert."

"All the shampoo products have been recalled from the three cities and shipped to the CDC. Mary Jenkins will have a report of her findings within seventy-two hours. They are working night and day on the thousands of bottles. That's one facet of the investigation."

"Margaret?"

"I contacted my resources in the three cities and learned a great deal. First of all, after examining copies of all the paperwork that was filed by the three right wing groups, I noted striking similarities in all three. Not only is the name of the rally, 'Pure American Days', the same in all three cities, but the method of payment is the same. A cashier's check issued by USABank in the amount required by all three cities was attached to the forms requesting approval for the parade and rally. Here is the kicker: USABank does not have any offices in the three cities. In fact, USABank has no office anywhere in the country. It is a bank with no physical presence. It is chartered in the Cayman Islands. So, we have no chance of finding out the details of the bank and its officers.

"But we do know that USABank can receive mail at a post office box in Alexandria, Virginia. However, we can't go barging into the post office and open the USABank box without reasonable cause and a document signed by a federal judge. The postal service takes seriously their obligation to protect the flow of mail from sender to designated recipient without interference from anyone. That anyone includes law enforcement organizations like the Bureau."

"Think like the officers of USABank to learn the reason behind their actions. Why does the bank want to conduct business in this country, yet have no brick-and-mortar support? Check the papers they filed with the Department of Treasury and Banking Governance. Then check their website. Those are good places to start. Work backwards in an effort to gain access to their communications. We'll need every shred of evidence to convince a federal judge and the postal service that it is in the national interest to learn who is responsible for the rent on the mailbox, so we can open it. I know it won't be easy, but you've come this far, and you must not stop now. You can do it. What else did you learn?"

"As I said, information on the forms was eerily similar beyond the designation: similar number of marchers, two hundred; similar start time, nine am; similar reason for the parade and rally, and here I quote, *'To demonstrate that the citizens of the U.S. of A will not fear terrorists based in the Middle East; to rally the American people to stand for national purity; to rally the American people to be on guard and to keep America SAFE!'* See how the word 'safe' is bold and in all caps like a rallying cry. It's weird, and I don't like the phrase national purity. That is a very frightening phrase. Hitler used a similar phrase and sentiments behind it during the thirties."

"And that same phrase is on each permit request?"

"Yes. It's looking more and more like a national conspiracy orchestrated by an overarching organization. Right?"

"Margaret, it's looking more and more like you were –and are –right in your overall assessment of the situation. Given that the date of the parades is fast approaching, you need to dig deeper and faster. We can't stop the marches and rallies, but we must learn as much as possible about them before and during the time they take place. Make sure each field office has at least one camera crew at each parade and at the rally. I particularly want to hear the speeches. We have to monitor all the marchers and the speakers at the rallies closely…as if we were watching grass grow. Something very evil seems to be brewing. You guys have done a great job…so far. Keep up the good work. You're making me look like a Rockstar for guiding you. Seriously, stay at it. Thanks."

They leave. David ponders the brilliant, hardworking people in his charge. They never had a chance to show what they could do when Barbara was in her office. This aspect of being a boss, decision-making, people-guiding, and leadership, he likes. This bit of newness is good. He begins to prepare a preliminary report for Fletcher and Jack. He is reminded of a song's lyrics, "what to leave in and what to leave out." It's Friday. The report can wait until Monday.

* * *

Another weekend with Rachel. They talk about what clothes, knick-knacks, and personal items they'll be shipping to their new home. Obviously, winter clothes, boots, and anything related to snowfall or cold weather will not be going to Eleuthera. But what furniture? A desk for each, maybe. No TVs. They will have an internet connection. They should buy a powerful radio. Should they have a garage sale or simply donate everything to The Salvation Army? David has always thought garage sales were inane: People buying other people's junk, so it could be resold a year later. But this time is different–they are on the seller side. He and Rachel decide to combine their items into one "Gigantic Garage Emporium," as they will call it. Sell clothing, china, glassware, kitchen items, living room furniture, and everything except that which is attached to the dwellings, like appliances and carpeting. What does not sell will be donated. They decide not to offer coffee and cold drinks to the tire kickers, as a ploy to keep them longer, in the hope that they buy more. Too much clean up.

They'll need permission from the homeowner's association for the sale and the signage they will need to post. Positioned as the conclusion of a life chapter and the beginning of another, the couple sees no problem with getting written permission. The association should be happy for them. Once the stuff is sold, they will hire cleaning crews to come and make the places move-in ready. The Gigantic Garage Emporium will happen after they have two signed contracts of sale, ideally. But they are not locked into that time frame for a sale. They have to

130

work backward from their desired departure date…two days after David's official retirement. Two months before that date seems like a good time to put the homes on the market. Again, they will have to notify the homeowners association of their intentions. Lots of planning. Lots of decisions. Take only bare essentials. The more they decide to keep, the more expensive the shipping. International shipping is not cheap.

The selected realtor must be told of their plans. Should they use one or two realtors? Two. Competition is a good thing. If one townhome sells before the other, they have leverage. They can pull the listing from the lesser aggressive agent and give it to the successful agent. Price. The similarities of the units are such that they should command a similar price. Bought years ago, there should be substantial equity in each. The banks have to be notified.

Rachel remarks that a similar size unit three streets over recently sold for about $385,000. If they could get that price or something near it, they will have sufficient funds for the first year of their new life.

"David, it's like we are newlyweds moving into our first home. Mom and Dad have offered us lots of stuff, most of which we don't want. Eleuthera is our new home, and it's already furnished, albeit in the mode of a Caribbean Spartan. Whatever we ship or buy, once we are on the island, will reflect the fact that our new home has new owners. We will give it our personal touch. You know, we've not named our new home. We'll need to name it and have signs posted by the driveway entrance, so everyone will know it. What do you think? Let's play the name game. I suggest 'Three Palms,' for the trees on the beach."

"Sorry dear, but that is mundane. What about 'Escape'? It's what we did."

"Too criminal. It hints of your job."

"Peaceful Place?"

"Sounds like a rest home."

"What about 'Triumph'?"

"Smacks of that Nazi film of the thirties. The film by Lena, what's her name."

"I got it, 'New Beginnings' because that's what it offers us."

"I like it, but let's not stop thinking about a name that reflects our life."

As they try to cover all the details of the sale and move, they fill numerous pages on two yellow tablets. People to call. They raise questions for which others must supply answers. All-in-all, the complex planning procedure consumes their weekend's waking hours.

* * *

David arrives at the office before Robert or Margaret. He is stuck on the word **SAFE** on the three requests for parade and rally permits. He stares at the computer hoping the answer to his unasked question leaps off the screen. It does not. Another failure of technology, like the non-existent overnight work gnome. Within the safety of his office, he asks out loud, "What is **SAFE**?" No answer.

On a hunch, he activates his computer, enters two passwords, and gains entry into the Bureau's archives. He enters Political Movement 2000-2010. Up pops a file containing a twelve- page list of movements, action groups, and anything tangentially associated with politics. The Bureau is particularly good at compiling lists. The listing is chronological. He rearranges it alphabetically and scrolls down to page eleven. There is a file on **SAFE**. He opens file logged as BMLR-10.04. (Baldwin Miller's Life Report, October 2004) and begins to read the sketchy and quite subjective file on Senator Baldwin Miller and **SAFE**.

The agent who compiled this report sat in the audience of the first rally and recorded the event, as well as observed Senator

132

Miller wherever he appeared during the following year. Much of the material therein was transcribed from recordings taken ad hoc.

- Senator Baldwin Miller began his grassroots campaign in Big Pass, Kansas on October 18, 2002. **SAFE** stood for a **S**ecure **A**merica **F**or **E**veryone.

- The original six points of Senator Baldwin's manifesto were on display:

One: Talk and listen to your spouse, children, and neighbors.

Two: Participate in government, in schools, and in your community.

Three: Demand security and safety from government.

Four: Demand control of weapons and dangerous substances.

Five: Demand the highest moral standards from leaders in all aspects of your life. Use background checks.

Six: Have faith in your higher power and guard against the charlatans and false prophets.

- The poster containing the platform or manifesto was huge, about 30 feet by 40 feet, and the darkly colored eagle gripping the panel with the six points is a powerful, almost threatening symbol. Miller was seeking a new constituency in a small Midwestern town. Every small town represented a part of a new constituency much broader than his in Pennsylvania. He was running for some office higher in the food chain than that of Senator.

- Prior to his oration, there was a prayer and the national anthem was sung. National pride runs deep in the heartland. There is a commonality to the look of the townsfolk. There is a sprinkling of teens in the assembled throng, but no small children.

(In so far as possible, Senator Miller was quoted when answering questions from the audience. The names of members of the audience have been redacted.)

- *"Welcome, ladies and gentlemen. How gratified I am to see such a huge turnout. Maybe we should have uplinked this event to all the high schools in the state. I hope that by now all of you understand the six points of the SAFE platform. We have taken the liberty to provide leaflets with the six points, our mission statement, and our telephone numbers. My team has given us this reminder poster behind me. I'll now take questions."*

- *"Senator Miller, my name is XXXXXXXXXXX. My wife, XXXXXXX, and I have three children and we are scared stiff. We see stuff on the television news. We call them the three Gees: Guns, Gangs, and Godlessness. My family wants to be safe and secure. But, how do we get there without more violence?"*

- *"Mr. XXXXXXXXXXX, I don't think this great nation of yours needs another revolution. I say, get involved in local governments. This is the entry port to the sea of political change. If you can influence local governments and the state government representatives who live in your town, they will influence the national government. The problem, as we see it, is that in the past fifty years, politics and political power have shifted away from the local, law-abiding citizenry to those who live in a non-responsive ivory tower called Washington D.C. New rules and laws have been handed down to you good citizens. To reclaim your rightful power from those presently in power is not easy because those in power will not go quietly into the night. But you good people know everything worth having is worth the effort. Plants don't grow without fighting the soil, elements, and vermin. It takes a lot of effort. It's the same with reclaiming your country. It's worth reclaiming, so it's worth the effort.*

- *"What I'd like to ask is, once we've begun the process, how do we know that the people in Washington won't just shut us out like they've done in the past? And second, do we need new laws?"*

- *"They won't shut you out, because these newly elected officials will know who elected them and that they can be run out of office if they don't meet the needs of the people...that's you. No new laws are needed. What is needed is firm enforcement of the laws already on the books. There are state and federal laws that regulate and control dangerous things like guns and drugs. There are state and federal laws that establish prosecutorial guidelines and punishments for abusers of the gun and drug laws. Let me ask you to think a minute about guns, because that's the thornier of the two subjects. The Second Amendment to the Constitution clearly states that gun ownership is based upon the need for a militia. "Let me quote: 'A well-regulated militia, being necessary to the security of a free state, the right of the people to keep and bear arms, shall not be infringed.' The militia would, in turn, act at the orders of and owe their allegiance to the body that allows them to exist...that's a government run by men and women you elect. At the time of the Constitution, this was the government's way of maintaining individual freedom and establishing a force to fight the British.*

- *"Today, there is not a right-thinking American among you who would call for the removal of hunting guns. Rifles and shotguns are for sport and acquiring food for your tables. Do we need automatic weapons? Do we really think it's a good idea to make automatic weapons available to children and the emotionally unstable? What's wrong with licensing these weapons, like we do cars, and doing background checks on the people who want to own them? These two steps would go a long way to ensure the safety and security of decent, honest citizens. We do not need the Posse Comitatus and the myriad paramilitary, neo-Nazi, white supremacist terror groups that feel they, and they alone, can protect us if we think like they think and do what they tell us. And we don't need street gangs to have access to automatic killing power.*

*   *"And we surely don't need the rampant drugs that are threatening the future of our youth. We have strict laws outlawing cocaine, crack, crank, meth, heroin and every other imported or homegrown destroyer. But our police have their hands tied by the judicial system that coddles the criminal. The police can't do this, and the police can't do that. The rights and freedoms of the criminals are held above the safety and security of society. We should implore the courts to use the laws that are on the books. Demand the courts to act without fear. If they will not, we will get new, responsible judges who will. Remember, the judges are elected by citizens like you or appointment by officials voted into office by citizens like you. They all owe their bench to someone and that someone ultimately is you. The future is in your hands .This is what we believe. What do you believe?"*

*   *"Senator Miller, God bless you and your wake-up call. How do we protect ourselves against the liars, deceivers, and charlatans?"*

*   *"Protection against charlatans requires vigilance. This country is blessed with the highest degree of technological expertise in the world. And because of a free market system, technology is expanding rapidly and becoming available to all of us. There is a wealth of*

information about places, companies, and people stored in files throughout the world. You can use this information for safety and security. You can be your own investigators. And, the sooner, the better.

- *"It's possible to establish a national clearinghouse of information –of personal files to be checked by your duly elected authorities. We have the system already in place. This single source contains more useable, important information than the Internal Revenue Service or the credit companies and it should be substantially more accessible to all you good folks. When we have accessed this data bank, we can control our destiny.*

- *"Thank you, my friends. I hope I'm not being too presumptuous to call you my friends. I am excited. I feel the energy of goodness. I feel the strength of conviction. I feel the concern. I know there is a better way, and you are the answer."*

- *During the evening, his voice gradually transitioned from warm and friendly to strident and demanding. With every answer, Miller won their hearts. He was hoping their votes would follow.*

(The following is a transcript of the Senator's television program interview/discussion.)

- The television news show features Pennsylvania Senator Baldwin Miller, the leader of the SAFE movement. His deep and pleasant voice starts calm and measured. Over the course of the show, his voice gradually increases in intensity and volume. The pleasant melody of a professional speaker becomes the fervent tone of a confrontational cheerleader. Staccato supplants modulation. Senator Miller is calling out the plethora of death and destruction that he and his followers have seen in the high schools around the nation. He has all the statistics, dates, and names. His marching orders. His rambling becomes ranting.

- *"You are either part of the problem or part of the solution."*

- *"How could these murderous events have occurred? How could children kill children? Who is the cause of this effect? Who is to blame? Who is accountable?"*

- *"The NRA and the loose gun laws make it too easy for anybody to have guns. And not just handguns and rifles but automatic weapons. The champions of unrestricted personal freedom without commensurate individual responsibility foolishly believe we all have the right to carry any weapon we choose. The Second Amendment to the Constitution allows people to carry guns if they belong to a well-regulated militia. Said militia, by definition, owes allegiance to a government. To what government do the White Brotherhood and the Voodoo Kings have allegiance?"*

- *"The entertainment industry foists death and destruction on all of us. They target the young and impressionable with movies and video games. Bigger and more powerful guns. Explosions in all shapes and intensities. Car chases, plane crashes and dismemberment by the dozen. Continual savagery and brutality now come in all shapes and sizes. All for the sake of money."*

- *"Pornographers are evil. Make no mistake about it, pornography is violence, and the pornographers are the purveyors of hatred. This is a travesty of humanity."*

- *"And how about the promoters and sellers of alcohol and the dealers of drugs. Wherever the emotionally insecure want to be, other than where they are, alcohol and drugs will send them. These malignancies*

138

take money away from children and families. Take resources away from our economy and destroy the workforce."

- *"The schools don't care about the children. They have forgotten that if they spare the rod they will spoil the child. School officials won't discipline. They adjust the world around the malcontent to make the malcontent happy or compliant. They're afraid of lawsuits from parents. But most of all, they are afraid of failing to be perfect. So, they do nothing and promote platitudes that are politically correct. Do you know that the first use of the term, 'Politically Correct', was by Chairman Mao? So, is being Politically Correct the first step in following a Communist Doctrine."*

- *"Professional athletes and their sports associations are the worst. The barely educated pro athletes, the ones who got out of high school to never graduate from college, want everyone to love them for their athletic deeds. But these same highly visible miscreants claim not to be role models. And the leagues say that whatever the jocks do, they should just not take steroids or kill anybody. If they do these two heinous things, the league will have to suspend them for two games and fine them a dollar."*

- *"And our government leadership is a bad joke. An incredibly sad, bad joke. The present administration, and the party that has run the country for the past sixteen years, have let the moral fiber of the country degenerate. Their tactics for re-election have been to favor and promote the various personal agenda. Everything today is done in the name of pleasure and for money."*

- *"But we the people are the solution to the problem. We must take back our lives, take back our communities, take back our nation, take back our government, and take back our rightful place as the moral leader of the free world. And we must do it now. We must establish a new life free from the threat of depravity. Our children must be kept safe."*

• *"Thank you. Now, we'll answer questions."*

(The Senator started off like the voice of reason and ended his spiel with morsels of truth slathered by the hysteria of near facts. As the news show returns, the moderator has a nervous smile.)

• *"Welcome back to Newsmakers, I'm your host, Bob Trumet. Today, we are talking with Senator Baldwin Miller of Pennsylvania. Our switchboard is completely lit up. But Senator Miller, before we go to the first caller, let me ask you two questions. First, what do you expect to get from SAFE? Second, how can the people learn more about SAFE?"*

• The Senator leans into the camera ever so slightly. He does not stare, but looks intensely as if he really, really cares. His dark blue suit, white shirt, and red and light blue striped tie flag his belief system. Dark hair, solid facial features, and subtle gesturing complete the communication of a strong father figure. The eagle at the top of the six-point platform, the same as the lapel pin worn by the Senator, is depicted in flight, wings spread, with beak and talons open. The bird is in raptor mode.

• *"Bob, **SAFE** is for the people and by the people. I am just bringing the issues to the attention of all Americans. It's the people who can solve the problems and be safe and secure. They have the power. They have the right. We want to hear from the people. **SAFE** will be an expression of the will of farmers, factory workers, clerical workers, teachers, retailers, all the hardworking*

140

*Americans who pay their taxes and who made this country great. America can be great again because these people will make it so for their children. Second, if the people want to learn more about **SAFE**, they should search their souls and talk to each other. Then tell us what you want. Call the 800 number on the screen behind me. We'll send you information. Do they want security and safety? Do they want to leave their children and their grandchildren a nation that is safe and secure?"*

- *"Thank you, Senator Miller. Now, let's hear from our first caller."*

- *"Bob, this is XXXXXXXX from Mechanicsburg, Pennsylvania. Senator Miller, it's about time somebody recognized what the working man and his family want. We want to be safe and our kids to be safe. I just want to say we want to help you in any way we can. Let us know how and we'll do it. We're in the telephone book, Senator. Thanks for looking after us."*

- *"Mister XXXXXXX, thank you for volunteering. It's volunteers, like you, that made this country great and can make it safe again. Please stay on the line and one of the aides will take your information."*

- *"Caller two, Senator."*

- *"Good morning, Bob. Senator Miller, you are right, so right. Where can I get copies of your six-point platform? I want to give them out in my neighborhood, at little XXXXX school, and at the plant where XXXXX, that's my husband of twenty-two years, and I work. I'd like to get the church involved, too. Do you have a mailing address? Oh, yes, this is XXXXXXXX from Moline, Illinois."*

- *"Thank you so much, XXXXXXX. If you stay on the line, one of the aides will take your name and address to send you some flyers. Now, will you do*

141

something for all America? Write and tell us how we can help you feel safe and secure?"

- *"Next caller, you're on the air with Senator Baldwin Miller."*

- *"Good morning, Senator. This is XXXXXXX from Biloxi, Mississippi. Let me ask you: How did we get in this state of moral decay to begin with? If we can learn how the problem started, we can learn how to correct it."*

- *"Your question deals with the root of the pervasive moral decay. We believe the root of the problem can be found in not caring. Over time, Americans cared just a little bit less. We didn't take responsibility for our own actions and lives. We let the other guy do it. We let the government take care of us. We let big business take care of us. Our lives had too much comfort stuff: cars, clothes, and self-gratification. All of this did not happen overnight. It happened almost imperceptibly over the last decades of prosperity. Like sand shifting almost invisibly in the desert wind. After a while, the sand has moved completely so that the dune that was on the right is now on the left. No one noticed the change. It just happened. Prosperity blinded us or made us look away. We let it happen to us. And we had many willing accomplices. For everything we gave up, there was someone who would take it. But Americans can take back their lives if they want to. Americans can take back their freedom, rights, and responsibilities."*

(Two years later. Transcript of a national news show taken over several days.)

- *Today on Capitol Hill, the Senate initiated an investigation into the allegations concerning Senator Baldwin Miller of Pennsylvania, his **SAFE** campaign, and the recent school shootings. This*

142

*investigation was hurriedly called based upon evidence provided by the FBI. This evidence dealt with the agency's investigation of the aborted shooting at Coastal Mesa, California. An unidentified source indicated that there is evidence to prove that the Senator knew of the shootings before they occurred. There is even speculation that the shootings were choreographed to be precursors of Senator Miller's **SAFE** rallies. The Senator's aides deny all the allegations and innuendoes, stating that this is a smear campaign initiated and driven by the President and his party. The Senator claims that the campaign to discredit him is preposterous and is the act of an obviously desperate political opponent. The ad hoc committee hearing starts tomorrow.*

• *The Senate hearings hit the ground running. Questions were designed to ensnare liars not to elicit facts because the facts are all in. Other activity in Washington and the rest of the country seems to be on hold. Two large notebooks of information and facts have been provided to each of the Senators. It's now time for the committee to ask questions about the reports. The accused government agents are the first to testify. A public gallows is built in this fashion. The committee promises that Senator Miller will testify tomorrow.*

• *News from Washington is that Senator Baldwin Miller has apparently taken his life. This evening at eight thirty-seven the body of Senator Baldwin Miller was found in his automobile, which was parked with its motor running near the Lincoln Memorial. Apparently, Senator Miller had committed suicide by firing a single large-caliber bullet into his head. The police stated that he appeared to have placed the gun barrel in his mouth. The explosion and impact removed the back of Senator Miller's head and shattered the rear window of the coupe.*

As of now, there are no other details. Speculation is that Senator Miller took his own life, rather than face the Senate Committee which was investigating his involvement in the recent rash of school shootings. Police have cordoned off the area and are combing it for clues. Neither Senator Miller's family nor his office is available for comment or elaboration.

End of report.

The report reads like a bad obit, is not well written, and is unsigned. David guesses that the report was compiled by a junior analyst because it is based mainly on tape recordings and transcripts from field agents but no investigations. It is impossible to know exactly what was in the documents that were the basis of the report. There was an obvious amount of editing and personal bias in the file. The author did not like Senator Baldwin and thus gave this document a damning hue. The brief and inflammatory national career of a junior Senator from Pennsylvania had ended and something, anything had to be in the Bureau's archives. More than likely, the junior analyst was told to "just put something in the files."

The Senator was a wolf in sheep's clothing. He was intent on a higher office and was willing to foment unrest and kill children to attain his goal. David recalls that there were many in the Bureau convinced that Baldwin's rallies were not reactions to the numerous attacks on children, but rather they were the ex post facto cause of the killings. Without the killings, there would be no reason for the rallies. To stoke the attendance and publicity of the rallies, there had to be children killing children.

David is not sure how, if at all, this applies to what they are looking at today. He recalls the rumors that Miller had a national network that went underground when he died. Is that network still functional? Has **SAFE** been reborn? Is there a connection between the poisonings and the marches and rallies?

144

The use of **SAFE** must be a hint. David will tell Robert or Margaret about **SAFE** as they continue their investigation. Learning more will be David's contribution to the overall work.

IX

Beneath the Sunday paper, with his eyes closed, David had hoped for a tranquil day. The buzzing of the phone ends that wish. There, on his Bureau cell, is the name, Robert Delcia.

"Hello, Robert. Why the call on Sunday afternoon? Let me rephrase that: How can I help you?"

"David, I just got off the phone with Mary Jenkins, you know, my contact at the CDC and they have finished examining all the bottles of shampoo from all three cities...15,560 of them. They found only one with a pin or needle prick near the bottom. And that one was from a CVS store in Minneapolis. They tested the contents and found DMSO and the super-rabies virus. Only one, and it was a killer bottle. I'm here with Margaret who is, sad to say, almost beaming. Now that we found one bottle that had

145

been tampered with in each of the three cities, she says we have the basis of a national conspiracy. What do we do next?"

"Have Ms. Jenkins email her findings, put them together with the investigation you and Margaret have conducted to date, print out the documents, and put the file on my desk. In the meantime, I'll arrange an early morning meeting tomorrow with Fletcher and Jack. Put me on speaker. Margaret, congratulations to you and Robert. When both of you are done, go home and get well-earned rest. If you sleep in tomorrow, I'll cover for you. Good job. I'll take it from here."

For the next hour, David reviews what he knows and how to position it to Fletcher and Jack. Whatever he puts forth must be logical and reflect the best thinking of his team. There can be no loose ends. The conclusion must be direct, simple, and clear. The next actions for the Bureau must be in the best interest of the nation's citizens and Beauty Brands. No rush to judgment. No panic stirring moves. Calm. Serious. Efficient. His mind is whirling. The options are myriad. As he thrashes through the details of this situation, pressure builds within him. Stop! He takes ten slow and deep breaths. Then, he presses the numbers of another Bureau cell.

"Fletcher, something important has come on to our radar screen. You, Jack, and I need to discuss what my team has uncovered. Can we meet in Jack's office, or yours, tomorrow before the rest of the people arrive? I need your expertise and guidance. Call me when you get this message. Thanks."

He needs a drink to calm down. Three ounces in a rocks glass. No rocks. Four swallows and the nectar is gone. He feels his body warm and begin to uncoil. His mind follows. Sitting on the couch and staring outside at the gentle sunlight, he is still. In his inner ear, he can hear his heart beating loudly. He feels his pulse rate. One hundred and thirty is unacceptable. The phone message undid the benefits of his breathing exercise. Relax. Relax, he tells himself, but he is not paying attention. Should he have one more drink to ensure sleep? He just sits and stares, not sure what is happening. He knows what he will recommend, but Jack will have the final say. His phone buzzes.

"David. Hey pal, you sound stressed out. What's the big mystery about?"

"We believe there is a connection between some product tampering and planned right wing marches and rallies scheduled for this upcoming weekend. These issues are complex, and the connections are tenuous. We need to review all the work that has led my team to this point. How about tomorrow at six in Jack's office?"

"Are you trying to scare me with some conspiracy theory?"

"It's not a theory. The facts are there for everyone to see. My team just pulled them together to make sense of it all."

"Jack's out of town this week. So, you and I can meet in my office and we can video conference Jack wherever he is. I'll find him tonight and alert him. How about six thirty in my office? Is that okay with you?"

"See you then. And thanks, Fletcher."

"Now, get some rest. You sound terrible."

One more drink to ensure deep sleep. He thinks of the scotch as medicinal. Another three ounces; he heads to the bedroom. He sips and strips. His thoughts bounce to everything that he is facing at work, not at work, and nearly at work. His thinking becomes illogical and fuzzy, and he laughs as he wonders if it's possible to slur your thoughts like you slur your speech when you've had a lot to drink. He sets the alarm and collapses onto his bed.

* * *

The meeting started well. Jack and Fletcher were interested in what David had to report and were not as dismissive as they had been previously. Given the apparent gravity of the situation, they agreed with David's decision to have the parades and speeches monitored by personnel in the appropriate field offices. Jack will call the president and CEO of Beauty Brands and explain the situation with product tampering. He will not mention anything about a possible right-wing conspiracy, because the dossier on Beauty Brands indicates that the company and its CEO are big supporters of conservative causes and the political candidates that champion them. A national recall and replacement will be suggested. All bottles returned to Paducah, Kentucky will be examined by company staff for leakage. Any bottles found with the telltale mark of tampering will be sent to the CDC for content analysis. Jack will also contact the head of the CDC and alert her to a possible influx of bottles over the next six weeks. Fletcher will contact the assistant director at each field office, outline the situation, and request their full support in monitoring and reporting back to David's team for review and analysis.

"Good job, David. You and your team may have stumbled across a big national issue."

Stumbled across...Jack was in true character: condescending prick. David knew that the two senior officers would take up this cause and, when it reached a tipping point, they would get out in front of it to the media and take full credit for leading the way in the investigation. So close to retirement, he won't fret about their headline grabbing and dismissive approach to those who do the work. This type of credit usurping is not new to this office. Robert and Margaret might get pissed. If sufficiently pissed, they could leave the Bureau in silent protest. They would be replaced by fresh faces willing to work in near obscurity. On the other hand, they most likely won't storm out of the Bureau because they didn't join the Bureau for public praise: they joined to serve a higher purpose.

The meeting is adjourned.

"David, good job. We'll take it from here. You and your team can go back to review, analyze, and distribute information... just not information about this situation."

Fletcher is just as condescending as Jack. When two people work closely for ten years and enjoy the same strange lifestyle outside of work, the lesser begins to sound and act like the greater. An homage to the leader. During the elevator ride to his floor, David decides on a plan for Robert and Margaret who are not yet in the office. They will arrive later in the morning after their well-earned rest. He heads for the cafeteria for breakfast and more coffee. The residual effects of last night's scotch call for food to quell his land-based *mal de mer*.

* * *

"Robert, can you round up the team and come to my office?"

They settle into their usual places in David's office.

"Margaret, please fill in Dinah and Jacob as to what you and Robert have uncovered."

Ten minutes later, Dinah and Jacob display concern about the discovery.

"OK. Let me bring everyone up to the minute. I had a meeting with Jack and Fletcher earlier this morning. They are in agreement that the situations in the three cities warrant the Bureau's full attention. Jack will do his thing in the upper stratosphere while Fletcher takes control at the field office level. They have requested that we stand down. I think that sucks. So here is what we need to do: You need to contact your resources at the three field offices and request that when they are monitoring the parades and rallies they use uplinks to our satellite. Tell the people who will be monitoring the events that what they upload to the satellite will be downloaded into our system for review and analysis during the next week and stored for posterity. In reality, the entire team will be seeing the activity in real time as it goes into a file.

"Why the real time analysis? My concern is that under normal procedures, the material would be dumped into the master file system and controlled by people other than you: controlled by Jack and Fletcher. Given their dismissive attitude toward your work in today's meeting, I think they think they have before them a gold mine of opportunity. If I am correct, they would want to parse and edit the three feeds into a simple five-minute video that fuels their need for congressional approval and public love. They would say, 'look what we uncovered,' 'look at how well we are protecting the citizens of this great country,' and now 'appropriate more money for us and don't interfere while we are protecting you.' They would lose the real truth of the events in an obfuscating snowstorm of self-aggrandizement.

"After the crowds have dispersed and the speakers are back in their cars, we will be here analyzing what we just witnessed. That's when our real work begins. As a first step, we will create a temporary report based on the rallies in Buffalo and Minneapolis. I suggest we start to develop the report with information from Buffalo. We can confirm, deny, add, and subtract the findings based on activity in Minneapolis and repeat the process with information from San Diego. That should make the report thorough, fast, and accurate. We will issue our report within twenty-four hours of reviewing all the videos. This rapid response will keep everyone upstairs on the straight and narrow path of truth. The two at the top won't be able to adjust the findings of our work to suit their agenda. We will hand them a friendly preemptive strike of objective unvarnished truth.

"Each of you will view and record the activities on his or her own monitor. The separate team approach will give us confirmation of any sighting or finding. Margaret, you take Buffalo. Robert, you and Dinah take Minneapolis. Jacob you've got San Diego. I'll alternate between Buffalo and San Diego.

150

Given the time zone differential, I can easily handle both. I expect everybody at their desks at seven am. That's when the monitoring of the pre-parade crowd will commence in Buffalo. We want to catch these events from the very beginning. When bathroom breaks are required, go one at a time. Come back and view what you missed. We cannot afford to miss anything.

"This means we will be working this weekend: a long Saturday and a wrap-up day on Sunday. Our report will be emailed to Jack and Fletcher before we go home on Sunday. So, be prepared. Comfortable clothes, snack bars, and bottled water are recommended. I'll be responsible for meals. So, I'll need your food orders before we start...lunch and dinner for Saturday. We'll deal with Sunday food later. Guys, we are on to something big. Great work so far."

David calls Rachel and tells her he has to work the weekend. He does not say why, and she doesn't ask. She trusts him. They agree she should call real estate agents and get a feel for the correct timing, how the agents will market the homes, how much the two homes are worth in today's market, and what to do if they don't sell prior to the couple's departure. She will also get cost and timing information from international shippers. She hopes they have one of those kits that tell people changing residence locations exactly what to do. That would make life easier. If they don't have the information, she will use the guidelines for domestic moves marketed by the postal service.

More reports to read. More forms that cry out for completion. It is difficult for him to focus on the trivia of his role. David is anxious about the weekend. He is not following protocol by preempting his bosses. They might resent his actions. His rationale will be that he wanted to get them the best report possible while the information was fresh. The report will have his name as author on every page and it will be in the central file. That will eliminate any actions on their part that might stem from their hidden agenda. Besides, he is about to retire. What can they do to him?

* * *

The Bureau has a firm policy against casual dress during the work week, given the fact that agents represent the Federal Government in service to the general public. Even on Saturday, casual means collared shirt, khakis, and leather shoes. Not today. Not David's team. Comfortable attire is the rule. He has never seen the four of them dressed as they would be at home on a Saturday. There they are...relaxed, but not sloppy. Cubicles are occupied, and monitors turned on.

The people have begun to arrive in Buffalo. The milling around slowly congeals into a crowd as the number of marchers grows rapidly. Anticipated start of the parade is nine am in the east... at least that's the time on the permit. Commentary from the agents indicates that the marchers are being watched. Small cameras located in hats and vests record the activity. Audio will be provided to Kansas City by means of a parabolic mic located in a van across the street from the staging area. The staging area is at the southern end of First Street. The march will be north twenty blocks on First to Solvay Park where they will hear a speech, enjoy family picnics, and visit with like-minded friends. The rally leaders have promised to leave the park as clean as they found it when they depart around two pm. There is no temporary stage. Whoever speaks will do so standing on a picnic table.

Wandering within the growing crowd are four men dressed in black from head to calf: black ball cap, black shirt, and black pants. Their boots are tan. Although the day is not yet brightly lit by the sun, the men are wearing large military sunglasses that partially obscure their faces. They smile at everyone they meet, say a few words, and hand each soon-to-be marcher what looks like a pamphlet. Margaret and David make note of these men. The field agents inserted in the crowd will send a pamphlet or two to Kansas City. First scanned to their phones and sent electronically. Hard copies will be sent via overnight pouches for Monday delivery. David will have the information before Fletcher or Jack. A storm of questions, with no answers, crashes in David's mind. These paramilitary men are the key to understanding the why of the rally and the who behind it. Two of these men go to a van and return to the crowd with a banner. Unfurled, the words on the banner read "Pure American Days." Several members of the throng stand at attention and insert a pole to hold the banner. They will lead the parade. The march begins. Marchers with smiling faces shout and wave to onlookers standing on the sidewalks. In another universe this would be an Independence Day parade in small town U.S.A. Not today. Not with the men in black paramilitary uniforms.

The stroll-like march takes two hours from first to last marcher. The crowd spills into Solvay Park which is already well populated with family and friends of the marchers. Blankets have been spread and tables are set for lunch. Margaret notices a half dozen more men in paramilitary dress. They appear to be standing guard at one of the pavilions. Inside the pavilion is a small group of men and women who are not dressed like their guards. The members of this second group are dressed in white shirts or blouses and dark blue pants or skirts. They must be leaders who are there to teach the throng and seek volunteers. The agents in the crowd and on its borders can now turn on their individual mics. Crowd noise is just that: David and Margaret's ears are flooded by a cacophony of conversations about myriad issues…bathrooms, food, sitting arrangements, location of lost children, and questions about what will happen now. The volume of the mics is turned down, but the conversations still overlap.

The second group comes from under the pavilion's roof, walks to a table in the front of the crowd, and steps up to the table-top platform. They are smiling a plastic near-grimace that begs the viewer to trust them. Just like a barracuda before it strikes. David and Margaret think the comments of these people will be key to their analysis.

"Ladies and gentlemen. Good, God-fearing, hardworking Americans of Buffalo. Thank you for coming out on such a beautiful God-given day and demonstrating how strongly you feel about keeping America secure and safe. I will be the only speaker."

A loud and favorable response.

"When I'm done with my three-hour speech…"

A loud groan and some boos from the audience.

"Just kidding. I'll be brief. Let me explain why we think a rally like this is needed in every city across this great land. First, internationally our embassies and military bases are under attack from Islamic jihadists who wish to rule a world without Christianity. Our men and women, your relatives, are being slaughtered and our government does nothing but frown and wring its hands. Our feeble feds do nothing. No military response for the numerous, evil attacks. No holding the jihadists responsible for over five hundred deaths in the last few months alone. The Federal Government speaks about increased diplomatic pressure and negotiations. How to you negotiate with terrorists? You, the good citizens of this great land here in Buffalo need to force the Federal Government to act not talk. An eye for an eye, as the good book says."

Cheering and applause.

"The second fact is equally disturbing. These Islamic jihadists have begun to infiltrate our homeland. There are fifty percent more mosques in the U.S.A. now than there were five years ago and one hundred and fifty percent more mosques in our country than before the attack of 9/11. The cancer is spreading across this great land. To make matters more frightening, the Islamic jihadists now number in the hundreds of thousands living and working in our own backyard. One estimate has the terrorist

154

population in this country to be over a million. That's potentially a big army of fighters bent on our destruction. And what is the Federal Government doing about this threat? They tell us they are negotiating. So, in reality they are doing nothing. Absolutely nothing. In World War Two, all people who were first or second-generation Germans or Japanese had to register with the federal government. Their actions were monitored. In fact, thousands of Japanese were placed in retention facilities, so they could do no damage in their adopted country...the U.S.A. We say make all the Muslims register with the Federal Government, put the jihadists in special camps, and monitor every Muslim closely."

Thunderous, applause, cheering, and whistling.

"The last point I would like to make deals with Sharia Law. This is the code of laws that governs the public and private lives of all Muslims. Sharia Law controls politics, banking, economics, and even the sex lives of all Muslims. Muslims have no freedom except that which is granted under Sharia Law. Sharia Law and the religious leaders that oversee its administration deny individual freedom of speech, freedom of religion, freedom of assembly, and all the other freedoms that make the U.S.A. the great country it is. The Islamic jihadists that are growing like a cancer in this great land want to impose Sharia Law on all of us. They want to deny us our God-given freedoms. I would rather die in battle with the camel jockeys, than give away my freedom. At the very least, I would know that I killed many of them before they got me. Do you feel the same way?"

Cheers, whistling, and "hell yes" are instantaneous.

"We know the terrorists are already here because they have begun to kill innocent citizens...non-combatants right here in Buffalo. Remember the police shooting of Eliot Brankow who lived at 3412 Woodmere Drive. The man had gone crazy and killed his wife and daughter before the police put him down like a rabid dog. We have it on good authority that Mr. Brankow had been poisoned before the shootout. He was poisoned by a mind-controlling drug.

He had no understanding of right and wrong. He only knew anger. How he was poisoned, no one will ever know. By whom he was poisoned, no one can be sure. But we have seen incidents similar to his death in major cities in Europe where the Islamic jihadists have established colonies. Was he a test case for further widespread poisoning in our sacred land? Could his death be the beginning of a bio-terrorism attack? Very likely. These devils are in the process of taking over the liberal countries in Europe: the ones that opened their borders and freely welcomed the terrorists. These countries are now suffering the consequences of their blind liberal thinking. Is the U.S.A. next?"

A chorus of "hell no" becomes a chant that echoes off the buildings around the park and down the streets. The speaker pauses for about two minutes until the chanting dies down. *"I was hoping you would feel that way. We see the problem in front of us and we know the path to solving the problem and keeping America secure and safe. I don't think this great nation of yours needs another revolution. I say, get involved in local governments. This is the entry port to the sea of political change. If you can influence local governments and the state government representatives who live in your town, they will influence the national government. The problem, as we see it, is that in the last fifty years, politics and political power have moved away from the local, law-abiding citizenry and moved to those who live in a non-responsive ivory tower called Washington. And new laws in which you had no voice or input have been handed down to you good citizens. You have been told to follow the new laws because they are the laws of the land. You must reclaim your God-given power of self-determination. To reclaim this power from those in power is not easy, because those in power will not go quietly into the night. But you good people know everything worth having is worth the effort. It's the same with reclaiming your country. It's worth reclaiming, so it's worth the effort.*

"Once the right men and women are elected, they won't shut you out of the government, because these newly elected officials will know who elected them and that they can be run out of office if they don't meet the needs of the people...that's you. No new laws are needed. What is needed is firm enforcement of the laws already on the books. There are federal laws that regulate and control immigration and citizenship. There are state and federal laws that establish prosecutorial guidelines and punishments for abusers of those laws.

"Protection against left-leaning charlatans requires vigilance. This country is blessed with the highest degree of technological expertise in the world. And because of a free market system, technology is expanding rapidly and becoming available to all of us. There is a wealth of information about places, companies, and people in files throughout the world. You can use this information for safety and security. You can be your own investigators. And, the sooner, the better.

"It's possible to establish a national clearinghouse of information: personal files to be checked by your duly elected authorities. We have the system in place. This single source contains more useable, important information than the Internal Revenue Service or the credit companies and it should be made more accessible to all you good folks. When we've loaded this data bank, we can control our destiny."

He pauses to bathe in the cheering accolades of his audience. His smile is friendly, and he waves to those whose eye he catches. After a few minutes, the crowd noise has died down.

"Thank you all for coming today. If you would like more information, please stop one of the gentlemen walking amongst you. They have pamphlets that can help you take the next step. Now, please have a pleasant picnic with your family. One word of caution: we have been told that we must clean up our space in the public park and be on our way by two o'clock. I guess our freedom to assemble is already being controlled by the bleeding-heart

liberals. We would appreciate it if you would put your trash in the large baskets and bags, so we can haul them away and keep the park clean. Enjoy your lunch."

More raucous cheering. The speaker and his four cleanly dressed cohorts quickly leave the platform, walk with purpose to a waiting van, enter, and leave the area. David immediately notes three things: The man never gave his name or the name of his organization; he referred to Mr. Brankow's death as a poisoning; and if David is correct there are large sections of the man's speech that can be found in the ranting of Senator Baldwin Miller over a decade ago. David's questioning mind responds: Why? How does he know that? This situation has become frightening. It's as if a dangerous dragon, once thought dead and buried, has emerged from its cave to wreak havoc on the land. David's anxiety level is on the rise. What he witnessed is not right. He and Margaret sit in his office and review what they saw and what they think this means. Once they have agreement, they must wait for Robert and Dinah to perform their analysis of the events in Minneapolis. David will request that Margaret, Robert, and Dinah compare notes on the marches and rallies. Before he watches the San Diego feed, David must wash his face in cold water in an effort to clear his head. He will also perform breathing and stretching exercises to calm his nerves. The five of them will have lunch when they have the time.

* * *

"What do we know, Margaret?"

"I am speaking for all of us now, so far our overall conclusion is that this is a grassroots movement controlled by an outside force. The speeches are nearly identical in Buffalo and Minneapolis. The hysteria created by misinformation, or flat out lies, speaks of a powerful force that is run by people who know how to manipulate the minds of everyday men and women. It is

158

interesting and that the speaker in both Buffalo and Minneapolis never gave his name. The guys in the black paramilitary uniforms and big sunglasses evoke images of storm troopers in a totalitarian state in Africa or South America. The poisoning was mentioned in Buffalo, but not in Minneapolis because we caught the tampered product before it could work its evil.

"Another interesting difference in the speeches in Buffalo versus Minneapolis is that the speaker in the Twin Cities mentioned the damage done to the Al Akbar Mosque. He said, and I quote:

'Windows were broken, pig's blood was splashed on the door, there was urine found in the fountain in which the attendees wash their hands, and anti-Muslim graffiti was spray painted on the walls inside. Some loyal Americans sent the terrorists a message that their kind...the kind that wants to rob us of life and liberty does not belong here. I think all God-fearing Americans should look at this example of how we treat our enemies and think long and hard about what they are doing to stop the Muslims from taking over this country.'

"If the speaker in San Diego mentions the murder/poisoning of Lisa Marie Buenaventura, we will have ironclad evidence of a national conspiracy. Two murders and an attempted murder. With the mentions of how to react against those who espouse Sharia Law plus the reference to the damage done to the mosque in Minneapolis, this group has gone well beyond fear mongering. They are into the onerous world of xenophobic hate speech that could be the precursor of hate crimes. Done in three states, the crimes fall within our jurisdiction. Anybody want to add to this?"

"Yes, I do. First, you guys have done a helluva job. But it has just begun. I will send each of you an archived file labeled BMLR-10.04 or Baldwin Miller's Life Report, written in October of 2004. Baldwin Miller, a junior Senator from Pennsylvania, was a political charlatan who went around the country promoting a movement called **SAFE** or a Secure America For Everyone. He found substantial acceptance in the small cities and towns throughout the nation. He was more than another rabble-rousing liar. He was deeply involved in the rash of school children killings that appeared in the early part of this century. The Bureau had solid evidence that Miller's speeches were planned to occur after each massacre. The dates of the rallies could not be planned unless Miller and his group knew when a school shooting had occurred. They had to control what appeared to be a variable. A Senate Committee was formed to investigate. But, before Miller was called in front of the august body, he blew out his brains. The **SAFE** campaign stopped without its leader. And not surprisingly, the school shootings stopped just as suddenly.

"When you examine the file on Miller, you will see numerous rambling quotes. I won't go into details. But much of what the speakers in Buffalo and Minneapolis said appear to be nearly direct lifts from Miller's ranting. You should read the file and compare the quotes. You will be led to ask, how is that possible? It can be possible if members of Miller's organization, his network, went underground upon the death of their leader only to resurface now. If it's reasonable to link the speakers' comments to Miller, then the big unknown is who was and is in the network. The answer to that question will require extensive exhuming of the past. If the network has resurfaced, they must be funded. By whom?

"While Jacob and I watch the rally in San Diego, you three dig into Baldwin Miller's past to determine his associates back then. Then trace these people up to the present. Simultaneously, go to the lab and run facial recognition on all the people who stood with the speakers before the crowds. I have a pass card you can use to get into the lab. We will reconvene for dinner at six. Good job, guys."

* * *

The rally in San Diego is more of the same. The speaker mentioned the murder/poisoning of the high-school girl. David is now fearfully convinced they are looking at a national conspiracy. The five meet in the small conference room.

"Did you three have any luck with finding Miller's compadres?"

"A few crumbs. We're trying to determine if the people we know of are alive today. That will take much more digging. We did notice this: The same two names were associated with two of the school massacres. Jean Blankenship and Harold Scharr. We have yet to find them, but we've just begun to look. We are also scouring the other mass murders for names other than those directly involved."

"Don't ignore the law enforcement officers. If Miller planned the school shootings, he had to have help from someone in authority at each location. If Miller could stage the attack then rail against violence, it is highly likely a cop was involved. This cop would be unable to find the killers because he was told to not find them. Or were the cops the killers of the killers on orders from Miller's organization? Don't overlook anyone. How about the facial recognition?"

"Nothing so far, but that program takes a while to scan for every person in our data base. Unfortunately, it is just that…our domestic criminal data base. Regardless of its size, it can't account for men and women who are beyond the criminal radar. And it cannot recognize international criminals. I input the faces and set the program to run automatically. If and when it finds a match, it will stop to print out the file, and then continue the process until all the faces have been analyzed. When ready, I will input Jacob's people."

"Nice work, Dinah. I never knew you were a closet techie."

She smiles: a rarity for her.

"Here is my proposal. We will go to our respective homes right after the sumptuous meal before us. We will allow the work of the day to percolate in our well-schooled and well-trained minds. The facial recognition program will run all night, finding people we don't know. I suggest someone put a note down there, so the system is not shut down by a well-meaning person. Tape my business card to the note to confirm the importance of your request. We will meet here tomorrow at ten to formulate and draft our report for Jack. Plus, we will see if we can discern any old associates of Millers and new faces from the rallies. On a personal note: I'm tired and I need to get some rest before tomorrow. Tomorrow will be just as tough as today. I want to send a final report to Jack and Fletcher before they arrive. I'll spring for lunch. You'll be home for dinner. And with that, I bid you a fond adieu."

Six ounces of Balvenie made David's journey to the land of nod faster than he could recite the alphabet backwards.

X

Showered, shaved, and groggy describes David as he enters the Bureau. He recognizes the fuzziness that has engulfed him and knows its cause. If asked its source, he will attribute it to the pressures of the job, work on Saturday, and a worrisome night's sleep. The lie will suffice. He must put on his teamwork demeanor. The four are already at their stations. Shit! It's eleven. Lunches are in a large bag. He enters the bull pen.

"Good morning, guys. Sorry for my late arrival. I forgot that I had a must do errand. Let's meet in the conference room to review what we learned while the world was sleeping."

"After running the facial recognition software on all fifteen people at the respective speakers' tables, I learned that only two are in our data bank: Paul Rhodes and Jerrod Frey. Rhodes did a nickel at Joliet for wire fraud. He was released four years ago and settled in Minneapolis. He works at a third-party administrator or TPA... A2Z Services. The TPA contracts with companies that offer retirement plans for backroom work, such as recordkeeping and administration. He is single and lives in downtown Minneapolis. While in Joliet, Rhodes became a member of the Aryan Brotherhood. He seems to have hidden this from his employer or resigned from the brotherhood without the usual rite of death inflicted upon those who wish to no longer be racist hate mongers. Or maybe he just went underground.

"Jerrod Frey also did a nickel in Sing Sing for computer hacking. He was so good at what he did, he bragged he could 'get into any computer system anywhere in the world.' Mr. Frey walked three years ago and works as an independent IT consultant in San Diego. Now, his mantra is that he 'can protect any system against any hacker.' Same coin, different side. He has been seen at several other right-wing rallies over the past two years but never standing with the speaker...always in the crowd. Frey is also single and lives near the beach.

"Conclusion? We have one ex-con who has extensive knowledge of computers and their systems and another ex-con who knows how to move money. This duo may be our link to USABank and any relayed accounts."

164

David grins as members of his team try to sound hard by using terms they think the KPD uses.

"Nice job, Dinah."

"As they say on late night TV…but wait there's more."

Chuckles all around.

"I also ran the system on the faces of Jean Blankenship and Harold Scharr. They both can be found in cemeteries. Ms. Blankenship is resting in New Orleans. Mr. Scharr is resting in St. Louis. Ms. Blankenship died in a one-car accident on I-10 on a clear dry night. She died three years ago. No other people involved. Mr. Scharr died of a self-inflicted gunshot five years ago. A suicide and an accidental death that may not have been an accident. Too coincidental. Hazarding a guess, I guess they were murdered. Reason for their deaths could be that someone is trying to cover up something by tying off loose ends. They appear to be the only known associates of Baldwin Miller that survived his death…so far. We still don't have a clue if there are others from the Miller network still alive. My guess is that there are. Also, be cautious. Just because we couldn't learn who the others were, does not mean they're innocents or newbies. They just haven't done something to warrant inclusion in the data base."

"Two in and two out. Good job. Going back to Mr. Rhodes: A third explanation of his ability to stay alive as a non-functional member of the Aryan Brotherhood is he is now under the protection of a group that is more powerful than the AB or at the very least, has a working relationship with them. He could work with this new organization with the approval of the AB. What about policemen from the past?"

"They are next on my to-do list."

The next hour is spent reconfirming what they saw on the video feeds and what they deduce from that.

"Guys, we have yet to get a handle on who or what is ultimately behind the rallies and the hate speeches. Who is the money? Who is the muscle? Who are the planners and schemers? How do we get that information? Robert?"

"We can monitor cyber activities of Rhodes and Frey. If they are involved in the money side of the operation, we'll know soon enough. That will confirm that USABank is in deep do-do."

"Good. How do we monitor without a court order?"

"Secretly."

"OK, but not just yet. Jacob?"

"David, I would come at this not from the bottom up, but from the top down. Who benefits the most from the movement behind the rallies and the hate speeches? I mean who drives an overarching organization? I would like to know if there is a shadow control group that is self-funded, or do they get money from another organization. So, I ask again who ultimately benefits the most if this movement is successful in stirring up the voters, if their candidates get elected, if they control the government. Control of the government would allow them to control the U.S. economy, and perhaps the world's economy. Eisenhower warned the country to be leery of the military industrial complex. Is that what we see today hidden behind multiple masks?"

"That's taking it to an extreme. But I like the thinking that deals with finding out who is the power behind the throne. Who is the modern-day Metternich? Your question of who benefits the most is one we must pursue. This must be part of our recommendation to Jack and Fletcher. We need to review your report by two, so we can get the final done and we can be out of here by four, at the latest."

* * *

The preliminary and the final reports are nearly identical, except for tightening of the language and the rearranging of the supporting findings. Margaret and Robert want the national conspiracy theory to be the primary conclusion because it is supported by the connection between the rallies and the product

166

tampering. They are leading the charge. The nearly verbatim similarities of the three speeches and the frightening lifts from Former Senator Baldwin's rants should be the first two corroborative major findings. Then facial recognition.

Recommended actions include requests for wire and cyber taps on Rhodes and Frey, securing cooperation of the U.S. Postal Inspector General to open and monitor the post office box of USABank, and securing cooperation of the Department of the Treasury for information about USABank.

The report is completed. The names of all the team members are recognized as authors. With a click of a button, the report is sent to Jack Strathmore, Fletcher Wilson, the team members and the archives. The five head for the door.

"David, will you join us for a celebratory drink?"

"Thanks. I am much older than you guys, so I need much more rest. See you tomorrow."

What he's really saying is that he wants to drink alone. During the drive home, David imagines how the Balvenie will taste...sweet and warm. How four ounces will make him feel...relaxed and happy as if there is nothing to worry about. The closer he gets to his house, the more he is concerned that he is falling back into an old and debilitating habit of drinking to escape. He fell into this habit when he knew Jennifer was unfaithful. He fell deeper after he killed the girl. Rachel has commented on his frequent and heavy drinking. From what does he want to escape? Not the pressure his new position. The situation is too new. The evil that lurks in newfound conspiracy? What about the images of Jack, Fletcher, Mitchell, and Stephanie on the flash drive in his lockbox? The details of uprooting his comfortable life to a paradise filled with unknowns? Well, he won't be a slave to the pressures. He won't be a slave to the anxiety. He won't be a slave to the scotch. Fuck it: he is the master of himself and will have one drink and that's all.

"David, can you come to Jack's office now."

Another urgent call from Fletcher. Another elevator ride to the rarified environment of major decisions. David approaches Jack's guardian troll. He gives her his plastic all teeth smile, knocks on one of the double doors, and enters.

"David, great report. You and your team nailed it. You must have worked all weekend. I am surprised and proud that you guys went beyond your normal job functions. Good for you for seizing the initiative. Fletcher, I told you David could bring a lot to the party. Barbara could never have done such incisive and detailed work. She never had command of the team. David, your team did a masterful job. And good for you, for giving them credit.

"Until now, no one knew anything about the rallies, how important they were, their similarities, and the link back to Baldwin Miller. We need to notify our field offices. I need to get on the horn and reach out to the Postal Inspector General and the Secretary of the Treasury. We must get permission from those two to learn more about USABank and who is behind it. Then, Fletcher will need to go to a federal judge for approval of all the necessary paperwork. I think we should bring Operations into the investigation. So, Fletcher, please alert Mitchell Davis and send him the report. Also, alert legal that something big is about to fall in their laps. Something that will demand immediate work. To give them a hint, send them the report.

"David, can I assume your team is still digging?"

"Yes sir, like pit bulls after buried bones."

"We all have much more work to do before we start naming names and calling on the appropriate people. Fletcher, make sure David has all the resources he and his team need, as well as the cooperation of everyone here and in the field offices."

"Will do."

168

"David, what's next?"

"As soon as we have additional definitive information, a report will be issued to all those who need to know. So, I'll need a list of people you wish to know what we know."

"Fletcher and I will compile the list and send it to you. Now, get back to work and get us more excellent but disturbing information."

"Thank you, gentlemen."

As he turns and heads for the door, he hears Jack whisper, "I told you our investment would pay dividends."

He gives the guardian troll his best sardonic grin as he passes her desk. Once back in his office, it takes a few minutes for his pulse rate to drop from one hundred and twenty to seventy. Why does he feel anxious about meeting with Jack and Fletcher? The contents of the damned flash drive. He knows what they know but they don't know what he knows. Enough! Stop!

He tells his troops about the meeting upstairs and particularly that Jack and Fletcher know their names and the superior quality of their work. Buoyed, the four return to their cubicles to continue the critical quests: find the former associates, check police records in towns that had suffered school children massacres, reexamine all the paperwork associated with the rallies, and determine who Rhodes and Frey really are. The team must wait to see what's in USABank's mailbox.

* * *

"David, over the past two days we found something interesting about who might be behind the rallies. Here goes: We checked the police forces of Carter, Wyoming: Menthen, New Hampshire; Lutztown, Pennsylvania; Ox Bow, Maryland; and Costal Mesa, California to learn who was on the respective forces at the time of the murders, who is still there, and why others left. I won't force you to sit through the extraneous information. Suffice it to say, most of the older officers at the time of the murders have retired. Some of these retirees are dead. A few of the older officers died before retirement. Most of the younger officers are still on the respective forces while a few left for other professions. Of particular interest are William Stowe from Carter, Martin Hofstadter of Lutztown, and Bernard Flato of Costal Mesa. All three of these men were under the age of thirty at the time of the murders, all left their respective forces, and all disappeared...only to show up as employees of Secure America Services. Information courtesy of a friend at the IRS. Too coincidental if one believed in coincidences–which we don't.

"So, we dug into this very private company. There are precious few public mentions of Secure America Services. The company is registered in Florida to operate nationally. Their location is in Tampa to be exact. The company is registered as a tax-exempt nonprofit organization under category 501(c) (3), exempt from federal income tax because the listed activities have the purposes of education and public safety. Yeah, right. There is no physical address, only a P.O. Box. The only telephone number is one for the company's agent, Umberto LaStrada. I looked him up. He's a lawyer who deals exclusively in corporate matters. I called his number and was sent straight to voicemail. Something is hinky.

"And we're just getting started. We looked deeper into the legal records of **SAFE,** over a decade ago, and learned that the following names appeared as some form of management team: Harry Forbes, Michael Thompson, and Joseph Campbell. Digging into the history of these names, we found that before working with Senator Baldwin, all three had been agents of the CIA. They all left the CIA at roughly the same time. They went off the grid for about a year and then resurfaced at **SAFE.** When **SAFE** dissolved, the three went off the grid again. But unless each has a doppelganger, these same three men are listed as management of

170

Secure America Services: Forbes is CEO, Thompson is COO, and Campbell is Logistics Director. Now, this is very hinky.

"We know that some former bad guys and six men of questionable virtue appear to be active in an organization that stands on the platform of an evil movement which seems to be promoting this evil across the country. We want to unearth all we can about the men…their pasts, their finances, and their families. We have photos of the three former police officers and want to subject the faces of the forty to fifty paramilitary personnel at the rallies to our facial recognition software. We'll probably get partial matches, which won't hold up in court, but will be enough to scare the crap out of anyone above them when they are questioned at our field offices."

"Great job, people. You are on to something big. Go get it. As soon as you're ready, we must prepare a follow-up report for Jack and Fletcher.

"Just want to say, David, it was you who suggested that we look into the police officers in the towns."

"It was you who did the work, I just made the suggestion. I could have been mistaken. It is to your credit that we have actionable information. Now, scoot. I have forms to complete and useless emails to ponder."

* * *

Saturday at ten am, David is still asleep on the couch. The TV is on, but the volume is low. A half-finished drink is on the table beside him. He stirs as he hears someone enter his house. Peering through one eye, he recognizes Rachel.

"David, are you OK? I called several times and got no answer, so I came over. Are you sick? Hurt?"

"Nope, I'm fine. Just tired. I needed my rest…to be undisturbed, so I turned my phone down."

"We were going to visit a few realtors today. Do you feel up to it?"

"Yeah, give me about an hour for a shower and breakfast. Wanna join me in both?"

Rachel has a pained expression.

"David, sweetie, you know I love you. So, what I'm about to say is based on that love. Just relax and listen. I am worried about you and have been ever since you found that damned flash drive and started to play gawd with the reporter, Peterson. You've lost weight, your skin is pale, and you're drinking way too much. I took a peek into your recyclable bin and saw four empty Balvenie bottles. There's another on the floor beside the couch. Five bottles are dangerously too much hard liquor for two weeks. I'm afraid you're falling back into an old habit as a result of all the pressures you must be under: upcoming retirement, the move and disposal of personal items of your last ten years, the new position at the Bureau, and whatever pressure cooker you're working on there. You're not eating enough of the right food. You and I haven't been to yoga for more than six weeks. I doubt you're running or working out at the gym. And we haven't made love in a month. Whatever is driving you is ruining your health. Selfishly, I don't want you to be so sick that you can't make the move. I want you with me happy and healthy for the next three decades. Is all this making sense to you?"

"Sadly, yes. As I once told you, I dove into the bottle during Jennifer's infidelity. That was about the time I shot and killed the young girl in Virginia. I just couldn't deal with those two events in a healthy way, so I hid under booze. I was functional at the Bureau during the day and dead drunk by nine pm. It worked for a while but then the booze became my master. With the help of AA and my psychiatrist, I quit drinking and worked my way back to health. I realized the biggest issue was my marriage failure. I came to understand that I was not responsible for it. So, I got better. I could cope with life without Jennifer. Then, I met you.

172

You helped me sustain my emotional and physical health. You're right. I now have the attitude of someone who has surrendered to the pressures."

Rachel is now sitting beside him with her arm around his shoulders. He sinks into her for solace and protection from himself.

"Rachel, tell me, what do we do now?"

"As you know, I am not a big fan of shrinks. I think they are readily available crutches for the vast majority of people who can straighten themselves out with meditation, diet, and exercise. And this is not an intervention. You don't need to go to AA or a shrink…unless you want to. So, we'll get you on a healthy regimen. I call it Rachel's Remedy. Step one will be to eat better food more often. For this, you will have dinner at my house Monday, Wednesday, and Friday. We'll have to find variations for cooking chicken breasts, seafood, and pasta. We will eat lots of salads. We will eat at your house Tuesday, Thursday and Saturday. Sunday will be our day apart: a day for reading and self-examination. Step two concerns your spirit: you were beginning to meditate when we were practicing yoga. You can do it again on Sundays, at the least. We'll return to our yoga classes on Wednesday and Saturday. Step three involves you getting back into healthy physical shape. You should plan to visit the Bureau's gym at least twice a week, ideally at lunch. Step four involves lowering work stress. During the work week, we will both leave the office around four. No late nights at the office. We may take some required reading home. To handle our respective workloads, we should be prepared to arrive at our offices before seven. How's that for a plan?"

David kisses her tenderly. She is his savior. His eyes are filled with tears of relief that someone is going to help him.

"The offer still stands."

"What offer?"

"Shower and breakfast with me before we interview real estate agents. You never know what might happen."

"Race ya."

Rachel sheds her clothes as she runs to the master bath with its shower stall for two. David remains groggy and slightly disoriented as he attempts to replicate her clothes removal routine while running down the hall. He stumbles twice trying to extricate himself from his pants. His head hurts. His tongue feels three inches thick. Entering the bathroom, he sees that Rachel awaits him in the shower. He gingerly steps into water that is too hot for his liking. But she likes it that way. He won't say a thing. Water temperature is a minor concession. They commence the ritual of body re-acquaintance: water, soap and face cloth, lather, wash, rinse. Repeat. They both giggle. During the repeat cycle, intimacy appears, runs assertively toward its logical conclusion amid deep and powerful kisses. Physical bliss arrives early for David. It's so intense, it's almost spiritual. She relishes his body inside her. He hangs on to Rachel. His tears are indistinguishable from the shower cascading over their heads. Towel dried and dressed they sit at the kitchen table for English muffins with peanut butter, coffee, and OJ. David tries to explain the many stressful forces inside his head, the confusion they cause him and how he sought escape in a familiar bottle. He has to work hard to hold back more tears. Clean and fed, they are out the door in two hours.

Off to their first stop: Estate Sales. The agent, Brenda Moyer, was very thorough. She showed the couple the price ranges for homes in the area: asking price as well as selling price. Plus, she had a record of all the homes that sold within the previous two years...asking versus selling. There was a seventy-five-thousand-dollar spread from the asking price of the most expensive home to the sales of the least expensive over the past two years. That range gave the couple an idea of what to expect and how to negotiate. She also suggested that she be responsible for the sale of both units. She explained they would be more likely to get their asking price if they put the homes on the market at least six weeks before their move date and market them as must sell by the date. She told them that houses like theirs move quickly. But as they got closer to the move date, they might have to come down in price. They should start the selling process next week. This tactic was to be expected. They told her they were just beginning to look for an agent and would get back to her one way or the other before next weekend.

At the next two agencies, Dream Homes and Neighborhood Living, David and Rachel heard much of the same. Repetition of the facts and tactics meant that a rapid sale was dependent on the aggressiveness of the agent and the willingness of the seller to bend on price. They head back to David's home for dinner. During the drive, they agree that they will contract with Ms. Moyer and Estate Sales. Rachel will call her tomorrow. They'll ask her to walk through the two homes next Saturday.

"What do you have that we can eat for dinner?"

"Not a whole helluva lot. I have spent money on other things and bought takeout for my meals."

"Then it's shopping, we will go as we start your wellness journey. Salad greens, tomatoes, cheese, dried fruit, nuts, and canned tuna splashed with balsamic vinaigrette and expertly tossed make a wonderful and healthy meal. We will also need rolls and butter. Tonight's salad will be large enough that we can take the remains to work tomorrow. One last item is ice cream. Your body will crave the sugar it enjoyed from the alcohol. Ice cream or gelato will be a good substitute for the time being. For both of us, there will be no beer, wine, or scotch. When you can honestly say you would like a drink and that you don't need one, we will discuss it. A subtle but critical difference. You are the decider, but I am your mentor. So, no lying to yourself or to me. Gottit?"

"Gottit. By the way, I like butter brickle with hot butterscotch sauce. How do you know all this? It's like you've been through it before."

"I have. I never told you and you never asked. I didn't want to hide my life with a substance abuser from you. I just referred to my ex as dead, so it never came up. I planned to tell you when we were on the island. But now is a more appropriate time. My husband, of long ago, dove into the bottle and was never able to get out, no matter how we both tried. He was unable to hold a job at one place for more than two years. He was very smart... almost a genius, but he brooked no interference in his work. He was a lousy team player. Within two years, this attitude would alienate everyone around and above him. So, he was let go for the good of the company. In most cases, the company treated him well. They claimed they were changing the position and he was not qualified for the new role, that way he could collect unemployment compensation as he tried to re-start his career.

"But he drank to hide his feeling of inadequacy. The children saw that he was not himself after dinner. He would disappear into the den to drink and read until he passed out in the chair. Numerous times they had to help him to bed. They were very worried. I was worried. We tried every known method of help, but nothing worked. I think that he had a deep-rooted wish to fail at life. And he worked hard to fulfill that wish. Booze ultimately killed him. He died of organ failure. But that's enough of wallowing in the pain of the past. My children got over it, as did I. That was then, and this is now. I am yours and you are mine. Now and forever. That's all that matters. Let's shop."

"After dinner, can we do that thing we did in the shower? I think I remember how it is supposed to be, but I need more practice to get it right."

Her grin is deeply rooted in hope for their future.

* * *

David's lunch is in a container that sits inside a small plastic bag which is inside his gym bag. He will work out then eat

176

at his desk. Barbara is not here to interrupt his closed-door time. He has two protein bars for snacks. Rachel saw to that. He thinks that today is the first day…blah, blah, blah. Monday is uncomfortable as he begins his tortuous return to health. Tuesday is slightly less uncomfortable, yet he trembles a little. He stays in his office as much as possible. Wednesday at eight am is team meeting time. The first time they will see the emerging new David.

"Dinah, what's on your plate for the week?"

"I'm looking into Umberto LaStrada with the help of the Tampa Field Office. Also, I'm trying to learn more about Secure America Services. The facial recognition software is through scanning the partials of the paramilitary people at each rally. I am now reviewing and further analyzing the several IDs for each partial. Then, we have to sort through them to see who might be connected to whom and why. Film at eleven."

Chuckles from the group.

"Jacob?"

"My new best friends are Frey and Rhodes. What are they up to, etc.? Information is scarce but it's out there."

"Great. Margaret?"

"Retired police officers Stowe, Hofstadter, and Flato are now officially under my microscope. So far, they are way off the grid."

"Try comparing their official PD pictures to the faces of the rally speakers. Now, Robert?"

"I'm digging into Forbes, Thompson, and Campbell of Secure America Services. I'll be working closely with Dinah. As she looks at corporate docs, tax returns, and activities, I'll be examining the lives of the three-headed hydra of management. Subpoenas would make all our tasks easier and the results better and faster. We could get information, as well as evidence from each of them."

"I'll ask Jack that the names of the men on our radar be named on any surveillance requests. That's as far as we can go as of this morning. Now, go and learn. We need to hit the ground running the minute the subpoenas are issued. We will have a lot more work. A word of caution: until they are issued, if you find anything of interest, it must be copied then erased from your computer. We can't have some crafty lawyer throwing out what we know because we learned it before we were legally permitted to learn it. Before you say anything, I never said what you didn't hear. OK?"

Jack responds positively to David's request for an expanded list of parties, and notes that the appropriate Bureau Field Offices will have the necessary subpoenas in hand within seventy-two hours. The legal unit is reviewing all the supporting information. He knows a federal judge who is sympathetic to the Bureau. The balance of David's day is filled with administrative activities, turning down the invitation for the annual softball weekend, and congratulations to a few recent promotions. David knows none of the people who were promoted. Not surprising, they are all under forty and don't work in his unit. It's getting to be time for the dinosaur to leave the Bureau. But he wants to close one more big case before he leaves. He wants to show everyone that he has what it takes to make a difference. He smiles at this macho crap. The promotions remind him he must recommend one of his team to assume his old position. His personal cell interrupts him.

"Drummer, this is Peterson. We need to have lunch to talk about what will happen soon."

"Can't do lunch. I'm up to my eyeballs in paperwork that has deadlines."

"Drinks after work."

"No can do. Have plans."

"When the hell can we meet? It's critical."

"I'm going to say this one time and one time only so pay close attention. We are never going to meet again. I did what I did to help you on your quest. I demand that you keep me out of your quest. Remember, I said I'm an anonymous force not a source. This force has lost its power. Whatever you plan to do, you'll have to do it without me. You're a good reporter. You can do it on your own. You don't need my blessing. Is that clear?"

"But I want to discuss what I'm about to do and how it might impact you."

"Nothing you can do could impact me. Our worlds are that far apart. So, I thank you for the call and wish you well. Goodbye."

One source of stress is eliminated. A small smile of relief.

XI

The far-reaching subpoenas have been issued. Soon, information will be flooding into various offices for analysis. Kansas City will get the major portion of the information. Jack will see to that. He wants the majority of the credit. Jack forwards electronic copies of the paperwork to David. While the individuals noted on the subpoenas are trying to explain their actions to FBI Field Agents, David's team can dig everywhere and anywhere the people and corporations live and work. David's team can lift all the rocks. The multi-headed Treasury Department can request information about USABank's dealings in the country. Their hurdle will be convincing the Ministry of Banking and Finance of the Caymans that the country's banking laws can be loosened for this one specific situation. Once sufficient information has been analyzed, the appropriate field offices will be able to issue arrest warrants to those named on the subpoenas. David's team will have successfully completed its work. The field office personnel will have long, not-too-friendly discussions with those arrested.

David calls the team into his office.

"While not earth shattering, I feel the need to tell you about my new work habits. I will be coming in early and leaving early. This is necessary for me to work on all the details of my departure which is fast approaching. The details involved in uprooting and moving out of the country are staggering. Every time we do something, three other items arise that must be added to our to-do list. So, rather than try to sneak personal issues in on my time at the office, I have decided to work on my next life adventure at home in the early evenings. Besides, you are all good at what you do, and you don't need me to be looking over your shoulders every day. You had enough of that during the past few years. You are good enough to know the urgency and gravity of this situation. If you honestly need to reach me after hours, call. You have my Bureau and personal cell numbers. Otherwise, email me an update of your work before you go home, and I'll read it before you get here in the morning. We can discuss it when you get in. If that makes sense to you, we're done here."

No reason to tell them the truth. It's personal, and it will not affect their work. The remainder of the week is spent in near silence as the four upload, download, and offload an incredible amount of information, both hard data and visuals. They will secure complete background information, as well as IRS filings for each target. The team will also look for links between the people they know about and any criminals or radical right-wing leaders. Periodically, they go into the small conference room and close the door. Discussions and problem solving for their ears only. The process seems to be never ending. Long hours for all but David. He must divorce himself from the pressure of their frenetic pace to avoid more anxiety for him. This is the type of investigation that will earn his team their bones: recognition within the Bureau nationwide, as well as possible promotions. They schedule a debriefing for Monday from eight to ten in the small conference room.

By the end of his first week on Rachel's Regimen, he is beginning to feel physically better and somewhat more mentally stable. David realizes this is just the beginning, and he is probably feeling the first glow of change. Or his mind is trying to trick him that it's okay to have a beer or a single glass of wine. He cannot let his guard down; he must stick with the program for the remainder of his time at the Bureau, then evaluate his mind and body. After each workout and yoga class, he feels physically and mentally energized. He wants to sustain this flood of endorphins on days without exercise. Is this a healthy addiction? Is he dreaming less about violence and confusion, or does he just not remember the dreams? He and Rachel make love more often. That's a flood of endorphins they both like. They have begun to experiment beyond the trusted norm. David often ponders the sexual appetite of his post-menopausal lover. The old joke is that for men, sex twice a week is not enough, but for women it's way too much. Not so with Rachel. No complaints from him. Saturday will be another day of planning, crossing off items from lists, and making more lists with many new items to be checked out or tasks to complete.

Sunday, as Rachel reminds him, is a day for reflection, napping, and prepping lunches for the week. The *Star* will be the blanket under which he can nap. But first, he must give the paper a cursory look. There is the headline at the top of the first page of the Metro Section.

Sex Scandal Rocks City and FBI

The Star *has uncovered evidence of pervasive sado-masochistic activities involving several of the city's civic and government leaders and a section chief of the FBI. This deviant lifestyle has been known to exist for at least the past three years. (Out of decency for our readers, we have altered photos of the participants in the deviant sex games.) The event that sparked this investigation was the murder of Barbara Wilkins, the Section Chief in Charge of Interagency Communications for the FBI in Kansas City. She was viciously murdered by Fatima Johansson who, it was alleged, had been a partner of Ms. Wilkins in deviant sex that went terribly awry. The investigation progressed to the downtown clubs that cater to a clientele wishing to partner with anyone whose sexual appetite includes: spanking, whipping, insertion of electric probes, and group bi-sexual activities.*

182

David does not need to read the article. He knows the events and the players, as well or better than Peterson. His eye catches a subhead: ***Killer Killed in Jail.*** He reads what follows. There are the names of Fatima Johansson and Roberta Mainway and how they knew each other. Plus, there was an attempt to explain what happened in the jail. Peterson hints at police involvement. That will really piss off Commander Anderson. In the last paragraph, Peterson notes his numerous and failed attempts to get a comment from the FBI. That will really piss off Jack, Fletcher, and Emily. Peterson is poking sticks at tigers, but he is protected by the First Amendment. The Bureau can get angry...but that's about all. The office will be buzzing tomorrow. The last line of the article is that this is part one of a three-part story. Sleep overcomes David.

* * *

The beginning of week two of his life reclamation. He is at his desk before seven am. The whiteboards are covered in the conference room. David's team prepped for today. The group filters in and they summon David to the small conference room.

"Dinah, will you start?"

She moves to a whiteboard and removes the paper. She is making an important presentation in the method of show and tell.

"Much of what I will tell you is the result of the combined efforts of Robert and me. The efforts were combined because they dovetailed in many instances. First, Mr. LaStrada was very cranky that we are asking numerous and embarrassing questions. Second, he was consistent with the no response to my questions, except for the sanctity of client-lawyer privilege. Third, he does not appear to have a traditional office. The Tampa Field Office confirmed numerous phone numbers ascribed to him and a DSL line in the house. I don't want to know how they found out about that. They began monitoring his cell phone calls and his use of the internet

183

earlier last week. They did this before our subpoenas were issued. I don't want to know how they got the authority. Immediately after Mr. LaStrada and I spoke, he made a telephone call to a number that is connected to Harry Forbes. Fortunately, we were monitoring Mr. Forbes's line. After the LaStrada call, Forbes called Michael Thompson and Joseph Campbell. Bingo! Proof of a connection, but nothing illegal. All the calls were made on cell phones in the hope of avoiding uninvited listeners. We don't know what they said. We just know they spoke. The calls were all about three minutes in length.

"As we later learned, Messrs. Forbes, Thompson, and Campbell are not in close proximity to each other. Robert will give us those details. They could be in separate office locations. Details on this in a moment. We think there is no central office. I think all four of these men work from their homes and cars. This would be the simplest way to avoid observation by uninvited guests like us. You can't hit what you can't see. Along those lines, our pals at the IRS forwarded the tax returns for these four for the most recent three years. All four earn five hundred thousand dollars each year. They are salaried employees of Security Investment Services. Changing subjects.

"So, what do we know about Secure America Services? It is a company in a very non-traditional sense. In reality, it is a shell consisting of four men working separately and paid by another company. Obviously, Security Investment Services wishes to remain out of the spotlight of investigation. Corporate banking records could shed more light on this company.

"I went over the corporate docs of Secure America Services and found no mention of Security Investment Services. I did find the names of all four men at whom we are looking. The docs appear to be in order.

"And that brings me to my next point. Mr. LaStrada made a second call that day. He called a number associated with Security Investment Services. Interesting...a phone call to a company that controls another company where he knows the management. We have not had an opportunity to dig into Security Investment Services. That is my top priority for today. Oh, sorry, one last item. The facial recognition software kicked out eighty-four possible matches for the thirty partials we input. This week, Jacob has volunteered to go through the list to determine if any of the people can be eliminated from further scrutiny. That way we'll have a workable list of targets."

"Nice job. OK. That's the first whiteboard. Robert?"

"My responsibility dealt with Forbes, Thompson, and Campbell, all of whom are former CIA agents. Forbes served twelve years, Thompson served ten, and Campbell seven. There is nothing distinguished about their careers. No memos of commendation or reprimand. No foreign posting. No major responsibilities. No big cases listed in their dossiers. They seemed to have been analysts working anonymously at Langley. Not unlike us. Just not as smart or good looking. None of the three is married or ever was married.

"Forbes graduated from Michigan, Thompson from Brown, and Campbell from Vanderbilt. I looked at their parents and any siblings. Those lines of inquiry netted nothing of interest that would tie them to any radical right-wing groups. The good news is that I learned where these three live, and it is nowhere near LaStrada. Forbes lives in Kearny, Nebraska, Thompson lives in the mountains north of Denver, and Campbell resides in Coral Gables, Florida. So, there can be no office to which these fine gentlemen go each day. They obviously conduct their business, whatever that is, from their homes and cars as noted by Dinah.

"I did learn that each has given substantial funds to other right-wing groups, such as the Sons of Liberty, America First, and Think Progress, as well as the NRA. The three of them have been photographed at Tea Party rallies and have donated funds in support of several local chapters of that organization."

"Jacob?"

"I am responsible for learning more about Paul Rhodes and Jerrod Frey. After their jail time, they bounced around from office job to office job. Never lasting more than two years, until now. Tax returns for each for the past three years show that they are paid a salary by Security Investment Services. The tax filing address for Rhodes is Beaumont, Texas and for Frey it is Tacoma, Washington. They each make seventy-five thousand dollars a year. That seems like a lot for a pair of guys who stand at the speaker's side during rallies. My guess is that when they are standing guard, they are armed in case someone in the crowd does something stupid. I'm not sure they know what's really going on. I'll bet they're happy to be drawing a paycheck and will do what is requested of them. My search didn't add much to what we already knew. I think they are in charge of moving money. More than likely, the money's first step is from Security Investment Services to Secure America Services. As of now, I don't know to whom these two send wire transfers. And I can't pin down where Security Investment Services gets its money. Treasury will help us there. In the meantime, because my workload is light, I'm volunteering to comb the list of the partially known faces from those spit out by the computer."

"Nice teamwork, Jacob. What about the speakers at the rallies?"

"Margaret will touch on that."

"Margaret?"

"Drum roll, please."

David is pleased to see and hear the four of them working so well together.

"OK. Here we go. I examined the worlds of William Stowe formerly of Carter, Wyoming PD, Martin Hofstadter formerly of Lutztown, Pennsylvania PD, and Bernard Flato formerly of Costal Mesa, California PD. All three had multiple reprimands in their jackets, violence on a member of the African American or Hispanic community. They all resigned from their posts, roughly three years ago, and promptly fell off the employment grid. However, their Federal Tax Return showed that last year each has been drawing a seventy-five-thousand dollar a year salary from Security Investment Services.

"Stowe now lives in Buffalo, Hofstadter lives in Minneapolis, and Flato lives in San Diego. Facial recognitions of the three are spot on matches to their official police department IDs. These three were the speakers at the three rallies. Coincident to the shampoo tampering? Not likely. I believe that the three speakers are the ones who tampered with the shampoo. Until now, they have stayed off all grids: social, political and criminal. Not so much as a parking ticket. They are acting as if they were choir boys. They're hiding in plain sight.

"These three were given the task of poisoning the shampoo bottles. But, because of the complexity of the super-rabies formula carried by DMSO, I doubt if any of them could have developed the poison. All three of them have only a high school education and no chemical or technical training after that. Add to this the geographic disparity of the poison attacks, and my considered conclusion is that the death delivering cocktail was created at a lab somewhere and distributed to the three for them to perform their tasks. If I had to make a second bet, I would bet that these delivery men have some of the poison mixture still in their possession. I seriously doubt the three of them received one fully loaded syringe and that's all. They most likely received some form of container and instructions on what was needed to do what had to be done. We need to find the address of the lab and who runs it. The homes of the three men will tell us a great deal."

"If I can be so bold, that is fantastic work. Now, you need to prepare a report that can support a sweep of all these characters. We don't want Jack involving so many of our agents at various locations on a hunch. He needs credibility for such an extensive action. Create the report with one simple recommended action, based on the volumes of work you have completed. Please be specific with the names and addresses of all concerned. Send me the report by three, and I will review it and send it upstairs."

"Sir…"

"Please, Dinah, never use the term *sir* in reference to me. I am David, god of the section. Vengeful gawd. Seriously…I'm David. The other word makes me feel old. A feeling I loathe."

Everyone chuckles.

"OK, David. If you check your inbox, you will see our report. We sent it to you right before we started the presentation. We request you read it and make any revisions deemed appropriate."

David is stunned. His young team is steps ahead of him. He must be old. Of course, he's old, that's why he is retiring. Old people retire.

"Holy crap! I'll look at it right away and get you my comments before noon, so it can be forwarded upstairs. Thanks to all of you for such great work."

* * *

"Mr. Drummer, please come to Mr. Strathmore's office immediately."

Stephanie, the protector troll, is not a warm person. She does what she is told with no human connection. David is only slightly concerned. On the elevator ride, his stomach begins to tense. As he walks toward Jack's office, he notices that Stephanie has her head down, engrossed in the information on the computer screen. He knocks on the door.

"Come in. David, great you could come so quickly. Fletcher and I were just discussing your report: another one out of the park. Right, Fletcher?"

"Right, Jack. We appreciate how your team tied all the players together. Because of the scope of the operation, we'll need a day to properly execute the legal intrusions."

"David, I'll be sending congratulatory notes to your team. The notes will be placed in their permanent records. Seems to me, you're heading up a team of real go-getters. We never saw that before. You've done a masterful job. I'd authorize more money for you, but can't, in light of your recent raise. You're really a solid team player. Fletcher and I appreciate that. We see you as someone who would never do anything to jeopardize the team here in K.C. We know we can count on you. OK, then that's about it. Let me do my thing to put your great work into action."

Again, beckoned and dismissed. The purpose of the meeting was not to discuss the report; it was to remind David that they bought his silence about the cover-up. It's obvious that they read the Sunday paper and Peterson's article scared the crap out of them. They must be aware of the four people not pictured in the article. David guesses that they spoke to Emily Knapp and Commander Anderson to formulate an action plan to deal with any fallout from the article. Their reactions to parts two and three of the article will be interesting.

Back at his desk, David calls another team meeting.

"I want you guys to figure out how to rotate days off over the next few weeks. I know each of you has accumulated approximately three weeks PTO. Here's what I suggest: Take five days of that time and spread it over eight to ten weeks. No more than two of you can be out of the office at a time. Take Mondays or Fridays for long weekends but set up a schedule for me to know in advance. You guys have all worked hard on this situation. So, make this upcoming weekend a long one and do something special. Get out of town. Pick weeds from your garden. Do whatever you wish but do it away from the office. My best guess is that the extensive sweep of arrests will occur next week with sit-downs occurring later that week. I'll arrange for us to receive transcripts and videos of the interviews. We can analyze them and form our own conclusions. Remember, the field office agents are like data collectors. We are the analysts. I am confident we'll learn a great deal from the interviews that will lead us to another level of this investigation. I want your PTO plans on my desk by tomorrow first thing. Now, scoot."

* * *

His personal cell vibrates relentlessly, interrupting his relaxation on the couch. Caller blocked. David answers.

"David Drummer?"

"Yes. And you are?"

"Louisa Cochran, we met a few times when I was working with Wendell Peterson of the *Star*."

"Yes, I remember you. You're the public defender whose clients included Fatima Johansson and Roberta Mainway. What can I do for you?"

"I'm sorry to bother you at home, but I need to know if you have heard from Wendell recently, I mean since his article was in the Sunday paper."

"No, I haven't spoken to Wendell for over a week. We had a brief conversation a while back, but it was very brief. Why do you ask?"

"I'm concerned for him. Immediately after the article was printed, he mentioned he received several strange calls. They would come in clusters. When he answered, there would be only silence at the other end. Plus, we have not spoken for the past few days. That's strange because we talked daily or more often when he was writing the article. I need to know where he is. I'm afraid he could be in some type of trouble."

"Did you speak to his editor at the paper?"

"No. Not yet. I plan to call him. I thought I'd try you first. He trusted you and spoke highly of you."

"Maybe Wendell simply decided to go into hiding for a few days. A little R and R after the story hit the public. I'm sure he needs the rest. Plus, he's smart enough to stay out of the public

190

eye until all the dust settles. He would want to avoid any confrontations or repercussions from the eight pictured, but unnamed, people. He knows who they are, and they know that. His survival mode is strong. He'll be fine. I'm sure of that."

"OK. Maybe you're right, and he is simply hiding until after the first installment of the article. Thanks for helping me understand."

"You're welcome."

In the silence that followed the phone disconnect, David thought he had calmed Louisa's nerves. In reality, he had taken her anxiety onto himself. He was beginning to worry. Is Peterson alive and hiding, or has something befallen him? If he has succumbed to a force, who is that force? More than likely, if Peterson has been attacked, it's by one of the unnamed players who recognized himself in the altered pictures. He stalked Wendell, then confronted him away from the newspaper and his home. Did the confrontation begin as verbal but escalate rapidly to something physical? Is all this David's fault? Gawd, no. David cannot accept that his actions to help the investigative reporter were careless and may have caused him harm. What Wendell did with the information was his responsibility. Now is the time David would normally reach for a scotch, but he cannot and will not. He'll call Rachel and discuss this issue. She'll share clarity of thought and impart strength to deal with the unknown, without taking responsibility for it.

* * *

Jacob is standing in the doorway to David's office. "Welcome to my humble work-cave. How may I serve you? Come in."

David is becoming giddy. Is this an emotional mask or a true feeling?

191

"As you may recall the facial recognition software spit out eighty-four faces and names of men who could have been dressed in paramilitary uniforms at the rallies. We were not sure who was who or which was which. I dug through the list of names and came up with a workable list by eliminating those who have died, are incarcerated, or are physically challenged. That narrowed the list to forty. I took another step. Assuming that the sponsors of the rallies would not be willing to transport the lowly order keepers from a long distance, I made a secondary list of the geographically inaccessible men to be eliminated from further investigation. Those are men who live more than two hundred miles from Buffalo, Minneapolis, and San Diego. I doubt that the rally organizers would pay for someone to drive that far for a morning, regardless of how important it was to the cause.

"This produced a final list of eighteen: a workable list. Since the total of partial faces was thirty, we now know that twelve of the faces are not in our active data bank of criminals. We may have their faces from airport or bus terminal cameras, or simply walking along on some downtown street, but they are not known criminals. They may have been recruited by other members of the paramilitary sub-set or they are recent volunteers for the event. Both of these options are disconcerting because they mean that Secure America Services is growing."

"Nice work, Jacob. Now, how do we learn the particulars about the eighteen and then the twelve newbies?"

"I'll have the current particulars about the eighteen by three this afternoon. Then, we can notify the appropriate field offices to include these men in the sweep. I spoke to legal, and they are sure our warrants will be broad enough to include the eighteen. During their interrogation, the field officers will probe each of them to learn if they know anyone else who was working the crowds with them. No doubt they will give up any names of the twelve that each knows."

"Great, issue a report of your diligent work up through the channels. Let Jack notify the appropriate field offices. He will be happy that he is controlling the situation. I've learned in working with Jack and Fletcher, if you give a little so they can get a lot, you will be rewarded. Please call your partners into my office."

Four faces are attentive.

"From here on, whenever you write a report about this investigation or have something that is critical to it that can be substantiated, please send the information to me, Fletcher, Jack, and Bureau Legal simultaneously. That will reduce the time needed to get buy in. Jack will forward the information to whomever he wants to in the field. Legal will forward the information to the federal attorney. The more ammunition the better. And the faster we get the guns loaded the better. Here is the crucial point, all facts and conclusions must be substantiated. No suppositions or conjectures. The information will be used to get the bad guys, and we don't want a smart-ass lawyer blowing a hole in the federal government's case because of faulty or slipshod analysis. Is that clear?"

"Yes."

David knows his team will be recognized as being major players in this investigation and prosecution. The entire Bureau will know their names and talents. Part of management is to get the people working for you recognized and promoted.

XII

David's telephone rings like an alarm. He catches a glimpse at the clock. It's six fifteen. Who the hell would call so early...and on Sunday?

"Hello? Yes, this is he. Yes, I remember you. How can I help you?" He is required to listen to someone tell him something he does not want to hear.

"Did you speak to anyone at the paper?"

"Call the editor again. I'm sure he knows more than he told you initially." More listening to a near rant.

"I wouldn't worry about it if I were you. Maybe the second installment is being delayed while the newspaper management has all the facts double checked. Remember, this is a dicey story that involves a number of the city's influential people. The paper doesn't want to print something that would get them sued. Fact checking is critical. If I may hazard a guess, perhaps one of the unnamed participants contacted the paper and threatened a libel suit. Or maybe, the paper decided to hold off with the second installment for another week to build interest and increase circulation. Either way, you can get the truth from his editor." The rant is over. The voice on the other end of the phone is calm.

"You're welcome. You have a nice day also."

"David, who was that at this ungodly hour?"

"Louisa Cochran. She is worried that something has happened to Wendell Peterson because the second installment of his tell-all article was not in today's paper. Plus, she has not heard from him for more than a week now. He's not answering his phone. I think she is overreacting. Does that make sense to you?"

"I agree that her reaction is a little over the top. And besides, sweetie, there's nothing you can do about any of this anyway. I agree with what I heard you say. The paper most likely got some heat from someone who recognized his or her picture. This led the paper to double check all the back-up information to be damned sure they were on solid footing. That's why there is no second installment today. I'll also bet a whole dollar that Peterson is in hiding to avoid confrontation with any participants."

"A whole dollar! Rachel, you must have insider knowledge to bet that much. Now that we're awake, let's have breakfast. I'll run to the deli for all the fixins while you make coffee. This also gives you time to shower and to start the paper. I'll be back in forty-five minutes. I need a kiss for the road."

David throws on some clothes and is out the door in five minutes. Breakfast is as robust as the conversation. David expresses concern over Peterson's absence. Rachel carefully enumerates all the reasons it is beyond his sphere of influence. Finally, he buys into her point. She rises, comes to him and kisses him tenderly on both cheeks.

"I'll call you later to chat."

What David hears is that she is not one hundred percent convinced that he has let go of the Peterson disappearance issue and wants to check in on him. Clean up is a breeze: everything not eaten goes into the bag and the bag gets pitched. While he is prepping his lunches for the week, he reads the paper and listens to

ESPN. In less than an hour, five lunches are ready, and tonight's dinner awaits the evening hour. He's beginning to enjoy this part of the overall process of life reclamation: small jobs completed regularly. Nothing too startling in the paper. It's now time for back-to-back-to-back *Thin Man* movies. Powell and Loy were wonderful together. To David, it is not funny how the director of these movies treated alcoholism as a joke. He settles down on the couch. Paper beside him. He starts the crossword puzzles as Nick Charles starts his second Martini. He begins to doze. Suddenly, the movie is interrupted by a news bulletin.

"Early this morning, state police discovered an abandoned car. In the car was the body of a man identified as Wendell Peterson of 689 West Willow Boulevard in Kansas City. Mr. Peterson was a reporter for the Kansas City Star *newspaper. The paper has yet to issue a statement about his death. Mr. Peterson died as the result of a gunshot wound. The police have yet to confirm if Mr. Peterson was murdered or committed suicide. The police will make their pronouncement after further investigation. We repeat…"*

David listens to the repeated message as tears well in his eyes and darkness creeps into his soul. He feels responsible for Wendell's death. A second innocent person has died because of David's actions.

* * *

The twisted truth. The lies. The hatred. The set-up. Who is the biggest liar? Who is behind all the killing? Who is the woman in my house? What does she want? Is she here to help me find Wendell's killers? Is she here to kill me? Will she lead me off the path of truth? Can I trust her? I can't trust the police or my bosses. I can't trust anyone in government. I dare not move. I cannot move. The images and noise from the television seem to move away. The sound

196

is so distant, it is almost not there. Sort of hollow like in a barrel, but there is no echo. The picture on the screen jumps. The motions are herky-jerky. Then they are in slow motion. The timbre of the voices vacillates with the changing picture. Black and white becomes color, which becomes black and white. This ebb and flow of sight, sound, and motion was disrupting but now is soothing. Hypnotic.

Am I trapped? Am I stuck on this couch? Why am I crying? I cannot hear my sobs. Can't feel the shudder. My pants are wet. Seat is wet. Did I spill my drink? I didn't have a drink. What is the mess? My arms are locked at my side. Who is this woman? Why is she standing before me? Is she yelling? I see her lips move, and she is gesturing frantically, but I can barely hear her. Her hands on my shoulders. She is holding me. Rocking me. Looking into my eyes. Trying to get a response. Did I respond? Her voice is far away. She is telling me to move my arms. Move my legs. Just move. I cannot. Am I dead? I don't think so. I really don't want to move and don't care to try. I have stopped. Is this death? I hope not.

The darkness surrounds us. No light from the TV. No lights in the room. Just waves of dark gray, like there is dust in the air. She shrinks and grows with the light. Now, she is shrinking. Her voice disappears. She tugs my arms and pulls me up. I stand, but do not move. Turn around to the couch and notice big dark stain on seat. Mine? My tears? My shirt is wet. I must have peed myself. She unbuckles my belt and removes my trousers and underpants. Then she walks me to the bedroom and sits me on the bed. I think this is not the right time for that now. When is the right time? She helps me with new pants and then leads me out of the bedroom to the garage.

A new bright light in my eye hurts. Some man explores my body to be sure of something. Does anyone really know what the doctor sees? His hands are gentle and firm. His voice is soothing. I can't understand what he is saying. He is too quiet. He needs to yell so I can hear him. A nurse is observing. The woman that brought me is not here. Did she deposit her trouble on the doorstep of another? Two pills and a small cup of tepid water. Why not a big glass of ice-cold spring water? The ceiling is low. The lights are flickering to my heartbeat. Fluorescent lights give me a headache and make me feel nauseated.

Two men uniformed in white help me down a hall to another room. Not my room where my wet pants are. My new room. Green and gray walls and ceiling. Very soft ceiling lighting. Not fluorescent. A bed and a chair. A window in front of me and the door behind me. Heavy metal grates on the window. Keep me in? Keep them out? The door has a small window in it. Will they watch me? What will they see me do? Am I to stay here for a long time? Forever? Will they feed me, clothe me, and bathe me. I don't think I can do all of that. And I don't really care. I am tired. I want to rest. What were those pills? The bed linen is fresh. There is something special about freshly cleaned and lightly starched bed linen. It is comforting to the skin. Cool, but not cold. I rest. I won't sleep. Not that tired. Head on pillow I can see the window in the door. I'll watch them watch me. Think about where I am and why.

The square route of pi is 1.7724531. Pi squared is 9.8695877. The rule of seventy-two predicts the doubling rate. It is a financial tool I learned from someone. Divide the earned interest or growth rate into the number seventy-two. The resultant number will approximate the time, expressed in number of years, it will take the value of that money to double. The sum of the squared values of the horizontal and vertical legs of an isosceles right triangle equals the squared value of the hypotenuse. The three four five rule. Why are there only three hundred sixty degrees in a complete circle? Why are there three hundred sixty-five and one-quarter days in a year? Who says? Time is an arbitrary measurement applied by mankind in an effort to make some sense out of the unknown. Why are there three hundred sixty-five days in a year and only three hundred and sixty degrees in a circle? Who says?

Do we really age faster in space? Does a Sherpa age faster than people who live at sea level? The tree falling in the forest does make a sound. We just don't hear it if we're not there. How strong is mother's love? Being rich is nice. But there is always someone who is richer. The same can't be said about happiness because there is no absolute measurement of joy. Happiness is relative. What constitutes a good parent or spouse? What is the proper balance between the influence of heredity and environment? When are choices programmed? 9.8695877 plus 1.7724531 equals 11.6420408. I knew that.

Light in the room comes from outside. This room is mine. I don't share it. Where is it located? Who is the doctor? The toucher? The pill giver? I was awakened and given pills to help me relax...sleep. How stupid is that? Why not give me the pills before lights out? That's when I need the pills? Are all these pills good for me or just a way to control me? I need to shower and shave. Get cleaned up. My crotch itches. Did I pee myself again? I am tired, but jittery. Where are the men who brought me to my room? Where am I? Two nurses lead me to the shower. I assume it's not a communal shower. Will they enter with me to wash my soiled body? They take my hospital garb. The towel is so fucking small it could barely cover my genitalia, and I'm not big. I get a new pair of hospital pajamas, a robe and paper slippers. The nurses take me to the end of the hall.

Examining rooms. I am deposited in room two and I wait. And wait. And wait. Am I waiting for Godot or the Iceman?

* * *

"Good morning, Mister Drummer, how do you feel?"

"A little groggy from all the meds you guys dumped in me. Where am I, what am I doing here, and when can I get out? Where are my real clothes? I look ridiculous in these baggy pajamas. Look, I'm well over twenty-one and I can come and go as I please. I please to leave. So, give me the forms to sign, my clothes, and I'll be on my way."

"Mister Drummer, you were brought to Saint Joseph's Hospital for observation. Miss Vincent brought you. She was very concerned. You had become catatonic. You were not responding to light, motion, or sound. She claimed to have found you in this state Sunday evening at your home. You had urinated on yourself and were sitting silently still in front of the television set. She was very worried. She could not reach you. She wanted professional advice. You've undergone the recommended observation. We must now decide whether to keep you here for more tests and treatment."

"I recommend that you let me go home. I may not be in picture-perfect health, but I'm not violent. I haven't hurt anyone, not even myself. So, I don't need to or want to be here. I will endure outpatient counseling and take whatever meds you script. But I will not stay here."

"Sir, that's not entirely your decision to make. It's the decision for you, Miss Vincent, and me to make."

His pronouncement rang like a large gong in David's ears. The vibrations stopped his body cold. Someone outside of his immediate and trusted circle was trying to assert control over his life. A doctor he didn't know held a vote. David was the mouse in the maze. The doctor had the corn and the keys to the doors. Better to be pliant and win than to be stubborn and stay here.

"Listen to me, doc. If I am being held under some state health act and you wish to hold me longer, you had better get a judge's order or a signed consent form from my next of kin. Who, by the way, live about a thousand miles from here. I make my own adult decisions, and I decide that I like me, and I want me to go home. OK? What forms must I sign? What promises must I make and keep? Tell me. I am not prone to violence or rage, but I can get very cranky if lied to or if someone tries to control me."

There was panic and power in David's voice and the Doctor sensed it. What he didn't know was why it was critical that David get out of the psychiatric wing, or *rest ranch* as the nurses call it. David had a retirement to enjoy. All of which could not happen if he were in lockdown.

"Miss Vincent is here. I'd like to talk to her before I make my decision."

The pompous, arrogant prick. The doctor wants me to be sure not to miss the fact that he is holding my balls in his iron grip. He leaves the examining room: the sterile, bright, and very unpleasant examining room. Two shades of the most bilious green. Apparently meant to calm the patients. It failed with David.

Hold on, big fella. Don't get buried in all the details of everything. That's how you got here in the first place. Holding minutia under a microscope. Examining a nit on a gnat's ass. Too fucking much detail and not enough perspective. He can't tell anyone what Rachel and he know. The Bureau would lock both of them in a hellhole forever. No one would believe the details of the conspiracy. Conspiracies are only good and fashionable among the lunatic fringe unless they are true and not theories. Is David part of the fringe? No, damn it. He must take the meds and see the doc. But no group. It's none of their business. Tell the doc only what he wants to hear. Work and retirement planning pressure built until the black cloud engulfed David. Then his self-preservation system shut off all reciprocal contact with the outside. Only temporarily. Just enough time for the psyche and soul to regroup and begin working in concert. Keep still and do as he is told. Rely on Rachel. She is his only true friend. He knows that to be an immutable truth.

Enter the angel of mercy and doctor putz.

"David, the doctor has decided that you can come home with me. You don't need to stay here any longer. We'll stop at the drug store and get these prescriptions filled. You're going to be all right. But you need rest and to learn how to deal with pressure. You've been going too fast and too hard."

"Mister Drummer, you have experienced a panic attack. While serious, it is not life threatening. It was episodic, not permanent. It was serious because it took over your mind and body. But I stress episodic, because in my professional opinion, this event was triggered by something presently outside of you, it is beyond your control, and is not a long-term, clinical situation. With rest, the proper medications, and therapy, you'll be able to understand the cause of the event. Once that occurs, we can deal with underlying issues. It's a process, Mister Drummer. So, the more aggressively we work at it, the faster we can resolve the issues. Do you understand what I am saying?"

"Shit, doc I'm not deaf or stupid…just panicky. Yes, I know I need help. I don't wish this event to recur. I'll do what is required."

"Good, you may get dressed, check out, and leave with Miss Vincent. For discharge purposes, we have designated her as the responsible adult. I'll give you a list of professionals, one of whom can guide you to recovery. You can make an appointment with one next week. We assumed that would be suitable for both of you."

* * *

On the ride home, the couple stops at the drugstore. David realizes for the first time that his pants don't fit. They're baggy. The waist is too big. His belt is hooked in the last hole. He will need to punch a new last hole. His pants hang on his hips like some latest teen fashion statement. How is that possible? He ate good food regularly. Slept well. Maybe he had been gaining weight before Rachel's Remedy, did not realize it, and just lost it. Maybe he lost a few pounds during his three-day stay at the hospital. David received three prescriptions: a maximum twice-daily dose of alprazolam for anxiety, methylphenidate for energy, and eszopiclone to help him sleep. He prefers generics because they are cheaper. A pill for every mood and occasion. Synthetic body and soul elements. Ain't modern chemistry grand?

"David, you must understand that your deep involvement in everything around you caused you to nearly implode. You took in all the disturbing facts and kept them bottled up until your mind wanted to get rid of the load. Like a data dump. Until we leave for the island, you will need a full-time aide…a guardian, if you will. More loving than the hospital staff. So, for the next few weeks, we will cohabitate. You will live with me under my guidelines in my house. We'll move a few of your clothes tonight. Thereafter, we will move some of what we want to take to our paradise. A little of your things each day will be moved into my house. We can move items that I will not be taking to your house at the same time. A gradual swap. We will hold our Grand Garage Emporium at your address. When the sale is completed, the cleaning crew will have ample time to clean your house first…before mine. My guess is that the two sales will occur after we are gone.

"I will be solely responsible for enhancing your health and wellbeing for the next few weeks. This way we can discuss anything that is troubling you anytime day or night. If you want to schedule an appointment with a shrink, please feel free to do so. When we were picking up your meds, I bought some protein powder and high potency vitamins. These will be part of your daily regimen. We'll shop together, cook together, and clean together until we both feel comfortable with your health. I stress both of us will make that decision. I don't mean to sound like Nurse Ratchet; it's just that what you endured was very harmful and you must be healthy enough to leave all this behind. Does this make sense?"

"Yes. We can do it. I feel like an enormous weight has been lifted from my shoulders. I understand that as of now I'm not ready to face my new life on my own. I have you and that's a really good thing. Question: what do I say at the office about my absence?"

"I called Fletcher Wilson and advised him that you had suffered food poisoning from fish and that you were too weak to be at the office. He told me to tell you to mend and come back soon. I told him the doctor indicated you would be ready for the office in a few days. You would be in on Monday. Your weight loss will corroborate the reaction to bad food. I suggest you make a joke about it."

"Bless you."

"I am not a saint. Part of my actions is based on selfishness. I don't want to lose our down payment, nor do I want to lose you before we get to the island."

"Thanks for putting the money aspect first. That tells me where I stand vis a vis your money. Do you plan to dump me once we get to the island? Trade me in for a much younger model?"

"Oh, shush. You know what I meant. Stop splitting hairs."

Smiles are tonics.

"Let me ask a troubling question. Do you think my panic attack is based on the material on the flash drive?"

"Yes, yes, yes, and damn it yes! You have been struck by the implied power, simultaneously negative and positive, of that damned device. With the videos on the flash drive, you could crush major players in the Bureau. But you dare not try because

204

you rightfully fear the retaliation of Jack and Fletcher. So, you teased them. Hinted to them that someone might have material that could destroy them. My first theory of the crime is that Jack panicked when he read the Sunday paper's first installment and saw the eight disguised photos of the deviant players. Black and white grainy head shots with a black bar superimposed over the person's eyes was a dramatic way of saying, 'I know who you are.' Jack interpreted this as a strong implication that Peterson knew who was *not* shown. Jack knew there were twelve. Fletcher showed him what he had retrieved from Barbara's house. Jack's a smart man. He can add two and two and read the result as four...the four missing pictures. Pictures lifted from the video files of the four members of the Bureaus who were involved in this deviant lifestyle. The first theory of the crime is that Jack had Peterson killed. You couldn't have known how far he would go to silence the story and its author.

"When you learned that Wendell died under strange circumstances, your guilt took over. Guilt produced your panic attack. You convinced yourself that you were responsible for Peterson's death. If you had not sent him the file of eight, he would not have pursued the people who are on the videos, he would not have learned who they were by visiting the clubs, he would not have used altered photos in the first installment, and then he would not have died. He did not know of the missing four. What got Wendell killed is the rage of someone who feared exposure."

"The second theory of the crime goes like this: Wendell could have been murdered by one of the people depicted in the first installment. Regardless of Wendell's attempt to disguise the men and women, they knew the reality of the story, and each could recognize his or her own picture. Undoubtedly, several of the eight have money and influence sufficient enough to be able to seek the vengeful preemptive strike of murder. The eight are not street thugs; they are high-level civilians who enjoy strange sex games.

205

So, they would hire someone to do the deed. How they would find someone like that is unknown because that type of person is outside their circle. My guess is that they could have quietly contacted Anderson. Regardless, there's no way any of these people could know that you are involved in exposing their shame. They know only Wendell Peterson's part. Since they don't know who you are, you are safe from their retribution. That's a second theory.

"The four not pictured know what they could lose if their identities were revealed. And, importantly, they must have a vague idea who gave Peterson the clues to find the eight. They think that Peterson had pictures of all twelve. I am fairly sure they are aware of your involvement and that you somehow have pictures of them. Maybe even Peterson has pictures of them provided by you. They have the wherewithal to protect their lives. A preemptive strike is well within their world. Listen very carefully, you are not responsible. Someone else killed Wendell. If it was one of the eight, we're safe. Because they don't have a clue about your involvement. If it was one of the four, we're not safe. We will never know for sure, but we must assume the worst and protect ourselves accordingly. End of analysis."

"Rachel. I believe Peterson was killed at Jack's request. He would have access to someone who could do that. I believe that when he saw the photos in the paper, he could easily compare the material on the disc and computer file with the eight photos. Then they could quickly, but erroneously deduce that Wendell also had seen their faces. At that time, he doesn't know why Peterson did not publish the other four pictures. Jack may have feared Peterson was waiting until the second installment. An installment meant to crucify the Bureau. So, he had to have the second installment killed. And second, he had to severely discourage the author from pursuing this matter. The first required a set of calls to Knight Ridder/McClatchy and the *Star*. Hell, the Bureau did it once to delay Peterson's story, so they could do it a second time.

My guess is that Emily Knapp made the calls. I am not sure they told her why. But I guess her life could now be in danger.

"The second installment was doomed from the start. Wendell wasn't about to give up his shot at a Pulitzer just because two guys didn't want their dirty laundry spread all over Kansas City and Washington, D.C. They could have surmised this. So, they had to have him killed, probably by someone local who would do it for a price. That means that Commander Anderson, with his knowledge of hit men in the area, would have to be involved more deeply than he already was. So, Anderson makes a call or two, settles on a price which Jack can easily pay out of Bureau petty cash, and Wendell is killed. By now, the killer is out of the country. If we are accurate in our analysis, there is a good chance we are in danger."

"Enough! We now have two big ugly theories of the crime which can't be pursued without more evidence. And we are not going to seek more evidence. We can hash and rehash the situation until it is diced into pieces the size of room dust. But we are not going to. We are going to let sleeping dogs lie. Understand?"

"Understood."

"To have dinner, we need to shop. After dinner, we'll go to your place, where you can pick up some clothes and your car. I'll make more space in the bedroom closet for your clothes. Any extra you can put in the linen closet. Also, you'll need your car to transport more of your goods to my house tomorrow, while I'm at work. In the evenings, we can figure out what of my stuff should be transported to your place for the sale. If we do a little bit at a time and discuss items other than clothes that we can swap out easily and quickly. By the way, I love you."

"I love you, too."

XIII

"David, great to see you back. How do you feel?"

"Thankful to be alive, but weak. It'll be a few days before I'm back to full strength. Suffice it to say, if the fish feels a little slimy, don't eat it. The only good thing that came out of my misadventure is that I lost some weight. The process was not quite what Jenny what's-her-name recommends, but in the end it's successful. Now guys, please bring me up to speed. What happened during the week I was lounging by the pool?"

"We learned, through unnamed sources, that the big sweep will be tomorrow. By Wednesday, all the players will have been brought in for questioning and some will be held as material witnesses but not arraigned. The small fish will be first, in hopes that they are willing to flip on the big fish. That phase may take several days...maybe even a week during which they will sit in small rooms and have lots of time to talk to lawyers. Although arrested in several different cities, the group will be arraigned in Atlanta. A friend of Jack's is a judge in that court, and he will preside over the trial. The arrested are being accused of violating numerous federal statutes, and Jack's friend in Atlanta takes those crimes very seriously."

"What else?"

"The Postal Inspector opened the USABank mailbox in Alexandria and uncovered correspondence from the home office in the Caymans and a ton of circulars and junk mail. There were no names on the correspondence from the home office of the bank. The P.O. branch also had a large box of nondescript items that had accumulated over the past three months. It seems no one regularly comes to empty the P.O. Box. It is just a place where bank stuff of no particular interest is sent. No help to us. This implies that most, if not all transactions are accomplished electronically. But the Postal Inspector will keep a watch on the box for the next ninety days."

"Our very own cybercrime unit...that's Dinah and Jacob...uncovered the activities of Frey and Rhodes, and they followed the money backward. It seems our assumptions were correct: Frey and Rhodes are the money movers for the bank. When someone, as yet unknown, wants to pay someone else or put them in funds either Rhodes or Frey simply accomplishes the transfer electronically. The money is labeled as being from Secure America Services to whomever. All of this is done within the

USABank system. So, the cybercrime team of two lifted the veil of Secure America Services and discovered that all four men who run the show have to authorize any payments. While that ensures their control of the money, it also tells us how much control these four have within the entire operation.

"But where does that money come from, you ask? It comes from quarterly infusions by Security Investment Services. The first of every quarter, Security Investment Services sends a wire transfer of eight million dollars to Secure America Services. Again, all within USABank. It's like taking money from one pocket of your pants and putting into another. The money never really leaves your person. It has just been placed in another area or in this case another bank account. The note on the transfer states that the amount is for services rendered. What services? And who subsidizes Security Investment Services?"

"So, money moves within USABank...to Security Investment Services, and then to Secure America Services, and then to Frey and Rhodes who send the money to someone who needs it or has asked for it. You're right, we need to know who puts the money in the bank at the beginning of the chain of events?"

"That's the unknown at this time, but we're working on it. It would be so easy if we could get the cooperation of the Ministry of Banking and Finance of the Caymans. But we all know, that ain't gonna happen. All we need is the account and routing numbers from the deposit. Then the piggy bank is open."

"Keep working on Security Investment Services. By the by, Dinah and Jacob, nice job. I never knew that the Interagency Communications Section had a cybercrime unit. I'm happy we do. Please excuse me, I've got about five hundred emails to review."

* * *

"Fletcher, would you have time to see me today?"

"Sure, David, how about now? Come on up."

On his way through the bullpen to the elevator, David glances up to one of the TV monitors. There is a politician throwing his hat in the ring for the Republican Nomination for President. David had lost track of the fact that the presidential election is fewer than eighteen months away. There, on the screen, in front of a huge billowing flag and flanked by his wife and two daughters is the former governor of Texas, Barry Nelson. David can't hear what the candidate is saying, but Nelson's broad smile, well-coiffed wavy hair, serious dark-rimmed glasses, light blue shirt with the sleeves rolled up to his elbows, and American flag tie tucked into his shirt create the right image of a hardworking white-collar candidate. Obviously, he is attempting to show voters that he is a regular guy: A regular guy who was born with a silver spoon in both hands, Yale educated, and lives off a huge trust fund. Regular guy, yeah sure. He does not point his finger at anyone or anything. But he does strike the air with a gentle fist to hammer home a particular point. David has seen this a dozen times from both parties. Why can't the candidate's advisers come up with some new type of gesturing?

Off the elevator. In a few steps, he is in Fletcher's office. He thinks it's strange that Fletcher's Executive Administrative Assistant, Marjorie, always smiles when David comes to see Fletcher. He attributes her upbeat, friendly attitude to the supposition that she has no dark and dirty secrets to hide.

David lays out the findings and conclusion of his team.

"Jesus, David, you're asking the Bureau to ask the Cayman Island Government, a British Overseas Territory, to violate their well established and accepted banking laws and give us all the particulars on a bank account that may or may not be involved in possible activities. Why not ask us to talk to the man in the moon?"

David had anticipated Fletcher's reaction. He has a history of histrionics and of saying NO to every request, except those that come from Jack. These are classic traits of a smallminded sycophant with a self-inflated ego who wants no part in anything that might include risk to him. His first thought always to protect his lofty position. David repeats the salient facts unearthed by his team. These facts, when laid out, make the request to take the next step in the investigation logical.

"Fletcher, we would be happy if we knew the source or sources of the deposits into the account of Security Investment Services. All we need is the name of any depositor during the last year. That's all."

"That's a helluva lot for any bank. What was the name again?"

"USABank. It is obvious from the name that the bank was established to do business with entities in the U.S., legitimate, questionable, or nefarious. Look at the names of the other banks on the big island: Cayman National Bank, Royal Bank, and Scotiabank. None of these looks like it would be for citizens of the U.S. Only the name USABank fits that bill. All we need is the name or names of the depositors into the account of Security Investment Services. We're the FBI, for Christ's sake. We're not some sheriff in rural Montana. Certainly, you must have enough pull to get that information. It would be a coup in the annals of the Bureau if you could get it. Do we need to go to State and ask them to get the information for us?"

"Relax. I have to figure out a way to get the bank to agree to this one request. I doubt the stick will work, so we have to use the carrot. We are monitoring the comings and goings in their P.O. Box in Virginia. So far, we have learned nothing from that effort. But they don't know that. If I tell them we will abandon our monitoring of their mail, if they give us the name or names of depositors, we might get what I ask for. Also, if we clear this with the Ministry of Banking and Finance beforehand, they might look the other way and make it easier for the bank to comply with our one-time request. I don't know. It's risky. Suppose we learn the

212

name or names and they mean nothing to your investigation; we wind up with egg on our...my...face."

David hears Fletcher's tell...self-protection.

"They won't know if what we learn is helpful or not, and we won't tell them. They will only know that they have cooperated with the U.S. Federal Government during a critical time. It's the thing friends do. They may even ask our government for a favor in the future. But that's a point for a later discussion."

"OK. Let me make a few calls today. I'll give you an update as soon as I have information."

"Great. What we find will be a big boost to our investigation."

"If they agree to it and if anything even shows up."

"They will, and it will."

"By the way, how do you feel?"

"Well, food poisoning is not something I want to revisit. But I'm over it now and will be one hundred percent in a few days. I'm energized by the investigation."

"Glad you're okay. Now, let me make the calls."

In the elevator ride down, David thinks how easy it is to lay out a set of logical steps and findings, and then ask someone with an ego the size of this building for help. David doubts Fletcher will tell Jack what he is about to try. He wants all the credit for himself. Unless the digging comes up empty. Then it's David's fault. The so-called update will come after Fletcher finds a way to ensure credit for himself without risk of blame.

* * *

It's been nearly ten days since David began his doctor prescribed daily medications. There are times during the day when he feels outside the events, and there are times during the day when he feels sluggish, or his tongue is three inches thick. He understands this is the result of the prescribed meds in combination. Too many tweaks to his psyche. During the times of uneasiness, he tries to remain in his office so that no one will notice his condition. He can hide only so long, hoping these dreaded feelings will pass. He is playing a game of hide and seek. Hopefully, no member of his team will find him until he is comfortable with himself.

Per Rachel's regimen, David arrives at his new, temporary home at five twenty-five. She is on the way. He turns on the TV. Now is the time he would have his first scotch. No more. Now it's lemonade or grapefruit juice. On the screen is former governor Nelson again. This time David can hear him.

"Internationally our embassies and military bases are under attack by Islamic jihadists who wish to rule a world without Christianity. Our boys are being slaughtered and our government does nothing but frown and wring its hands. Our feeble feds do nothing. No response for the numerous, heinous attacks. No holding the jihadists responsible for over five hundred deaths in just the last three months. I say what the good book says...an eye for an eye.

"These Islamic jihadists have begun to infiltrate our homeland. There are many more mosques in the U.S.A. now than there were before the attack of 9/11. That attack signaled their invasion of our country. The cancer is spreading across this great land. To make matters more frightening, the Islamic terrorists now number in the millions in your own backyard. That's potentially a big army of fighters bent on our destruction. And what is the Federal Government doing about this threat? Nothing. Absolutely nothing. In World War Two, the government required that all people of German and Japanese heritage register. Their actions were monitored. In fact, thousands of Japanese were placed in detention facilities, so they could do no damage in their adopted country...the U.S.A. I say make all Muslims register with the Federal Government, put the terrorists in special camps, and monitor all Muslims closely. Those who have no documentation should be shipped back to their native lands...immediately, if not

sooner. We are at war and must treat our enemy accordingly. We must also close our borders. Electrified fences, 24/7 air surveillance, guards with high-powered guns, and angry dogs are signs of our desire to remain safe and secure.

"The last point I would like to make deals with Sharia Law. This is the code that governs the public and private lives of all Muslims. Sharia Law covers politics, banking, economics, and even the sex lives of all Muslims. Muslims have no freedom except that which is granted under Sharia Law. Sharia Law and the religious leaders that oversee its administration deny individual freedom of speech, freedom of religion, freedom of assembly, and all the other freedoms that make the U.S.A. the great country it is. The Islamic jihadists that are growing like a cancer in our great land want to impose Sharia Law on all of us. They want to deny us our God-given freedoms. I would rather die in a gun battle, than give away my freedom. At the very least, I would know that I killed many of them before they got me. That's the way I feel. Do you feel the same way?"

The cheering is boisterous.

"We are holding a 'Question and Answer' session tomorrow on Fox News. Please watch. If you have any questions for me, call in. God bless you, and God bless the U.S.A."

David almost screams. He gets a chill. His pulse jumps to well over one hundred and thirty. A Gordian knot has taken over his stomach. He sits frozen in terror. An epiphany leaves him dumbfounded. Barry Nelson just repeated the sentiments and many of the words of the speakers at the three rallies. David sees the grand motive: The election of an ultra-conservative president who espouses America first and America only. It's all frighteningly clear. Election of a president who rides the wave of hatred and fear of the unknown into the Oval Office. The grassroots movement now has a national face. Which came first…a national plan tested on a local basis or a local movement co-opted by a national movement? David settles on the former.

There are huge, logical, and very disturbing connections among all the moving parts.

He takes one of his mood enhancement pills and calls Dinah.

"Sorry to interrupt your work, but I'm glad you haven't left the office. I need you to a big job for all of us. Barry Nelson just held a brief rally explaining why he's running for President. I want you to download his speech. Then, you need to compare his words with the words of the speakers at the rallies. I suggest you create a split screen and play his announcement on one side and the speaker from Buffalo on the other side. They won't synch up precisely, but they will be close enough to demonstrate the straight-line connection. I'll set up an appointment with Fletcher for tomorrow at seven thirty. You can show him what you uncovered at that time. Does that make sense?"

"Yes, I guess. I know I can do that. What am I looking for?"

"You'll know it when you see the two videos side by side. See you tomorrow."

He calls Fletcher who reluctantly agrees to the morning meeting. He wants to know the purpose of the meeting. David tells him to wait and see. Tonight, David will be with his love. His mouth is dry. Anxiety. The mood enhancer will help when he explains all this to Rachel.

"David, you'd better be careful. You may be entering a world that is extremely protective and therefore dangerous. They may do anything to protect their movement and the face of that movement from besmirching by the Bureau."

"I understand. That's why I'm involving Fletcher at this stage. He can be the face of our investigation. If he wants to involve Jack, that's his call...not mine. I'll show him what we know, propose a course of action, and step out of Fletcher's way. I will function as support only."

"Now to the most important question: how do you feel about all this?"

"There's a large part of me that wants to run with it and a smaller part that wants to walk away and avoid the pressure of the investigation. For my own wellbeing, I will be a counselor on the outside of the arena. This decision was reached with the help of your strength and a dose of modern pharmacological technology."

"Good. Let's eat. I am famished."

* * *

"David, that's amazing. This is the work of your team?"

"Not really, it's the work of Dinah Smith."

"Well, Dinah…may I call you Dinah?"

"Yes, please do."

"Well, Dinah, this is masterful. It leads me to think that we may not have to go through the bank to get the information we discussed yesterday, David. Obviously, Mr. Nelson's candidacy is being funded by someone or some entity like a Super PAC. All Super PAC information has to be on his filing papers and reported quarterly to the Federal Board of Elections. The board, if asked, will reveal the source of his money. Once we know the source, we will see clearer connections amongst all the moving parts. That's my job. David, I'd like to show Jack what Dinah has discovered. I'll set a meeting for later today. I want both of you in the meeting. I'll call with a time. Thanks for the great work."

When the elevator doors close, Dinah lets out a small but pronounced whoop and fist thrust. David grins.

* * *

"Jack, allow me to introduce Dinah Smith, an analyst in David's group. David came to me yesterday and indicated that he was concerned about the connection between USABank in the Caymans and the two shell companies that have been on our radar

217

screen. He wanted to know if we could access the bank's records to see the income and outgo of money. I told him there was no way we could violate the banking laws of a British Overseas Territory. When I saw Barry Nelson's TV appearance, it reminded me of the rally speeches in Buffalo, Minneapolis and San Diego. So, I asked him to compare the Nelson speech with the speech at the rally in Buffalo as best he could. And his team did a masterful job of fulfilling my request. Take a look at the similarities between the speaker in Buffalo a few weeks ago and Mr. Nelson last night. Dinah, please run the video."

Four sets of eyes are glued to the big screen TV in the conference room off Jack's office. At the end of the speeches, Dinah reveals a list of all the similar phrases to lock down the comparison.

"Holy crap! It's like they are both reading the same talking points at different times and from different places. But what good is this knowledge, Fletcher?"

"Nelson gets money from somewhere other than the tens and twenties from the little people. Most likely from a documented Super PAC. When we ask the Federal Board of Elections, they will tell us the composition of any Super PAC. Then we'll be able to work backwards to determine where the Super PAC money comes from. Once we know that, the hate crimes statute becomes a secondary weapon. The primary weapon will be the RICO Statute. This will be considered to fall under the Racketeer Influenced and Corrupt Organization Statute. The two predicate felonies are the poisonings and the promotion of violence against lawful American citizens. We can make this latter one out to be a hate crime. The RICO Statute provides for extended criminal penalties for acts performed as part of an ongoing criminal enterprise. Prosecution under RICO can be much more far reaching than the Hate Crimes Statute and it has larger, sharper teeth. If you agree Jack, I'd like to get the ball rolling today."

"Get confirmation of the prosecution under the RICO Act from our lawyers. Get all the material to them and ask for an opinion. In the meantime, learn what you can about any Super PAC. Drilling down might be difficult, but I have confidence in your leadership and David's team. Now, go for it."

Jack leaves and goes into his office.

"Dinah, thanks for your help on this. David, I'll keep you in the loop and bring your team in when I need something."

Fletcher shakes their hands. He holds Dinah's hand a little too long as he looks into her eyes. The silence of the elevator ride down to reality is broken by Dinah's whisper.

"They're both assholes. One is a pompous overlord, and one is a lecherous sycophant. They are both assholes."

David can only smile internally at Dinah's insight.

"Dinah, please come into my office for a second. I want to be sure that you fully understand what went on in the conference room."

"I'm OK. I'd rather not have to work with those two more than is absolutely necessary. They make my skin crawl. How do you put up with them? Did you see the way Jack was staring at me? The bastard was trying to undress me with his eyes. Creepy is too kind a word for that. And if Fletcher touches me again, I'll rip off his fingers and shove them up his nose."

"First of all, Jack, knows full well that nothing in that meeting was Fletcher's idea. Fletcher hasn't had an original thought for decades. Hell, his wife lays out his clothes each morning. Jack's management philosophy is to surround himself with people who are just smart enough to take orders, not ask questions, and complete simple tasks. Fletcher fits the mold perfectly. He is a toady. So, Jack knows the video comparison came from our team…you. Second, both men are serious lechers. You are right to feel uncomfortable around them. Now that you are aware of the beasts that lurk within our house you can guard yourself accordingly. Be cordial, but cautious."

"I thought you told Jacob *if you give a little, so they can get a lot, you will be rewarded.*"

"I did, and you did. Jack will look to you for help in the future. Most likely, it will be after I retire. He will call you directly. He won't go through the prescribed channel of consulting Fletcher or the new section chief before contacting you. You could become an important resource for him and his ambition. But you'll have to be on your guard against any ulterior motive. I know you can do it.

"I told you when I hired you that part of my job is to protect you, and the others on the team, from the slings and arrows of outrageous fortune. You have just experienced outrageous fortune. I'm sorry I could not protect you in the meeting. Perhaps it's better that you saw the crap, so you know how to deal with it after I retire. Here is the best way to get back at Fletcher, while making Jack happy: send a form request to the Federal Board of Elections asking for Super PAC information for all the candidates from both parties. It's a simple and standard request because it does not single out any one candidate. When you get the information, you will lead the team in dissecting it. We will have our answers before Fletcher tells us he needs us to do anything."

"One question: what is your management style?"

"I look for people who are smarter than me, hire them, and impart my experience so that they can do my job but do it better. You four fit that bill."

She smiles.

"You are politically clever. One could almost say you are devious. I like that in a boss. I never knew you had it in you."

"I am more than just a pretty face. I'm doing what any good section chief would do. After a thousand years on the job, I understand the players. Besides, when you present your information to Jack, we'll have fun watching Fletcher squirm and try to take credit for it."

* * *

220

He returns to the emails and forms that clog his computer and mind.

"Hello, may I speak to the officer in charge of the Wendell Peterson death investigation?"

"Yes, sorry, I am David Drummer, Section Chief of the FBI Interagency Communications unit, badge number 59036."

"Hello, Sergeant Sweatt. I'm David Drummer, FBI. My badge number is 59036. I am seeking information about the death of Wendell Peterson."

"No, this is not an official call. I met Wendell in a professional capacity, and we became friends. I was wondering if you had determined whether his death was self-inflicted, or was he murdered?"

"One to the chest and one to each eye. Whoever shot him was serious."

"Do you have an idea where he was murdered?"

"Not where his body was found."

"Who was the other person who inquired?"

"A public defender named Cochran. Do you know her?"

"Yes, I know Ms. Cochran. I have reason to believe the two of them were working together on some investigation."

"Do you know what kind of investigation?"

"I have no idea. Thank you for the information and your time today, sergeant."

David stares at the computer screen. A single twenty-five caliber shot to Wendell's chest and one to each eye certainly rules out suicide. A twenty-five-caliber gun is the choice of many professional killers. Street thugs think that the larger the caliber the better the gun. In the show and tell stage of confrontation, a .45 doesn't look any more imposing than a long barrel twenty-five. They both can scare the hell out of anybody. But for killing, a twenty-five is more accurate, deadlier, and quieter. Critical factors for professional hits. Three twenty-five caliber slugs constitute over kill. Obviously, the shooter felt that the one to the chest was insufficient. But one in each eye? The small caliber slugs enter the brain through the eyes socket, then they ricochet off the bone and turn the brain to oatmeal. Death is guaranteed. Anger is not the mark of a professional. Caliber vs. anger creates a conflict in the killer's profile. Or the killer is simply a psycho who has a signature kill. David guesses Wendell was ambushed and killed somewhere safe. And then he and his car were driven outside the city and left for anyone to find. If he was ambushed, that would mean he was meeting someone he needed to talk to about his story. STOP! This mess is in the hands of the state police. There is nothing David can, or should do, except stop analyzing and anguishing over it.

He will tell Rachel what he has learned today. The conversation will help get the mess out of his head. She will share the emotional load while objectively ensuring he sees the truth.

* * *

Sunday. The day of rest. David is still swapping loads of 'don't need stuff,' as he calls it from Rachel's house to his and 'must keep stuff' from his house to Rachel's. He is constantly amazed at how much don't need stuff he has. This shedding of the unimportant is good therapy. The Gigantic Garage Emporium will abound with items in the one to five-dollar range. Sell the stuff quickly is the mantra. He breaks for lunch and to scan the paper.

In the Perspective section, he sees a full-page four-color ad featuring the pre-nomination candidate, Barry Nelson and family. The flag billowing behind the happy family. The headline in red reads, "**They Are All Around Us.**" The page reads like a manifesto.

"We open our arms to the displaced of the world... 'give us your poor, your tired, your yearning to breathe free.' Generally, this is a noble concept. We accepted our brothers from

222

Europe and the slaves brought here from Africa. But there is a new immigrant force flooding America...a force that wishes to destroy us. The force covers most points of the economic spectrum: shopkeepers and restaurant workers to scientists at our major universities and the heads of major businesses. But make no mistake, this force wants to usurp control of America. The immigrants and their whelps are the enemy among us. They collect information about the cities in which they live and send that information back to their masters in the Middle East. The information covers such subjects as public transportation schedules, police force weaknesses and strengths, and any form of defensive infrastructure to protect against attack.

"The intellectual elite that learn chemistry, physics, and all forms of science up to and including bio-terrorism will take this knowledge back to their leaders when their student and teaching visas expire. If they don't return to their homeland, they will simply disappear by blending into society. The knowledge they acquire and pass along can be used against the nation that opened its arms to them.

"These elements of the threatening force are like cancers growing within America. I think it is time we excise the cancers. To excise a cancer, surgeons must go to the core. We must be militarily strong enough to take the fight to their home. They made criminal statements by attacking our embassies and killing five hundred or more people who were in their countries on peaceful missions. If they can ignore the compacts between our nations, why should we be duty-bound to honor them? I say we must have the moral courage to close down their embassies and send the phony diplomats home.

"I say it's time we respond to the destruction of our embassies and the mass killing of our people. I say it's time we use our technology to reclaim our rights in the Middle East.

"That's what I say. What do you say?"

223

At the bottom of the ad is a single line: *This space was purchased by the Barry Nelson election committee. For further information, e-mail BNCAMPAIGN@gmail.com.*

David assumes that this ad is running in newspapers throughout the country. This would be expensive for anyone, particularly someone who has just announced his candidacy, unless that person was well funded. Money drives politics. David sees saber rattling eighteen months before the election and this *uber* hawk doesn't even have his party's nomination. He has staked out his territory for the upcoming debates.

XIV

"Dinah, what do you have for me?"

"After we received the Super PAC information from the Federal Board of Elections, Jacob and I scoured every candidate's information. But first, some context:

"*Super PACs cannot spend money in concert or cooperation with, or at the request or suggestion of, any candidate. Super PACs are prohibited from donating money directly to political candidates, a candidate, the candidate's campaign or a political party. Technically known as independent expenditure-only committees, Super PACs may raise unlimited sums of money from corporations, unions, associations and individuals, and then spend unlimited sums to overtly advocate for or against political candidates. Super PACs must, however, report their donors to the Federal Election Commission on a monthly or quarterly basis–the Super PAC's choice -- as a traditional PAC would.*

"Please hold those thoughts. We'll come back to them. Jacob?"

"After reviewing the Super PACs for the announced candidates, we didn't see anything out of the ordinary. The ideologies of the contributors matched the politics of the candidates, except the candidates were publicly less virulent than the contributors. Understandable. Barry Nelson's Super PAC is named Safety and Freedom. This is when our exploration got interesting. When we looked for contributors to Safety and Freedom we found four. Three smaller contributors: the NRA, Freedom First, and Progress Horizon each gave a million dollars.

These are not big contributions for a Super PAC. The level of contributions looks like seed money. If the candidate walks and talks the way the contributors wish, they may contribute more money. But we discovered a very substantial contributor to Safety and Freedom…World Enterprise. The initial World Enterprise contribution to Nelson's Super PAC was forty million dollars. That is not seed money. It's money that exerts or attempts to exert control over the candidate. When World Enterprise speaks, Nelson listens. That's not kosher.

"The four-page color ad that ran Sunday in the *Star* seems to have run in every Sunday paper in the country. That's roughly eight hundred Sunday newspapers from Portland to Portland. We estimate the cost for such a kickoff to a campaign to be approximately five million dollars. We looked into who made the media buy and learned that the space orders and materials were provided by Media 123. Media 123 is a buying service located in Dallas, Texas. When we called Media 123 to inquire about their client list, we were stonewalled. So, we asked that our field office personnel pay them a friendly visit with subpoena in hand. Before anyone could say, 'Oh golly look what we found,' a Mr. Dryer of Media 123 gave us his company's list of clients. There, lo and behold, was the name Safety and Freedom.

"So, the field guys asked Mr. Dryer the name of his client contact. He claimed not to know a specific name because his company received all communications via blind email, text, and anonymous telephone messages. When Media 123 tried to contact this client, the phone calls went dead…as if there were no one at the other end. He had never met anyone face to face. But the client paid its bills on time. The money was transferred electronically from a bank in the Caymans…USABank. Mr. Dryer said that his company simply took orders, did what it was told to do, and was paid. I think he knows more than he is telling.

"We tried to find out the names and addresses of people involved in the organization known as Safety and Freedom.

226

Another stonewall. Obviously, whoever runs Safety and Freedom works hard to remain anonymous. But we do know that USABank is the centerpiece of the overall enterprise. Dinah?"

"Remember when I told you to hold the thoughts dealing with the definition of and guidelines for a Super PAC? Remember the following words? *Super PACs cannot spend money in concert or cooperation with, or at the request or suggestion of, any candidate. Super PACs are prohibited from donating money directly to political candidates, a candidate, the candidate's campaign or a political party.*

"As you can deduce, Safety and Freedom is in direct violation of the guideline, to wit, they paid for the ad that launched Barry Nelson's campaign. The donated money went directly to a candidate's campaign. Based on this, we could close down Safety and Freedom, if we could only find them. At the very least, we can stop Media 123 from running any more advertising for Nelson."

"Great work, you two. I think our Dallas field office personnel should make a return visit to Media 123 and do two things: first advise them that they may be liable for federal prosecution for purchasing newspaper space for the ad, given that the ad was illegally funded by a third party. That should facilitate their cooperation. Second, have our guys retrieve any emails, text messages, and telephone numbers through which Media 123 have received communications from Safety and Freedom. Ask our field people to send the information back to our special cybercrime unit. Then you guys tear the numbers apart to find out where this force dwells."

"Will do. I wish the field people had done that at the first meeting."

"Easy, they did what they were told to do and that gave you two new avenues to explore. You are analysts. They are field operatives. They are hunters and gatherers, and you are preparers of reports based on what they gather. Going back to Media 123 with the threat of federal prosecution will quickly open up their minds and hearts, and we will get what we are looking for. Now, go and do."

* * *

"Margaret. Robert. Come in."

"David, things seem to be falling into place. The eighteen faces on the lowest rung of the ladder were brought in for chats. They gave up names of the other men who were in uniform. Their role was crowd control and direction. They were also required to mingle with the audiences and pass out literature. It seems that the men in Buffalo were hired by William Stowe, those in Minneapolis were hired by Martin Hofstadter, and the paramilitary troops in San Diego were there because Bernard Flato hired them. The three speakers. Once they were hired, the paramilitary troops were provided clothes and boots to wear during each event. They were told to keep the uniforms and foot gear clean, in preparation for more work. They would be contacted via phone. They claimed they were paid two hundred dollars, in cash, for the day. After the rally, they dispersed and went to their respective homes.

"Based on this direct connection, the field agents went to the homes of Stowe, Hofstadter, and Flato with search warrants and discovered that Stowe and Flato each had stashed away a small box containing a hypodermic needle and a partially filled vial of a clear liquid. The field people sent the needles and vials to the CDC for analysis. We had the results in a day. The lab found the super rabies virus and DMSO in both items. That links Stowe and Flato directly to the deaths in their respective cities. Hofstadter wanted to murder someone, but his efforts fell short when Beauty Brands withdrew the product.

"And here is the best part. Hofstadter kept the FedEx envelope in which he received his little bundle of death. The envelope contained the name and address of the sender. The agents in Minneapolis notified agents in Chattanooga that they had probable cause for a subpoena and possibly an arrest warrant. The agents in Chattanooga went to 456 East Tremont Avenue to search the premises for incriminating evidence. There they met a Mr. Melvin Winters. Mr. Winters is an out-of-work biochemist. After he was confronted, he spewed any and all information requested by the agents. In the basement of the house, the agents found what appeared to be his personal laboratory. Mr. Winters admitted he had created the super virus and seemed to be proud of his accomplishment. He sent the vials containing the poison and hypodermic needles to the homes of the men in the three cities. He said he was hired by a man he met online. This man claimed his name was Bill Smith. Mr. Smith electronically sent him $10,000 to create and mail the virus. Winters never asked questions. He just took the money for a job. He needed the money. He was arrested for unlawful possession of poisonous material, operating a lab in his house, murder and attempted murder.

"Back to the original three: we have two for murder and one for attempted murder. After informing the men in the three cities that poison was found at their homes, each was arrested and immediately asked for a lawyer. Each made a call to the same number. Our pal LaStrada was supposed to be on the other end. Unfortunately, he could not help them, because he was consulting with his lawyer about the charges against him. The field agents are talking to the three about these charges, hoping to move up the food chain and learn who ordered them to poison the shampoo. Another guess, we will have new names in two days. A big question remains: why that brand of shampoo? My best guess? A choice made by Winters. Maybe he will tell us. Otherwise, it was simply dumb bad luck for the brand."

"Be sure to let Fletcher, Jack, and legal know what you know."

* * *

Home in time for the early evening news. Immediately after the intro tease, Barry Nelson is on the screen. His wife and children are by his side. The billowing American flag is behind the platform. And standing on either side of the candidate's family are four men dressed in black, from ball cap to ankle. Their boots are tan. The image of military power. Nelson speaks.

"My fellow Christian Americans, it is time for us to do what the Bible instructs and take care of the sick, the displaced, the oppressed, and the hungry. It is time for the United States of America to reach out to the people of the Middle East. It is time to give aid and succor to the millions who think they have nothing to live for. Give aid to the millions who are witnesses to daily violence, beheadings, and mass torture. Give aid to the millions who wish to enjoy life within a duly constructed democratic government.

"My fellow Christian Americans, it is time to exercise stewardship, and help the millions of good, God-fearing, and industrious people of the Middle East. It is time to assist them in throwing off the yoke of tyranny that has plagued the region for hundreds of years. It is time to help these people retake the land of their ancestors that was stolen from them by dictators. It is time we act. That's what I think. What do you think?

This time was purchased by the Barry Nelson election committee. For further information, e-mail BNCAMPAIGN@gmail.com.

* * *

The offices of Media 123 had been closed and padlocked while the Bureau went through the company's files.

David immediately calls Dinah to spur her into action.

"Get the commercial that ran at the intro of the news and look at all the people on the speaker's platform."

"David, we're already on it. We will run the eight mugs through facial recognition and have answers by tomorrow morning. Got it covered. Have a good night."

As he hangs up, he realizes his team is well trained. Given Barbara's heavy thumb, he concludes they were self-trained. He is happy for them. The small part that makes him feel unhappy is with their training and high level of intelligence, they are beginning to not need him. The dinosaur smiles. Dinosaurs became extinct. He will retire. He recalls a similar case of melancholy. He had mixed feelings when his children went to college. He and Jennifer drove each one to Brown University and unloaded the SUV that contained what they needed to start their freshman year. On the way home, he felt that his children had made good choices and were in a good place. For their sophomore year, the children simply left in their own cars. That's when he felt the void of worthlessness. His melancholy was dispelled every time one or both of the children came home for a surprise visit. He knew that they wanted to be sure their parents were alright.

* * *

David leaves the office at five fifteen and immediately falls in line with the crush of commuter traffic. Sometimes, the cars exceed the speed limit for a short stretch to compensate for the miles of suffering in fifteen-to-twenty miles per hour traffic on the interstate. He just goes with the flow. Although the air is cool, he cannot drive with the windows open. The pollen in the air, compounded by the exhaust fumes on the interstate, hit his nose, lungs, and eyes hard. So, he drives in air-conditioned comfort. He recognizes a few cars and pick-up trucks he has seen over the past few weeks at this time of day. They must have jobs on the same schedule as his. He tries to imagine what these people do, what they listen to on the radio, and what awaits them at home. He is cognizant of those around him, and his analyst's training is always on. He signals as he approaches his exit. An indistinguishable black sedan, three cars behind him, also exits and follows him down the ramp. He has seen this car before. Was it mirroring his actions during every commute? Evenings and mornings? Or just evenings.

The windows of the following car are well tinted, so David can't distinguish the driver. The two cars make the same turns onto the same main, and several side, streets. Only when David turns onto Valley Boulevard, the other car does not turn with him. He wants to wave good-bye, but the black sedan disappears. The driver must be a fellow resident of the community, or he uses the residential streets as a way to avoid more interstate traffic. He could enter the neighborhood through the main gate and exit through the back gate a few streets past David's. He thinks it's interesting that the same driver is on the same path at the same time as he is.

Interesting indeed! It is not serendipity. David is being followed. By whom? Why? How often has he been followed? Every day? The driver must have a plan. Is David paranoid? He remembers some joke he heard years ago: *Just because you're not paranoid, doesn't mean someone's not following you.* He fears that someone at the Bureau is responsible for the car that is following him. Who? Jack! David decides to conduct an experiment in an effort to determine if someone at the Bureau is involved. He won't tell Rachel about his fear or his experiment.

Tonight, the couple will complete the move of items to be sold in the Gigantic Garage Emporium. The kitchen is nearly bare, there are no books on the shelves, or artwork on the walls, and the throw rugs are gone. All items, except large pieces of furniture, are crammed into David's house. Some of his summer clothes hang in Rachel's closets. His blazer and shirts for work hang on broom handles between two chairs. His shoes are boxed, and his beloved neckties are on the kitchen towel rack. He was so proud of his necktie collection. They were expensive. They were his sartorial extravagance. He will rent a truck and hire three boys from the neighborhood to help move Rachel's chest of drawers, bookshelves, couch, and other living room furniture. The bed stays until the last day.

Pricing the items is like trying to determine how many angels fit on the head of a pin. He and Rachel want to price all items for quick sales but are torn by the emotion of giving away their earthly treasures. Their pricing strategy is simple. Guess at an amount, print a label, and be ready negotiate down to a sale. It hurts him to price all his neckties at one dollar each. It hurts her to price her personal library of more than two hundred hardcovers at one dollar per book. Shirts and blouses are two dollars. Men's and women's work attire is priced at five dollars. Furniture prices start at twenty-five dollars, while kitchen items are grouped and priced from two to ten dollars. They both admit the process of pricing and labeling is almost like a precursor to selling children. He would like a beer. She says not yet.

* * *

Monday is the first day of his driving experiment. David leaves the office at ten after five. As he approaches the proper off-ramp, he checks his mirror. There is his tag along pal. Tuesday, David leaves the office at five twenty-five. His unknown new BFF exits the interstate behind him. Wednesday, he leaves at four forty-five and once again he is followed. David wonders if the person in the black sedan wants to be noticed following him or if the guy in the black sedan is a rank amateur and this is his first job of tailing.

On Thursday, David calls a brief team meeting at four thirty, rehashes what everyone already knows, and excuses himself to leave a little bit early. He heads toward the elevator but makes a detour to the men's room where he stays for twenty minutes. The anticipation of this ruse starts his pulse on its inexorable climb to one hundred twenty and beyond, a level it maintains for the last five minutes in the second stall. He is overheated when he returns to his desk and retrieves his case with tonight's reading. As he walks through the bullpen on his true departure, he passes the four cubicles of his team. He hears Dinah whispering into her phone.

"I don't know where he is. He left twenty minutes ago like I told you."

His heart sinks. Something is dreadfully wrong. If what he fears is true, tonight he must act.

He drives within the speed limit. The sedan is three cars behind him. He is sure both drivers can see each other. David speeds up and appears as if he will pass the exit ramp. The sedan pulls out to pass the cars between him and David. At the last second, David swerves and drives down the ramp. At a greater rate of speed, the sedan cuts in front of the line of traffic and races down the exit ramp in an effort to catch up to David. As the sedan approaches, David slams on his brakes. The sedan cannot stop in time and hits David's rear bumper and trunk. There are shards of headlamp glass confirming the hit. David throws his car into park and leaps out to confront the other driver. Just as suddenly, the other car backs up, cuts a sharp turn, and roars away. But not before David notes the make and model of the car and the last digit of the first sequence and all the digits of the second sequence: **D 804** of the license. Tomorrow he will learn the identity of the car's owner and driver.

* * *

"Dinah, would you come to my office, I need your advice."

"How can I help you?"

"You can answer a few questions for me."

"Who is Tim Holland?"

"I don't know any Tim Holland."

"Yesterday when you thought I was leaving early, I did not. I came back to my office and heard you whispering on the phone... '*I don't know where he is. He left twenty minutes ago like I told you.*' To whom were you speaking?"

"You must be mistaken. I wasn't talking on my phone."

"OK. You are now two for two in the lie department. I know that Tim Holland drives a 2010 Lexus GS sedan. I know that because I know his license plate is *AJD 804*. I know that because he drove his car into mine last evening on my way home and then fled the scene of the accident. He has been following me for at least two weeks that I am aware of. Maybe longer. I will have Tim Holland arrested, by the state police, and questioned about the accident and why he has been following me. I'm sure he will gladly give up your name, rather than take the full load all by himself and go to jail for menacing. What do you think?"

The silence in David's office with the door closed is so intense he thinks he can hear his pulse beat.

"Oh, yes, I forgot to mention something important for you: your involvement in the crime of menacing. When found guilty, you also will be sentenced to two years. Once you are released you will find it nearly impossible to get any type of decent paying job. You will find employment in the food service industry flipping burgers and making fifteen dollars an hour if you're lucky. How does all that sound to you?"

Tears have welled up in Dinah's eyes and she trembled slightly. "OK. What are you offering?"

"Nada. Zip. Zilch. Nil. Nothing. Confess and clear your conscience. That's it."

"It was not my idea. I was told to have you followed. Tim is my lover. He's been out of work for about a year. The money we were offered was too good to turn down. We needed the money. We had no idea why we were asked to follow you. We just took the money and kept quiet."

"Who told you to have me followed?"

"Jack. Jack Strathmore. Remember you said he would reach out to me in the near future to be a resource for him. Well, he reached out over a month ago...well before that day and offered me a thousand dollars a week to have you followed and to report on what I learned. Tim was also to follow some woman named Louisa Cochran. I think she's a public defender. We just kept tabs on you two. We did what I was asked. I never questioned Jack's motive. Why would I? How could I? I simply took the cash every Monday. The plan was for me to call Tim as you were leaving, and he would follow you as you drove to your home. He did not follow you every day. Some days, he followed Ms. Cochran. He would go to Ms. Cochran's office and wait for her to leave. Then, he would follow her. It seemed simple and harmless."

"Simple? Yes. Harmless? No. Menacing is a crime. But that's it for you today and forever at the Bureau. You will pack up your personal items and meet me in HR in thirty minutes. There, you will tell them that you are resigning for personal reasons and your resignation is effective immediately. They will ask you the standard questions. I will lament your departure. I will even help you to your car with the box of your personal items. You will get in your car and leave forever. You can use HR as a reference for your talents. They will never know the real reason for your sudden departure. I will be retired soon, so I won't reveal the real reason. Now, here is my promise: if you contact Jack, or he contacts you, before I retire and you two discuss my knowledge of your activities, I will be damned sure that you and Tim are prosecuted to the fullest extent of the law. Is all that clear?"

"Yes."

"Clear out your desk. And talk to no one while you are packing up. I'll see you in HR."

* * *

"That's what I know, Rachel. Jack is in deep *caca*. I know he knows a lot about Wendell Peterson's murder. He is afraid that Louisa, because of her relationship with Wendell, will pursue his killer. I know he's sure I have videos of him frolicking with Barbara Wilkins. Therefore, both Louisa and I are potential threats to his safety and security. But Jack is smart and crafty. He won't do anything that could cause him to lose all he has built in his twenty years of service. Plus, what he would lose in a nasty, expensive divorce. Therefore, Louisa and I are safe for the time being. Jack just wants to keep tabs on us until I retire, and she gives up. Plus, he wants me to know that someone is watching me and that someone could do to me what happened to Wendell. I doubt if Louisa has reached the same conclusion and I don't want to tell her. In this case ignorance is bliss."

"How can you be sure Jack won't do something to ensure you and Louisa remain quiet?"

"Assuming for the moment that Jack had Wendell killed, my guess is that Jack also had Wendell's home or apartment ransacked to find the video files. My guess is that he now has the abridged version of the master file. He does not know what I have. He may not have been squeamish about having a reporter killed, but he won't want to risk the aggressive investigation of the murder of a second section chief. Sooner or later, the trail would lead to Jack and his world would end. He knows that. So, he will do nothing, hoping that I will take all of this mess to my island and ultimately to my well-earned dirt nap."

"I think you're giving him too much credit. I think you're taking too big a risk with your life and my future."

"I understand how you feel but believe me I know the beast. Jack and I are like two dogs each clutching an end of a big bone and pulling it. Neither one of us will let go and lose the prize. We growl a lot as we hold our end of the bone and tug. That's Jack and me as of now. He wants the last four files, and I want to keep them for my safety...our safety. The tug of war is serious because the risk and reward are so great. As long as I do not lose control of the four damaging videos, I will walk away with the prize of retirement."

"I think I get your bizarre analogy. How can you be sure that he will rely on you to not reveal the videos…ever?"

"I know Jack. He is not brave. He is a bully, and he is smart. He's sure I can read the signals of Peterson's death and being followed. He knows that I know he knows. He knows that I know I have been threatened…twice. He knows I will be silent. And I will."

"I'm still not one hundred percent convinced you're right and that you and I are safe. That said: I have to trust your assessment of the situation, and I do trust your judgment. Now, let's get down to the task at hand: the list of duties and actions to ensure a successful move."

"OK. What is item twenty-three on our to-do list?"

* * *

"This is not a project status meeting. It is an explanation meeting. As you have noticed, Dinah is no longer working as part of our team. She left the Bureau last evening for personal reasons."

"That's it?"

"Not quite, Jacob. Let me explain. There often is seen a Machiavellian practice in many large organizations like the Bureau. This particular practice involves a member of upper management who wishes to keep tabs on a certain member of the organization that upper management fears for whatever reason: mostly not well-grounded fear, just unfounded paranoia. To keep tabs on this employee requires the complicity of an ambitious worker to spy on the activities of the target and report back to upper management. So long as the individual who is being spied upon doesn't realize what's happening, everything is fine.

However, once this individual recognizes the spying activity, and confronts the spy, the game is over. The spy must leave because he or she is no longer useful to upper management and cannot be trusted by fellow workers. Does that make sense?"

Stunned silence.

"You three are now the team until, and if, we find someone to replace Dinah. As you all know, I have never demanded blind loyalty. I hoped that you were honest at all times because that's how we deliver the best work. That's enough of the morose. Let's get to work. What did we learn from the facial recognition software last night? Jacob?"

"Dinah and I had been working on that phase. I have the report. None of the eight men dressed in paramilitary garb is a known criminal. Four of the eight are former Texas Rangers. All left the Rangers on their own volition within the past two years. None of these men has any black marks in their jackets. The other four also appear to be clean: two are former members of the Houston PD who left the department within the past two years...ironically on the same date. The remaining two have been on the former governor's staff for his two terms in office. They are obviously loyal to Nelson and may be the leaders of the bodyguards. We'll watch for their appearance at Nelson's rallies."

"Once again, our cybercrime unit comes through."

A faint smile creases Jacob's lips.

"Stay at it, you guys. For sanity's sake, let's not discuss Dinah or her sudden departure any further. Back to work. We must find out who controls World Enterprise and why the organization is the financial muscle behind this entire damned mess. We need to find the path from the poisonings to the paramilitary thugs at the rallies, to Secure America Services, to Security Investment Services, to Safety and Freedom, and finally to Barry Nelson. We must make some sense of this convoluted situation. Until now, we have snapshots of the various points that don't seem to be related, yet lead to another point, which indicates another. We need a video…a timeline from Point A to Point Z. We need to provide supportable facts to the prosecutors, so they can end this crap."

XV

The pollen count has risen in the past week. To the unfortunate like David, air poison season is in full bloom. David must take his OTC allergy meds every day or suffer more aggressive sneezing and more frequent throat clearing and snarking–the unfortunate manifestations of this malady. Very unpleasant at the office. So far, the many diverse medications he is taking seem to be functioning together with no obvious adverse effects. The Gigantic Garage Emporium will be on July 16. To-do lists must be reviewed at least thrice more before then. All of David's clothing he wishes to take to his new home is hanging in Rachel's closets: four pairs of khakis, two pairs of jeans, four pairs of Bermuda shorts, six short sleeved shirts, eight collared pullovers, and eleven tee-shirts. His three pairs of sneakers, a casual pair of slip-ons, and an old pair of sandals rest on the floor. Socks, underwear, and several swimming or running shorts are crammed in the bottom drawer of a small chest. He is convinced he can pack all these items and his toiletries in two bags. He must be sure to have at least a few months' supply of toothpaste, deodorant, shampoo and other sundries. Whatever else he needs to wear or use daily, he will buy when he is on the island. He wants to make a total sartorial break from the adult uniform of his career. His new uniform will be like those who have no uniform.

He stares in amazement at what Rachel considers the bare essentials she plans to take. He has to gnaw on his tongue and not suggest she may need two steamer trunks. She must understand that there will be no need for dress shoes, blouses, and dress slacks. He hopes that when she sees his clothing, she will rethink hers. If not, they will manage, and she can dispose of the unnecessary items once they set up their new house. He has learned, over the years, to never comment on what a woman packs for a trip. It is a discussion that can escalate into an argument that man cannot win.

"David, are all the small kitchen items over at your place properly priced. I want to sell them. The Salvation Army has no need for items like that."

"Yep."

"Do we have any more things to move?"

"Nope. Your place already looks bare without the furniture, bookshelves, and art. My place looks like a warehouse for a movie production company."

"Then I guess that's it. Now all we have to do is wait. Oh, yes, did you remember to call The Salvation Army and schedule a pick-up."

"Yes, it's scheduled for the morning after the sale. They will take whatever remains unsold. Then, my place will be bare and ready for the cleaning crew. I've scheduled the crew to be there the day after The Salvation Army."

"Then the myriad home seekers can see the real potential of your space, and by inference mine. Brenda said she's having a difficult time generating serious interest from potential buyers because of the helter-skelter look of both places. But she is convinced that when the places are ready, she can call four of them who were vaguely interested to take another walk through.

She asked if we were flexible on the prices. I told her yes once we hear an offer. No sense in showing our hand before that time. What do you think is a reasonable reduction?"

"Let's not get ahead of ourselves. Negotiation is a game of brinkmanship. We have enough money to move without lowering the asking prices to fire sale levels. We can probably wait nine months to a year, but I would like to close before that. I am confident once we're out of the houses, and they are cleaned, they'll sell."

"You're right. I'm just excited and anxious at the same time."

"Crap!"

"What?"

"I forgot a small item that must be removed from my place. My lockbox is still there. It's for sale but its contents are not. While I remember it, I'd better retrieve it. I'll be back shortly."

"The damned flash drive in that box has cast an evil spell over everything and caused a lot of heartache for many people. I hope you destroy it before we leave."

He arrives at his former residence and walks directly to the lockbox. He must turn in his government issue .45 when he signs the last of his exit papers. That's scheduled for his last day, the day before they take flight. The .9 will be sold to a pawn shop on the day his place is being cleaned. David and Rachel will have no need for guns on the island.

When he's in Rachel's home, he gets the feeling of early marriage: a Spartan environment to be made livable over time. They settle in for dinner and to watch the rain and lightning of a summer storm. Tomorrow is another day in the countdown.

* * *

Work is winding down for him but not his team. They are diligently digging into World Enterprises. If they learn who is behind the organization before he leaves, great. If not, one of them will issue the report to Fletcher, Jack, and Bureau Legal. He's almost at the stage of not caring one iota. His major task over the next few days is to write the recommendation for his replacement as senior special agent. None of them is ready for the jump to section chief. Whomever he recommends will be happy, while the other two might feel unloved. This is the problem with promoting one from within a well-functioning group of talented people. But it's not his problem. He stares at the three files on his desk, hoping something will leap from them to make his decision for him. No such luck. The rain from the storm continued until right after lunch.

On the drive home, he opens his car windows to let in some fresh air scrubbed clean by the rain. The drive is taken almost by rote. He has to come to an abrupt slow down as he is about to exit. The car in front of him, has sharply hit its brakes, and come to a complete stop on the ramp. He sneezes and reflexively snaps his body forward. Despite the heavy rain, pollen is still in the air. Simultaneous with the sneeze, he hears a metallic *thunk*, feels a sharp pain in his right shoulder, and is pushed against the driver's side door. Muscle spasm? His right arm throbs at the same time that his right hand begins to tingle. He has a difficult time holding the steering wheel with it. He puts his left hand on the pain point and feels moisture. His hand is covered with blood. Startled, he eases the car onto the emergency lane. Blood is now running down his arm onto everything beneath it...his pants, the driver's seat, and the car floor. He retrieves his cell phone and calls 911. The state police arrive in less than five minutes. He waits, squeezing the wound to slow down the bleeding.

"Mr. Drummer, the bullet grazed your right arm above your bicep, close to your shoulder, and appears to have lodged in

244

the driver's side door. We also noticed that a bullet struck the outside of the passenger door. We will need to find both bullets. That will require that we remove the inside upholstery of both front doors. To do this, we'll have to take your car to our impound lot. The ambulance will take you to St. Mark's ER. Your wound does not appear to be serious, but the professionals are better trained to determine that."

State Police Officer Childs is performing her incident scene duties as she has been trained. Her voice is well modulated and calm. David is placed on a gurney, but before he is loaded into the ambulance he wants answers.

"What the hell just happened? Officer, as you can see from my ID I'm an FBI agent. What can you tell me about this attack?"

"Every year or so, some not too bright teenage boys who have access to hunting rifles like to practice their craft on cars rolling by on the interstate. They lie in wait on hilltops near the road, like that one over there, and target cars as they slow down for the exit. To them it's just sport. To the drivers and to the police, it's life threatening. Judging from the hits on the cars and you, my initial assumption is that there were at least two boys on the hilltop. Maybe three. We'll check the site. They don't always collect their brass. Then, we'll begin an aggressive investigation. We caught two boys two years ago. We'll catch the shooters this year. Is there anyone you want to call?"

"Yes, I'd like to call my friend."

"Rachel, I'm about to be admitted into St. Mark's ER. There has been an accident on my drive home. No, I'm fine. The EMS just wants to have me checked out. Can you meet me there in about an hour? Love you, too."

"Yours was not the only car to have been hit by rifle fire. The car in front of you was hit. We know some of the boys previously involved. We'll catch these shooters. That's all I can say for now."

* * *

"Mr. Drummer, you'll be fine. The bullet grazed the fleshy part of your upper arm. No bone-damage. Minor muscle damage. Tissue damage and a lot of blood. You're fortunate. If the bullet had hit you three inches higher, it would have entered your neck or head. Somehow, your shoulder was raised, and your upper arm took the slug."

"I sneezed as a reaction to pollen."

"I've never heard of giving credit to pollen and a sneeze for preventing major bodily damage. This is a first. No surgery is required. We cleaned both the entry and exit sites and applied several butterflies and a wrap. We'll write you a prescription for an antibiotic to be sure there's no infection. You should wear a sling to keep the wound immobilized while it heals. Your arm and shoulder will be stiff and thus sore. I suggest that beginning in two days, you regularly flex that arm to loosen the muscle. The sling can be discarded in three-to-five days, depending on how quickly you heal and how strong you feel. You're not in much pain now because of the anesthetic we use. But you will feel the pain in about a half an hour. If you think pain will be an issue in the next two days, we can script you a small amount of Percocet. If the pain becomes an issue after that, call your doctor and he can give you a prescription for heavy-duty pain pills."

"Thanks anyway. I'll stick to the antibiotics and extra strength OTC pills. As the Navy Seals say, 'Pain is nature's way of telling you're alive.' I can live with discomfort."

David sees no reason to explain all the psycho-meds he is taking. Interaction of all the medications is not something he wants to discuss.

"There's someone here to see you."

"David, how do you feel?"

246

"Sore and pissed off. Some little rat bastards use cars for target practice for hunting season. They hit the car in front of me, and then my car, as we were on the exit ramp. The state police will get the little shits. Now, I want to go home."

"What about your car?"

"The police will return it to me once they have gone over it to find the slugs. I'll need to rent a car for the next week or so. My insurance will cover repair. But I don't want it back. I just want to get rid of it. I'll have no need for a car when we're on the island. I might as well let the insurance company give me a cash buy out and let them worry about clean up and sale. I'll make the call when we are home. Now, let me sign the release forms so we can get the hell out of here. I find hospitals, particularly ERs, to be depressing. Necessary, but depressing. That reminds me, when do you sell your car?"

"The day after the sale. Then, I will be stripped of a big reminder of my soon to be former life."

Walking toward the ER exit, David feels a tad woozy. He squeezes Rachel's arm to steady himself. In that one action, he realizes how much he relies on her: She is his strength, his rock. During his panic attack, his dealings with the mess at the Bureau, and now at the ER, she was at his side propping him up, so he could neither fall nor fail. He stops walking, turns to face her, and kisses her tenderly on the lips and both cheeks.

"What was that all about?"

"I wanted you to know how much I love you and how much I appreciate your loving me."

"I do love you."

* * *

Enterprise picks David up at eight thirty that night. Driving home left-handed is not easy, but he manages by driving slowly. On his way back to Rachel's he wonders…what if this was not a random shooting. What if he was the target, and the car in front of him was used as a decoy by the shooters to confirm distance and angle? When the car in front stopped, David had to stop. The shooter could then have a stationary target...David. That would mean that someone hired the shooter or shooters to kill him. That could be only one person...Jack. That miserable prick! He's trying to tie up this last threatening loose end under the guise of a teen prank. Crap! Stop! It is best for David not to slide into this pit. Just let the issue go away. He turns on the TV. There is News4You.

This just in to our news desk. State police are investigating the shooting of two cars on Interstate 80 near Exit 23-North. A spokesperson for the state police said that this is not the first time that shooters have targeted cars as they slow down to exit the interstate. The shooters seem to be practicing for the hunting season. Normally, the shooters hit cars. This time they struck a motorist who was taken to St. Mark's Hospital. The police have discovered the location where the shooters did their dirty work. The hilltop is approximately three hundred yards from the roadway. Police are following several leads. As we know more, you will know more of this breaking story.

In his anonymity, he is almost famous.

"How does my road warrior feel?"

"A tad sore and very pissed. Let me put forth a theory."

He lays his wound and car damage at Jack's feet.

"Dear, that's not crazy, it's scary. Why would Jack want you dead? You have told me, time and again, that he has nothing to gain from your death given you're so close to leaving the country. But if someone somehow links your shooting with the death of Wendell Peterson, they could deduce that Jack may be at the center of all things evil."

"If I'm dead, he eliminates any threat of my exposing his dirty dancing with Barbara. He eliminates any threat of dismissal and loss of benefits. He eliminates the ugliness of an expensive

248

divorce. But mine is only a theory, perhaps not worth considering further."

"Yes. No further discussion of that subject."

* * *

"Good morning, may I speak to Officer Riata Childs?"

"Good morning, Officer Childs, this is David Drummer, the highway shooting victim of two days ago. I'm calling to get a professional courtesy update on your investigation."

"Good morning, Mr. Drummer. How are you recovering?"

"Very nicely, thank you. The sling is a drag, but I anticipate having mobility in a few days. What have you learned?"

"We examined the slug from inside the driver's side door and the one that hit the exterior of the passenger door. They were partially mashed, but we learned that they were both 7.62s. Those are the so-called NATO rounds. And that's strange because when this has happened before, the slugs were .30-06 or .30-30. Those are the rifles commonly used in medium to large game hunting. This time the slugs are those normally associated with military snipers. An interesting note is that the slug that grazed you, and the one in the passenger side door, vaguely appear to have been fired from different rifles. This is not certain, because they were smashed but it seems plausible because a few of the LANs and grooves are not similar. If accurate, that means there were at least two shooters on the hilltop."

"One more question: was I the only civilian shot?"

"Now that you ask, yes. And that's interesting because the driver of the car in front of you also had his windows down. Given the number of shots in both cars, time to eject the spent cartridge and get another round in the chamber, adjust the sight if necessary, and fire, we have to assume the shooters were proficient at their craft. Yours was the only car have only one hit in the door and one on the inside."

"Next question: did you find any brass at the shooting site?"

"No, we did not. The shooters must have picked up all the evidence that would have their fingerprints."

"My last question: when will my car be ready?"

"Tomorrow. Have you notified your insurance carrier?"

"Yes. I have decided to let my insurance company pick up the car and dispose of it as they see fit. I am leaving Kansas City and will have no need for a car. Where can I tell the insurance to go to retrieve my car?"

"Our impound lot is located at 15098 Benderman Road. That's off State Road 46 just past the Westland Shopping Center."

"I'm not sure when they will come to get their car."

"I'll notify the impound lot of your plans. Your insurance company will need the case number to properly identify themselves. The case number is 620-RC-4915. Make sure whomever they send has this number. I hope your healing progresses fast and that you are whole very soon."

"Thank you, Officer Childs. You've been extremely helpful."

As David hangs up the phone, he flashes back more than a decade. The rifle he used at the compound was a M24 SWS that fired 7.62 x 51mm rounds. This has been the established sniper rifle and ammunition of the Bureau for years. Now, one word bounces around in his heart, lungs, and mouth…Jack. That prick is at the center of murders and mayhem. Strathmore must be very worried about the evidence David controls. So worried, he has become desperate. Is he desperate enough to try again before David leaves for the island? Or will he simply let the issue drop? David hopes the latter. Perhaps the event was meant to ensure David's silence. David and Rachel must be on their guard. Heightened security will be his responsibility. He must tell Rachel because her life may be in jeopardy.

At the second play-by-play, she finds David's theory to be nearly terrifying. She wants to know what they can do to be safe for the next few days. His plan is simple. He and Rachel must appear to be joined at the hip. She will drive him to and from work. They will use the rental car for all transportation because Jack doesn't know that make and model. She can turn in her car to the dealer a few days earlier than planned. They'll eat lunch at their desks and stay indoors as much as possible when not at their respective offices. Food shopping and other errands will be done as a couple. He tells her they will always have to be with at least one other person...ideally more than one. They are not to avoid crowds. They are to join crowds whenever possible. Blend in to be invisible. She trusts David's plan. Besides, it's only a short time until they are gone for good. This is not how David had hoped the last days of his time at the Bureau would be spent. But it's necessary.

* * *

From the bullpen, he hears one of the TV monitors.

"This is a breaking story from News4You. Earlier today, police found the nude body of a woman, Louisa Cochran, in the swimming pool of her apartment complex. She apparently drowned overnight. Police were called to the scene by a maintenance worker who was scheduled to make sure the pool was ready for the day. We now go live to Brett Peters. Brett, what can you add?"

'Well, Jane, I am about to interview Harry Goldenrod, the maintenance worker who discovered the body. Mr. Goldenrod, what can you tell our viewers?'

'Well, as I was comin' to the pool to check it before I opened it, I noticed this body floating face down in the middle of the pool. The body was surrounded by brown water. Then, I seen it was a naked lady. So, I called the police. I don't get paid enough

to handle dead bodies. When the police and fire rescue were taking the body from the pool, I noticed something very strange. The lady's eyes were totally black. That's not normal. Then, the police wrapped the body in a bag and put the bag into an EMT van. That's all I know. Now, I have to leave and get back to work. Damn, now I'll have to drain and scrub the pool before I refill it for the residents to use.'

'Thank you, Mr. Goldenrod. We have yet to speak to the police for amplification of the event and their actions. They have not been forthcoming. When I can find someone in charge, I'll let you know.'

"This much the station has learned: Ms. Cochran was employed by the city as a public defender. As of now, there are no further details. When we know more, you'll know more."

A knot begins to tighten in David's stomach. His pulse rate quickens. Jack is now a confirmed murderer. He won't tell Rachel. If she asks, he will dismiss the coincidence. Maybe she just went skinny dipping and drowned. No connection to Jack. Hopefully, Rachel will not see through David's ruse.

"Margaret, you called this meeting. So, tell us what you know."

"Before we begin, speaking for the three of us, what happened?"

"I was victimized by some teens who decided it would be fun to shoot at cars on the interstate. Nothing life threatening. Just a grazing wound that will be totally healed before my last day. Looking at the event philosophically, I can say this is a not very subtle hint that it's time to get out of Kansas City and retire. Now, on with the show."

"As you know, our primary goal of the past few days was to learn who is behind World Enterprise, and why and how they are financing Governor Nelson's Super PAC, Safety and Freedom. On this whiteboard, we have schematically connected all the organizations. As you can see, World Enterprise has an account with USABank. So electronic deposits and withdrawals are to be expected and perfectly legal. We gained access to World Enterprise's banking records, thanks to a friend at the Treasury Department who shall remain anonymous. Yes, we also have friends in high places. What we discovered was a pattern of wire transfers in and out. Each wire transfer in was in the two to three-million-dollar range, while the transfers out were much larger. The transfers in seem to come from various domestic banks...mostly in Texas, Oklahoma, and Alaska. Why is that important? These are large oil producing states. Hold that thought. Jacob?"

"We parsed Governor Nelson's latest advertising. Of particular interest are these words: '*It is time to assist them in throwing off the yoke of tyranny that has plagued the region for a hundred years. It is time to help these people retake the land of their fathers that was stolen from them by dictators.*' This is a thinly disguised call for intervention by the U.S. military...for an invasion. Revolt from the bottom up, and attack from the top down: a two-pronged approach to rid the region of terrorist regimes that don't like the U.S. They particularly don't like the fact that big foreign oil companies historically have held a large measure of sway over the royal families that ran the region for the past centuries. Revenue from the oil in the region would fund global expansion of the jihad. The jihadists are convinced that the U.S. oil companies have exploited the land and its people. So, the terrorists initiated and expanded their campaign to recapture the oil producing land and facilities. The recent attacks on our embassies are the clearest examples of how bold they have become. Nelson is calling for an invasion of the area to recapture the resources that have been taken from the very U.S. oil companies that support him. The connection is complicated but not invisible.

"Three months ago, the U.S. Air Force launched drone strikes against the four camps of el Jahdiq: strikes in Chadar, near Riatta in Qratri, near Basjar, and Najret. The men, women, children, buildings, and munitions were completely erased from the desert. The military rationale was that these attacks were in response to the previous attacks on the embassies in the region. Their justification was that the public was outraged at the slaughter of hundreds of U.S. citizens. That's crap. The public never heard of the drone attacks. Why were they kept secret? Why not tout our power in the region? We believe the retaliatory strikes were kept secret to avoid international condemnation of these obvious acts of aggression.

"But there is an interesting twist. No one in the entourage of el Jahdiq claimed credit for the attacks on the embassies that instigated the drone strikes. Taking credit for the embassy attacks would have been a real morale booster and strong recruiting tool, but el Jahdiq said nothing. This indicates, to us, that the jihadists had nothing to do with the slaughter of our people. Our guess is that someone else executed the embassy attacks and wanted to publicly blame the jihadists. Our guess is that the military knows who. Our further guess is that someone on high ordered the sacrifice of the people in the embassies for the greater good. That good being economic. A black ops paramilitary organization is most likely responsible for the attacks.

"The secret retaliatory strikes were ordered and executed for a military purpose: to cut the head off the snake so that a full-scale invasion would be easier...safer. If the snake has no head, it can't strike. If it cannot strike, any invasion by the U.S. to free the people and to reclaim the oil fields would be met with little or no resistance and supported by cooperation from the people who have suffered under el Jahdiq. And who wants the oil from the region? The big oil companies here in the U.S. We believe there exists an extensive conspiracy, using the military, to further the economic goals of the private sector in this country...the oil industry. Governor Nelson is the public and political face of that conspiracy. Robert?"

"The money to pay for Nelson's campaign effort is deposited regularly. After the huge amount noted previously, a quarterly wire transfer sends the money from the World Enterprise account to the account of Safety and Freedom. Safety and Freedom then redistributes the funds electronically to the USABank accounts of Security Investment Services and Secure America Services. From these two accounts, funds are transferred to banks in various cities throughout the country. These accounts appear to be for local businesses, such as an auto dealership in Denver, a carpet cleaning company in Buffalo, and a lawn service in San Diego, and a chain of dry cleaners in the Twin Cities. These enterprises withdraw cash on an as-needed basis: like paying the paramilitary people at parades and rallies. The cash withdrawn is never over ten thousand dollars and never in the same amount each time. The people who withdraw the funds are good at disguising their activities. That's the money stream. From big oil to a shell organization, to a Super PAC, and right down to local organizers. Back to Margaret."

"We know the flow. We had to find names of those responsible for managing the funding of this hierarchy of evil. Three names are listed on the legal documents of World Enterprise: Malcolm Simmons Whyte, William Raymond Carley, and Winthrop Carter Bashere."

The knot in David's stomach stretched from his pubis to his collar bone. His former father-in-law is up to his neck in murder and evil. Somehow this is not completely surprising. Frightening, but not surprising.

"We have begun digging into the personal lives of these three men. But we think we have enough evidence and can sufficiently connect all the dots to allow our field agents to have educational sit-downs with these three. Before that, our plan is for you to get this in front of Bureau Legal and then let them get in front of the Federal Prosecutor while we lift a few more stones. What do you think?"

"Holy crap! That's a lot to digest. The theory is strange, but your facts support it. I'm sure you're correct. Why not forward the report to legal yourself? Before you do, you must know that Winthrop Carter Bashere is my former father-in-law. I was married to his daughter, with whom I had two children who are now adult. I tell you this so there are no surprises. Thus, I request that you do not include my name on any future reports. By the way, I never liked that pompous butthead."

"We will honor your request. I assume you will be recusing yourself from all further investigating."

"Yes, I will be recused to Eleuthera."

"All of that said, we wanted to give you this final report as a going away present. We have been privileged to work with you...notice I did not say *for* you...more than we could express with stupid retirement gifts. You taught us an incredible amount. You gave us the freedom and responsibility to dig on our own. You have shared credit when that is not the norm in this building. We're going to really miss you. We thought it would be fitting that your name is on the report that ends this cabal. But at your request, we will not include your name."

"Thank you for all your great work. Also, please be sure all the files are up to date and linked. I am sure the federal prosecutor will be contacting you for additional information in the coming months."

Tears are in David's eyes as he enters his office. His stomach knot has been supplanted by the warmth of pride: pride in the accomplishments of the team and pride in his ability to bring out the best he knew was there. Now to anger: Bashere, that conniving rotten bastard. David could forgive the old man for siding with Jennifer, his daughter during the divorce. He was protecting his own, with no regard for the truth. But now, he has gone too far in pursuing his own agenda. Stop! David cannot wallow in the past. He looks to the sun-drenched future as he writes his recommendation for Margaret's promotion. The Bureau will bring in a section chief of their choosing.

Before Rachel comes to retrieve him, David goes to the mailroom for supplies. He fills out a request form for his homework supplies.

XVI

The big day is here. The Gigantic Garage Emporium is open for business at seven am. David and Rachel had not planned to start that early. They were there to set up the card tables and make sure all items were properly displayed and labeled. But two cars with four buyers each arrived, and they had many questions about items, the reason for the sale, and price negotiation. It seemed that more cars arrived every half hour. The power of advertising. Kitchen items were picked over more often than shrimp at a buffet restaurant. At first, the couple tried to meet and greet everyone. That became futile as savvy shoppers headed straight for the items they had hoped to find. These seasoned garage sale shoppers just walked around David and Rachel, like hungry lions avoiding a hunter to get to the fallen prey.

They ultimately had to see Rachel stationed at the mouth of the driveway with the cashbox. A pennant marked her realm as cashier. The purchase process was simple. All items under twenty-five dollars were sold and taken. The tag from any large item valued over twenty-five dollars would be presented to Rachel for payment. The customer would then sign the price sticker marked **SOLD** and replace it on the large item. The buyer would come back later in the day to pick up the piece. All sold and re-stickered items were to be picked up by six. If not, they would remain the property of David and Rachel until The Salvation Army took them away. There are no refunds for stranded merchandise.

"How much for the bureau?"

"Let me check."

"The price is marked on the sticker."

"Yah, but what would you really take for the bureau?"

"The price is fifty dollars. That's what I'll really take."

"How about twenty-five?"

"How about seventy-five?"

"Wait, you just went up in price. That's not negotiating."

"It's my method of negotiating. Sooner or later, you will agree to my price. Tell you what, let's split the difference and settle on fifty dollars."

The woman glares at David while all around them, people are happily chatting about items, the nice weather, and retirement.

"How about forty dollars?"

258

"How about sixty dollars? Or we can settle on the mid-point between those two amounts…fifty dollars."

More glaring.

"OK. Fifty it is."

"Thank you, ma'am. Please take the sticker to the lovely lady with the cash box and pay her."

"Who's going to help me get this to my truck?"

"I don't know."

"How about you?"

"Ma'am, once you buy an item, it's yours. If I were to help you take your item to your truck, I would have to charge you a delivery fee of ten dollars."

"That's robbery!"

"No, ma'am, that's good business."

"I'll call my son to come and help me."

"Good. In the meantime, be sure to replace the price sticker on the bureau once the woman at the cash box has you sign it and it is stamped with the word, **SOLD**. That way no one will try to buy your bureau. Please be sure your son picks up the bureau before six. Have a super day. Excuse me, I must attend to other customers."

Glare intensified.

"Well, I never…"

David strolls casually through the burgeoning crowd.

"Excuse me, may I use your bathroom."

"Sorry, the water has been turned off because we are closing the house."

He hopes no one calls his bluff.

Inexorably, the items on display disappear. His keen eye watches for pilferage. He checks his temporary tie rack and sees that it's almost as full as when the day started. The kitchen is nearly bare. Several bookshelves, and most of the living room furniture, are tagged as sold and will be picked up later today.

Around four in the afternoon, the crowd has thinned to the last few diehards. Suddenly, a van pulls up and out step three couples all in their seventies or eighties. They attack the remaining items like vultures attacking roadkill.

"Is this all there is?"

"Yes, sir. We had a very productive day. What you see is what you get."

"Not much here."

"True."

"What if my wife and I give you two hundred dollars for the whole lot?"

"That would not be tempting. Without looking to confirm the details, my guess is that inclusive of the unsold furniture inside, the value of the remaining items is approximately eight hundred dollars."

"OK. How about four hundred?"

"Eight is firm. What we don't sell we will donate to The Salvation Army Thrift Store and get a charitable deduction. They are already scheduled to come here tomorrow. Until then, the unsold items will sit in the house."

"Six hundred?"

"Eight hundred and everything not marked as sold is yours to take away."

"Seven hundred?"

"Sorry, eight hundred is the lowest I will go."

"OK. Eight hundred it is. I'll pay you tomorrow when we come back to pick up our goods."

"Sorry, the Gigantic Garage Emporium closes at six tonight. Items not sold, or sold but not picked up, will be donated to The Salvation Army tomorrow. From now until that pick up, the items will be stored in the house."

"How the hell am I supposed to load and leave with all the items by seven?"

"Closing is at six. If you can't, you can't, and we don't have a deal."

"Why can't you hold the items for me until tomorrow?"

"Sorry, the Emporium's policy is that this is a one day, as is, take it or leave it sale."

"Well, that sucks. Belinda, we're leaving."

By six pm, all the sold items were removed, and the folding tables were put back in the house. Small items were boxed. David checks the bathroom. Someone called his bluff without a courtesy flush. He locks all the doors, checks the windows, and activates the alarm.

"Dinner, my dear?"

"Yessir. No cooking for this cashier. Where?"

"I have a hankering for barbecue. Does that sound good to you?"

"Yes. Let's go to the **BIG PIG PIT** and get the meal to go. I need comfort food and to be comfortable while I eat it."

"I'll call ahead."

* * *

Sitting on the floor, in what once was her dining room, they devour ribs, chicken, fries, slaw, and soft rolls. No conversation is exchanged until they have eaten most of their meal.

"Oh, cashier, how much did we make today?"

"Over two thousand dollars is my guess. I haven't taken a final tally."

"Holy crap! We're rich."

"How large a charitable deduction do you think we can reasonable expect from the Army?"

"About two grand."

"While those two numbers make me happy, they pale in comparison to what we paid for all the stuff."

"Can't look back. Must look forward."

"You're right…but still."

"In a short time, all of this will be behind us. I don't about you, but I am exhausted, and my tummy is full. The next step is to shower and get into bed."

* * *

As he exits the elevator, David notices the toilet paper that covers the entrance to his office. As he enters, he sees the TP has been wrapped around everything: desk, lamp, computer, table, and chairs. Even the wastebasket. His heart swells with happiness. He removes nothing. He's ready for his eight am exit meeting with Fletcher and Jack. The only other visit is with HR to get the retirement package for him to review and sign on the last day. The elevator ride to the floor of decisions is pleasant because it's his last.

"Good morning, short-timer."

"Good morning, Jack. Fletcher."

"How is your arm?"

"On the mend. I discarded the sling a couple of days ago. The therapist has me doing some exercise to limber up the bruised tissue. Thanks for asking. I'm great."

"Really nasty thing those kids did."

"Yeah, kids and their rifles. A bad combination."

"Have you checked with the police? Do they have any leads?"

"I don't know, and without sounding snotty, I really don't care. It's in the past."

"On to business. Fletcher and I have read your recommendation for the senior analyst slot, and we agree. We will get HR's buy in and make it so before you leave. HR has given us a list of candidates for section chief. We're still mulling over the credentials of the people on the list. Frankly, whomever we select will have a tough time filling your shoes. You have done a great job, thus confirming our trust in you. I'm sorry that you and your talents will be leaving the Bureau. And I speak for Fletcher when I say this: we are envious of your retirement plans. When is your meeting with HR?"

"Tomorrow, I sign all the releases and turn in my gun and ID. Thanks for your time, Jack. Fletcher. My team is ready for whomever you put in that slot."

The three men rise, and David shakes two hands. The physical pain is masked by his happiness that he won't have to see these two conniving pricks after this week. Jack smiles his plastic grimace of pseudo-happiness. When David exits the big office, he looks directly at Stephanie. He does not smile. He stares though her and notes her discomfort as she shifts in her chair. He wants to say something. But does not. She is suffering enough.

* * *

"Margaret, can you come in here?"

"Yes, oh exalted short-timer."

"I want you to know that I recommended you for the position of senior special agent...my former position. Jack and Fletcher agree with my recommendation and will push it through HR this week. You will get this office and a fifteen percent bump in salary. I recommended you because you have the drive and intelligence to lead. Furthermore, Jacob and Robert respect you as you do them. Congratulations."

"Thank you. I deeply appreciate your recommendation and I'm honored to follow in your footsteps."

"As to the footsteps thing, remember that your role will also require you to work well with whomever the Bureau brings in as the new section chief. You will be the linchpin between that person and your two, soon to be three, compatriots. On that note, you will work with HR to determine the best replacement for Dinah."

"Do you have any idea who will be the new section chief?"

"None whatsoever and frankly Margaret, I don't give a damn."

"Again, thank you. Would it be permissible to give you a hug?"

"Close the door. Not for my reputation, but for yours."

Margaret leans into David with an auntie hug.

"This must be kept quiet until Jack announces it. OK?"

"OK."

"Now back to the salt mines, young lady."

Margaret smiles broadly.

David wants to finish some electronic paperwork before his last day. He owes that to his team. Forms are his to fill out. Requests for information will be sent to Margaret immediately. She might as well get used to the minutia.

* * *

The last day of work contains one meeting: HR at ten.

"Good morning, Mr. Drummer. Have you read the material we provided?"

"Yes. Here are the forms, my badge, ID, and side arm."

"Thank you. I want to be sure you understand your benefits package. It can be confusing. Basically, you will receive health insurance coverage for the remainder of your life. You will be expected to pay a small quarterly premium, which in your case is one hundred and seventy-five dollars. This coverage is for you alone. Should your marital status change in the future, you will have to have your spouse complete an application and undergo a physical. If the carrier accepts your spouse as an insured, your premiums will be adjusted upward."

"Gottit."

"You will receive a government pension for the remainder of your life. The yearly pension level is derived using a formula that includes your average salary plus bonus for the final five years of employment and total years of service."

"Gottit."

"One last item is compensation for unused personal days. It seems you did not take much time off over the past three years. You have accumulated sixty-seven unused days of PTO. That's the equivalent to slightly more than thirteen work weeks. Here is a check for the amount, minus the proper tax and insurance deductions."

"Thank you."

"Do you have any questions for me?"

"No. You have been most helpful."

What he really wanted to say was that she was mundane, repetitive, and tedious. But he won't get bitchy; she was just doing her job and posting him out of the Bureau according to the HR handbook section on exit interviews.

Back in his office he calls Rachel.

"You ready to get out from under?"

"You betcha. See you out front in thirty minutes."

He walks through the bullpen one last time. He shakes the hands of each team member. Margaret grins broadly as tears roll down her cheeks. Rachel is waiting for him in the car, parked in front of the building. He gets in and kisses her gently on the cheek. They drive off into the new world.

* * *

The Salvation Army truck was on time, the men loaded the goods, and they drove to Rachel's to pick up the balance of the couple's items. The driver gave him a blank receipt for tax purposes. The cleaning crew was also punctual. When they were done, his man cave nearly sparkled. Rachel's house is scheduled for a deep cleaning tomorrow…after they've gone. Then it's up to Brenda Moyer to sell the two places. David tosses his unused meds, prescribed by the shrink, as well as their possible refills, in a commercial dumpster. Not legal, but he does not care. No need for them in paradise. The couple arrives at the airport. He has all he needs in two bags. Rachel has three large bags. She obviously saw the folly in taking so many useless items.

They board the plane and sit in silence during takeoff, until David loudly speaks. "I understand that Alaska is nice this time of year. Are you going to Alaska, too?"

Rachel can't contain herself and breaks out in peels of belly throbbing laughter. Her happiness is contagious. David laughs loudly. Everyone around them stares. David stands up and turns toward the people behind them. "I want you all to know that my love and I are retiring, by that I don't mean shy. We are retiring to the island of Eleuthera after enduring the grist mill of modern commerce. So, yes, we are happy. Perhaps even giddy. For flying with us to Miami, all the passengers win a prize: one free drink of their choice to be paid for by me. So, enjoy. We will."

Applause and cheers ring out from the entire plane.

* * *

Upon arrival in Miami, they retrace their steps of a few months ago. It's like a real second honeymoon. In the morning, before leaving the airport Marriot, David mails eight small cushioned manila envelopes: one each to the homes of Jack Strathmore, Fletcher Wilson, Stephanie Azaub, and Mitchell Davis and four to the Bureau's home office, one to the Director, one each to two Senior Deputy Directors, and one to the Deputy Director of Professional Conduct. David is not dead like the protagonist in the play, but he just rolled over and kicked some serious ass. Off to Eleuthera.

On the island, they find the same taxi driver they employed on their last visit to take them shopping for dinner and breakfast items. He is happy to see the generous couple again. There will be time tomorrow, and the next day, to stock the larder. For tonight, they will have appetizers and wine. David's first drink of alcohol in a long time hits him hard. They fall asleep in each other's arms.

It takes two weeks in paradise to make their nest comfortable...unpack, stock larder, and move furniture into the right place. After that, they could determine what else they needed and what must be ordered from the main island. Although physically separated from the "civilized world," they both have cell phones with international capabilities, and they can access what they left behind via the World Wide Web. David goes online to read his subscription to the *New York Times*. The big story of the day is the one dealing with federal indictments handed down against the people his team uncovered. The list of men reflects an extensive hierarchy from the foot soldiers up to the three-headed Hydra that bankrolled the show. The reporter lists the charges, occupations, and alleged roles in the morass of evil for: Frey, Rhodes, Stowe, Hofstadter, Flato, Winters, LaStrada, Forbes, Thompson, Campbell, Whyte, Carley and Bashere. He also lists several other names that David does not recognize: men whose names were most likely provided by others in exchange for leniency. Governor Nelson could not be reached for a comment. His office said that the candidate was in Africa on a month-long safari.

The reporter notes that because of the number of indicted and their lawyers, there was no room in the court for the general public. Just room enough for several key TV and newspaper reporters. All of the accused had a lawyer, while the three at the top of the moral dung heap each had three. All pleaded innocent and were held over on high levels of bail. David notes comments about the great work of the Bureau in bringing down this cabal. The newly appointed Deputy Director of Community Communications, William Davis, assumed the moral high ground and would not comment on the activity in Kansas City. David chuckles…the bitch got bit. He guesses that Emily Knapp is seeking employment outside the government. Perhaps in another line of work. David then logs on to the website of the *Kansas City Star* to read a story about the shake up in the Bureau's local office: the sudden departure of three high ranking officers. Also mentioned is the early retirement of Police Commander Anderson. David whispers, 'Gotcha!' That's enough of the tumultuous world that's far behind him.

Life is blissful. Fresh fruit and vegetables are brought to their door every Monday and Thursday. Fish is sold by one of the many mongers in downtown stalls. Bread, wine, and other meal requirements can be purchased at one of the three grocery stores. David has yet to try his hand at surf casting. They swim daily and are learning to sail. Plans call for the purchase of a thirty-foot vessel a year from now…after much teaching and training. The couple has purchased a bicycle for each and a motor scooter for the pair. All three vehicles have baskets of sufficient size to carry goods from the stores.

Days gently morph into weeks and weeks into months. David is writing, an exercise to exorcise the demons that have resided in his soul for decades. With each chapter, he senses his anger is lessened. Rachel is working on a large canvas depicting their new home named Paradise Found. Painting supplies can be ordered from an art and hobby shop in Nassau and can be picked up at the local dock within a few days. Focusing on their therapeutic indulgences is their "me time." They don't discuss any work in progress. When they feel comfortable with their work, they will share it.

Monday, there is the usual knock on the front door.

268

"Hello, fresh fruits and vegetables."

Rachel goes to the door to see what she would like to buy. As she opens the screen door, she is yanked outside, aggressively spun around, and grabbed around the neck. As he pushes her inside, the plain black man of average height and weight utters a malevolent whisper.

"Be quiet or I'll break your neck. Where is your husband?"

"In the den."

"Let's find him."

Using her as a shield, they awkwardly walk in lockstep down the narrow hall. Abruptly, she shouts.

"David, something is terribly wrong. Watch out."

The next noise is the crushing of her throat. She slumps, and the man tosses the dead weight aside like a wet paper bag. David, in the doorway to the den, is immediately shot. Clutching his chest, he falls to the floor and feebly attempts to crawl to Rachel. Two more shots...one in each eye socket. David's death is ensured by this signature kill. As the man starts to leave, he fires one shot into each of Rachel's eye sockets and drops the gun in the hall. Exiting the house, he tosses the basket of fruits and vegetables, left by the door, onto the body of a black man in the bushes next to the road. He, too, has been shot in both eyes. The average looking black man pedals David's bicycle to the harbor, where he blends into the crowd boarding the next boat to Nassau. From there, he will take a plane to Miami and then fly back to Kansas City where he will hide in plain sight. Three bodies remain on the property. Someone will find the victims long after the assassin is gone.

John Andes

John Andes was born and raised in Central Pennsylvania and received a degree in philosophy from Brown University. John has written B2C and B2B advertising and marketing communications his entire career. He has two adult sons, is retired, and lives on Florida's Gulf Coast.

John coaches Little League Football, mentors small business owners and entrepreneurs, and teaches creative writing. John's writing is based on the premise that each of us struggles against forces thrust upon us in situations beyond our normal lives. By struggling, individuals have the opportunity to create a new and better persona.

John has authored *Farmer in the Tal*, *Hidden Agenda*, *Suffer the Children*, *Icarus*, *Matryoshka*, *Jacob's Ladder*, *Loose Ends*, *Control is Jack*, *Revenge*, *Adventures in House Sitting*, *He Who Builds with Skulls*, and *Street Cleaners*. *Scruffs* was his second print of *Suffer the Children* with HAVAH Publishing.

His web page is www.crimenovelsonline.com

John Andes

www.ingramcontent.com/pod-product-compliance
Lightning Source LLC
Chambersburg PA
CBHW030657260626
47157CB00007B/2689